AN
ACCIDENTAL
PIRATE

AN ACCIDENTAL PIRATE

the possibly true adventures of Fanny Campbell

BROOKS ALMY

BOLD STORY PRESS

WASHINGTON, DC

Bold Story Press, Washington, DC 20016
www.boldstorypress.com

Copyright © 2023 by Brooks Almy

All rights reserved. No part of this book may be reproduced or used in any manner without written permission of the copyright owner except for the use of quotations in a book review. Requests for permission or further information should be submitted to info@boldstorypress.com.

This is a work of fiction. Names, characters, places, and incidents are either the product of the author's imagination or are used fictitiously. Any resemblance to actual persons, living or dead, events, or locales is entirely coincidental.

First edition published April 2023

Library of Congress Control Number: 2022913521

ISBN: 978-1-954805-36-1 (paperback)
ISBN: 978-1-954805-37-8 (e-book)

Text and cover design by KP Design
Author photo on page 311 © 2009 Mikel Healey Photography. All rights reserved.
Author photo on back cover by Maurizio Papalia

Printed in the United States of America
10 9 8 7 6 5 4 3 2 1

For Mon Fox
Fanny would have been your favorite girl

CONTENTS

Prologue . . . 1

ONE Late Summer . . . 3
TWO The Aunties . . . 9
THREE Training Day Race . . . 14
FOUR Will's Story . . . 22
FIVE Will Appears . . . 30
SIX Gerald & Graham Campbell . . . 37
SEVEN Nate & Sara . . . 49
EIGHT Into Town . . . 57
NINE Tea with Biddy & Maude . . . 70
TEN A Magic Chestnut Tree . . . 74
ELEVEN Best Christmas Ever . . . 79
TWELVE The Proposal . . . 90
THIRTEEN Wedding Day, Early Morning . . . 96
FOURTEEN Wedding Day, Late Morning . . . 106
FIFTEEN The Wedding & Beyond . . . 110
SIXTEEN The Goodbye . . . 121
SEVENTEEN A Different Christmas . . . 129
EIGHTEEN The Plan . . . 142
NINETEEN Aboard the *Mary of Leeds* . . . 150
TWENTY A Losing Battle . . . 153

CONTENTS

TWENTY-ONE	The *Bloody Rose*	... 163
TWENTY-TWO	The Long Journey to Smuggler's Cove	... 172
TWENTY-THREE	Thorne & Q	... 182
TWENTY-FOUR	The Escape	... 188
TWENTY-FIVE	The Storm	... 198
TWENTY-SIX	Cumberland Island	... 208
TWENTY-SEVEN	Ghost Ship	... 216
TWENTY-EIGHT	A Hero Lost	... 224
TWENTY-NINE	The Vote	... 231
THIRTY	The Jail in Cuba	... 235
THIRTY-ONE	Becalmed	... 238
THIRTY-TWO	On to Cuba	... 251
THIRTY-THREE	Through the Jungle	... 260
THIRTY-FOUR	A Secret Village	... 266
THIRTY-FIVE	A Priest & a Prison	... 278
THIRTY-SIX	Celebration & Revelation	... 286
THIRTY-SEVEN	Back to the Jungle, Back to the Sea	... 298

AUTHOR'S NOTE

FANNY CAMPBELL APPEARED on the literary scene in 1844 in a novel by Maturin Murray Ballou. She was an extremely popular character and continued to be written about in novels and magazines over the years as though she were real. Some readers took her tale to heart: Sara Edmonds fought in the Civil War as a man; Maud Buckley captained a schooner on the Great Lakes that she called the Fanny Campbell.

I found Fanny included in a collection about female pirates in a museum bookshop, but she only rated one short paragraph. From that bit of information, I created my own story of Fanny Campbell. If she were real, I think she would have liked it.

PROLOGUE

FANNY KNEW SHE shouldn't be scared. If she were discovered, she would undoubtedly be thrown into the sea. Sailors were a superstitious lot, and a woman on board ranked very high for bad luck and disaster. But there was nothing to give her away. Her father had taught her everything about sailing. She was strong and as agile as a monkey. She knew how to climb the ropes and haul a mainsheet. He had also made sure she could wield a cutlass or a broadsword with the best of them.

The wind whipped her newly shorn hair hard against the side of her face. She pushed it back into the knob at her neck. Her eyes watered. She wiped the tears off her cheek with the rough sleeve of her uniform and focused on the horizon.

No sails now, but if she missed one, she would surely be flogged, and then all would be lost. The merchant ship *Mary of Leeds* had seen a pirate vessel far behind them. It disappeared, and it was her job to give the first alarm if it appeared again. If she failed, she would never see her Will again. *Quit that*, she told herself. *You have already been at sea three months. You will not fail. You will not be found out. You are a Campbell.*

ONE

LATE SUMMER

THE GIRL HAULED at the sheets, and her boat came about in a slamming turn. It sped over the blue water like a leaf in front of a hurricane. In the crook of the bay, the church steeple of Lymington, Rhode Island, was visible off to the right. To the left was a narrow beach, a high green hill covered with trees, and a split-rail fence. The little craft heeled over, nearly perpendicular to the sea. In the 1770s girls did not behave this way, but she didn't care. She fearlessly hung over the opposite side, her long red hair brushing the water. A huge black dog barked as the boom swung past its nose. It seemed that the boat was sure to capsize, but then, just as quickly as it started, the crisis was over. The boat settled back on its keel. The dog shook the water from her fur. The girl laughed and did the same with her hair.

"That's it, Dolly," she said, swinging her hair. "Shake yourself again. Good dog." Dolly obliged, and the girl sat back, her hand on the tiller. As she came about, she spotted a large ship just outside the mouth of the bay. A pirate ship? Her heart jumped. But then she spotted the British flag. "Fiddlesticks!" she muttered under her breath, clearly disappointed. "Come on, girl. No pirates today. We must get to plowing, or there will be no winter crops this year. We will all starve and then who will feed you?" As they neared shore, Dolly jumped into the bay and headed toward the beach, her shiny black head gliding through the water. "It was a joke, Dolly," the girl called out, guiding her boat in the dog's wake. She beached it high up on the sand, and she and Dolly ran up the hill to a large field ringed with trees. Late summer in Rhode Island was magical. The trees were leafy green, touched with red and gold, blowing in the light breeze, and wildflowers covered the hillside. The view of the bay, deep blue with light waves shimmering on its surface, never failed to put Fanny in a good mood. With a last glance back, she crested the hill and headed toward a large brown field.

A split-rail fence enclosed the field's borders. It was clear save for one large hole. Fanny jumped in. Hours later, all that could be seen was a head of tangled red hair. "Come on, you piece of garbage, move." The tall, lithe girl kicked the giant tree stump and fell back. "Very smart, Fanny Campbell," she said out loud. "Break your foot and there will be no fall planting this year at all." The enormous black retriever sat near the edge of the hole, paws crossed, yawning.

"Oh, I am so sorry, Miss Dolly," she said crossly. "Why don't you help? You love to dig." Dolly jumped in the hole, rolled on her back, and shut her eyes. "Thank you so much for your help, you big silly!" Fanny sat down again and took out her lunch: a piece of fresh bread, a small hunk of cheese from their own sheep, and an apple. She finished, tossed the core to Dolly, who was delighted, and took out a leather skin from her sack. She poured a bit of water into a small wooden bowl, put it down for Dolly, and then took a long drink herself.

"Alright, Dolly, a little rest and then back to work." Fanny closed her eyes for what she thought was a minute, but when she opened them again, the sun was low in the sky. "Tarnation and corruption!" she said, using her father's favorite expletive. He always said that swearing was the last bastion of ignorance, but that this was not swearing—it was creative anger. "I can't believe we have lost so much of the day. Back to work, Fanny, you laggard!" It was unusually hot that day, so Fanny wrapped the chain in an old petticoat so as not to burn her hands. She had spent the better part of an hour forcing the chain under and around the giant stump. "Finish this last one and I'll be ready to plow," she remarked to herself. "Don't worry, Fiona, you beauty," she said to the white horse standing under a spreading oak. "I won't make you work in this heat." She pushed her damp hair back, ready to pull again, when she heard Dolly growl.

"Do you need some help?" Fanny started at the sound and almost fell. There was a dark-haired man in a blue coat standing at the edge.

"No, thank you. I'd much prefer to break my back alone." He didn't move.

"Don't stand there like a big dumb ox. Come, put your brawn to some use."

He dropped the sack he was carrying, took off his jacket, and jumped into the hole. "Who could refuse such a charming invitation? What about the dog?"

"Oh, she won't hurt you unless I tell her to. Stay, Dolly." Fanny had used a lighthearted tone, but the man knew she was serious.

He picked up one end of the chain. "Shall we?" As they hauled at the chain together, the stump began to inch out of the ground.

"Is this your farm?"

"No. Yes. Keep pulling."

The stump flipped over the edge, and they both fell back on the ground. Fanny dropped the chain and jumped out of the hole, brushing the dirt from her skirt. The man followed. "Yes, it's mine," she repeated firmly. "What is your name?"

"William Marston Lowell."

"Well, Mr. William Marston Lowell, you had better stop staring at me and get on about your business, or I will be forced to throw you back in that hole."

He spread his hands in a gesture of surrender. "I'm sorry, miss. It's just that you are uncommon beautiful and strong."

She looked down at her calloused hands and felt the blood rush to her cheeks. "And you are uncommon fresh. Best get yourself back into Lymington, where you can find a girl who cares for that sort of balderdash."

"Ah, miss, my apologies for sure. I've only just returned today from two years at sea, and my manners are still rough."

She turned her back and began to fuss with the chain. "You see, my ship was damaged and is now in drydock at the shipyard." He waited and then began to walk away. Then he turned. "I'll be going now, but may I ask one question?"

She glared up at him and became aware of how very tall he was. "One, then."

"Do you have a name?"

"Yes."

"May I know it?"

"That's two questions."

"You are quite right. I apologize again for my impertinence. Good day, miss." He walked toward the road.

"Campbell."

He turned back. It occurred to her that his eyes were the same blue as today's sea.

"Fanny Campbell."

"A pleasure, Miss Campbell. May I call on you tomorrow? We could finish off that stump."

She waited. He waited. "Fine, then," she said. "But not tomorrow. Tomorrow is Training Day."

"And what, pray tell, is Training Day?"

"Come to the edge of town and see. And if you return here next week, work begins at sunup. Don't be late." As he walked away, she wondered what in a crooked smile could make her knees quiver like that.

TWO

THE AUNTIES

AFTER FANNY'S PARENTS died, she grieved deeply, but then went back to running the farm. Helping her were Nate and Sara, an escaped slave couple her father had taken in when Fanny was young. She considered them her family. Their son, Joshua, eight, followed Fanny everywhere. Working together, this odd little family group grew corn and flax in the fields and vegetables in the garden. With the flax, they produced beautiful cloth, brightly colored with the help of Sara's knowledge of how to make dyes from roots and flowers. Sara was currently trying to teach Fanny to weave, but this endeavor had so far failed, as Fanny could not sit still long enough to learn the difference between warp and woof.

Fanny was hot and dirty, but she couldn't wait to talk to Sara, so she tied Fiona to the rail out front and ran straight into the house without washing up. She pulled up short when she saw the table set for tea, her aunts Biddy and Maude sitting primly on the edge of their chairs, and Sara smiling brightly.

"Look who dropped by for tea," said Sara with a wink.

Aunt Biddy smiled sweetly. "Look, Maude, she looks just like Elspeth, right down to the smudges of dirt. Your mother was just as rambunctious as you." She rose and hugged Fanny tightly. Aunt Biddy was a tiny woman, all pink cheeks and grey curls. She never had a cross word for anyone and could find a ray of sunshine on the worst day.

"Aunt Biddy, you'll get all dirty!"

"Don't care, dear girl. I miss you too much. Why don't you come into town more often?"

"Yes," sniffed Aunt Maude. "Why is that?" Maude was the opposite of her sister. Tall and thin, with her hair skinned back in a tight bun, taciturn to a fault, with a face that barely moved, masking her innate kindness. Even so, like her sister, she loved their niece and feared for her future. After the death of their baby sister, Elspeth, and her husband, Gerald, the aunts had insisted that Fanny move into town with them and learn to be a lady, so as to find a suitable husband.

Fanny said, much to their dismay, that finding a husband was not on her list of things to do, and besides, she had a farm to run. She was not going over all that again now, so she just smiled and shrugged her shoulders. "Let me wash up and I'll tell you all about my day while we have tea."

She made her escape out the door and ran down to the pump. She washed the dirt from her face, twisted her hair back into a bun, and tried unsuccessfully to brush some of the dirt off her skirt. Joshua popped out from behind the horse trough with a loud shout, his impish brown eyes snapping.

"Aha! Look out! I am a pirate."

"Fine, Mr. Pirate Man. I am ever so scared, but could you please help me out and take Fiona to the barn?" Joshua took the reins, pleased to be given a grown-up task. "Aunt Biddy gave me a sweet. She said not to tell Aunt Maude."

"Did she now? And what did you say?"

"I said, 'Thank you so very much, ma'am.'"

"Good job, Joshua. What a grown-up you are! You are learning manners much faster than I ever did." She gave him a hug, pushed him toward the barn and marched resolutely up the stairs.

Inside, Aunt Biddy was on her second piece of cake. "Sara, I don't know how you get this so light and airy. Maude's cakes are like doorstops."

Sara looked at Maude who might have smiled although it was hard to tell.

"Biddy finishes every single one, so they can't be that bad."

"Not bad at all, Maudie, just dense."

"Who is dense?" asked Fanny from the door.

"No one, dear, sit down, please. Biddy and I have an idea for you." Fanny groaned inside but sat and took two slices of cake.

"Mrs. Fallon, the midwife, do you remember her?" Fanny nodded, her mouth full of cake. "Well, she is getting ready to retire and needs an apprentice. We, Biddy and I, think this would be a great opportunity for you. You could live in town and have your own business. We know you want to be independent, and this is a way to do that." Fanny contemplated another piece of cake. "Well, what do you think?" Maude asked impatiently, tapping her foot.

"Oh, Auntie, I am sure I couldn't do that. All that blood and screaming, I would surely faint."

"Faint? You?" Maude might have looked skeptical although, as usual, it was hard to tell. Fanny hadn't figured out how to cover this obvious lie, but Sara jumped to the rescue.

"Oh, Miss Maude, you should see her on birthing day with the sheep. She runs away with her hand over her mouth, and Nate and I have to finish alone."

"Oh, pish," said Maude. "Then clearly this will not work. Not to worry, Fanny. We will find you a suitable activity, you can be sure."

"Thank you, aunties. I am grateful for your concern." Fanny's fists were clenched under the table, but her face was serene.

"Well, we must be off. Fanny, I want you to know that, legally, we can compel you to come live with us. You are still a girl." With that, she swept out of the cabin. "Sara, would you ask Nate to bring around the wagon and take us home?" she said over her shoulder. Biddy bustled out after Maude. Nate helped them up onto the wagon, and Fanny watched them go from the door, waving.

Keep thy head, Fanny, she said to herself as she collapsed in front of the fire. "Sara, can she really do that?" Sara joined her, unraveled Fanny's bun, and began to smooth and braid her hair.

"I don't think so, but we will check. Don't worry, dear one. They will keep having ideas, but nothing will ever pry you from this farm and that is a very good thing for us all."

"Sara, I met a man today."

"What? Where? How? Who is he? And why are your cheeks turning red?"

"Sara, stop!" Fanny laughed. "It's nothing. He showed up in the field and helped me pull out that stump. Here is what I know: He is off a big ship in the drydock in town; He has blue eyes and is very tall; Oh, and he is English, but that can't be helped."

Sara's eyes twinkled mischievously. "Will he be coming back, do you think?"

"No! I don't know. Maybe. I hope so!"

THREE

TRAINING DAY RACE

THE PIRATE'S BREATH was hot on Fanny's cheek. He was so close a bit of his beard touched her lip. She spit it out and breathed in sharply. She felt a terrible cold on her neck. Had his blade found its mark? Her eyes snapped open. "Yikes, Dolly! Get your nose off me."

The huge black dog stood over Fanny on her sleeping pallet. Fanny gave her a shove. "I curse the day I taught you to climb that ladder," she whispered. "Now, get downstairs and let me dress."

Dolly licked Fanny's face with such vigor it felt like a wet slap. She then turned and picked her way down the ladder, front paws first, her plumed tail the last thing to disappear over the edge of the loft. Fanny lay back, chuckling softly, and sat up again so fast she barely missed slamming her forehead into the low beam above her head. Training Day! How could she have forgotten? As far as Fanny was concerned, this was the best day of the whole month.

Training Day, the last Saturday of every month, was like a small country fair. Everyone in town and from the surrounding farms would take off from working for a whole morning and gather to share food, fun, news of the day, and gossip. There were strength contests, log throws, boulder hefts, boxing matches, foot races, and, of course, the horse race. Ladies would bring their finest jams and conserves with fresh bread, and, when in season, there might be huge baskets of steamed clams and grilled fish. All in all, it was a great day.

At the northernmost edge of town, a five-foot stone pillar marked the road. It bore the inscription, "Lymington, Free and Faire." No one was sure who had erected it, but all agreed it was an apt description of their town. North of the town marker, as it was called, was a large field, bordered on three sides by forest and by the road on the fourth. Its owner, widower Donald Almy, had no use for it. It was too rocky to graze, and the soil was too thin to plant. He donated it to the town once a month and got many benefits in return for his generosity: fresh eggs, a side of ham, hot bread, seeds for his garden, and, best of all, company. Since his wife died, he had little reason to leave his cabin in the far corner of his land. He never came into town, and would never admit to being lonely, but Training Day gave him an excuse to mingle.

Fanny never got tired of the smells of cooking and the bustle of the townspeople. She always made it a point to search out Donald Almy and give him a hug and some of Sara's jam. She loved the sparkle that came into his faded blue eyes. But her favorite event was the quarter-mile horse race. Farmers, shopkeepers—anyone with a horse—could enter, so the field was always varied. The prize was sometimes a chicken or maybe a coin, but everyone raced as though it were for a fortune. Fanny would stand by the side of the road holding her breath as the horses pounded by, manes streaming, on their way to the finish at the town marker. More often than not, farm boys on nags bringing up the rear would bounce off the back of their rides and fall in the dusty road, causing much hilarity from the watching crowd. Fanny loved it all but was quite resentful of the fact that girls didn't participate. Nobody ever said they couldn't; it just wasn't done.

But this Training Day would be different. This day, Fanny had a plan. She hadn't told a soul. Did she dare? she wondered. What would people think? What about Aunt Maude? *"Almost eighteen and still not spoken for. She has ruined her chances. Tsk, tsk."* Fanny heard Aunt Maude's disapproving voice loudly invading her thoughts. Fanny shook her head. *I don't care. Everyone already expects me to be an old maid. I might as well do what suits me. Couldn't get worse, and it will be fun*, she thought.

Fanny let a tiny smile begin. It widened to a grin. Then she clapped her hand over her mouth to hold back a whoop of delight. This will be the best Training Day yet. She sat up in bed and pulled on her woolen hose. She dropped her skirts and petticoats over her head with practiced skill and scrambled down the ladder. The rest of the family was still asleep, but Fanny knew it was only moments before Sara woke to stir the banked embers in the fireplace to a flame and start breakfast. She had to move quickly if she was going to avoid questions. She moved silently in the faint light and took her hand-knitted sweater from the hook by the door. Her mother had made it in reds and oranges. Fanny said it made her feel like she was wearing a sunset. Wearing it made her feel close to both of her parents. She looked over her shoulder and tucked her boots under her arm. She lifted the latch, eased open the door, and slipped outside, Dolly a shiny shadow at her heels.

In the stable, Fanny took down Fiona's tack, rubbed her nose, and gave her a carrot from her skirt pocket. "Today is our day, my girl," she whispered. She took down her father's saddle. Age had softened the leather and given it a beautiful, dull sheen. As she ran her hand over it, she could hear her father's voice: "Never forget who you are, my bonnie rascal. We are Campbells. We are never slaves to the dictates of tyrants nor the opinions of idiots."

"Well, Fiona, we shall see whether there are tyrants or idiots at the race today. Maybe both!" She snorted with laughter and clapped her hand over her mouth again. "Shush you! We have to get there early so we can hide in the trees.

Come on, girls!" Dolly and Fiona followed her out of the stable and into the pale light. It was what her father had called a nautical light. She could see just enough to make her way through the woods towards the road to town. The woods smelled deeply of balsam fir with a hint of apples. She kicked at the dry leaves and pulled her sweater tightly around her against the predawn chill.

Fanny arrived at the back of the field just as a few early risers started to set up their wagons. She made her way deep into the copse of trees and settled down to wait. She didn't have to wait long. John Steadman, the blacksmith, roped off a boxing ring. Men from the shipyard brought long planks to make tables and the ladies of the town began to cover them with strawberry and blueberry jam, pickled radishes, conserves, and all manner of breads and cakes. A few minutes later, Mr. Woodson, the owner of the shipyard, bustled to the marker with two of his workers. He was sponsoring the race this year and had offered a gold coin as prize. His men brought out the stakes to mark the start and finish of the race, and riders began to drift toward them. She watched as the town boys, slick and arrogant, gathered in one group, and the farm boys, all shaggy hair and boisterous laughter, gathered in another. The town boys had better horses, but the farm boys had more fun. Ever since Fanny and Dolly had won all the herding trials last season, both groups would have nothing to do with her. She didn't really care, but she couldn't wait to rub their animosity right back in their faces.

They were all a bit afraid of her anyway. She could drive a fence post and toss a hay bale as well as any of them, and they were not used to strong girls. There was also a rumor going around that she had fought off a mountain lion with nothing but a spade. It was rubbish, of course. The truth was that it was very young, and she had flung it over the fence by its tail so as not to hurt it.

Twenty horses were in a roiling group at the start marker. Mr. Woodson stood at the side with a red flag in his hand. The townspeople lined the track, shouting and waving to their sons and fathers. From her hiding place, Fanny could see exactly where she would join the group. They all tended to move toward the right at the first turn. She would go left and pass them all. That was the plan anyway. Fanny mounted Fiona and buried her face in her silky mane. "Don't worry, girl, I promise this is going to be fun. Dolly, you wait until the end, alright?" Dolly lay down, tipped her head, and folded her paws. "Good girl! See you at the finish line."

Mr. Woodson dropped the flag and the horses surged forward. The crowd shouted and laughed and then gasped. From the left came a white streak. Fiona was at a full gallop, Fanny's skirts flapping, her red hair streaming behind her like a flag. As they made the first turn, Fiona lengthened her stride even further and pulled out in front. The other riders realized what was happening and urged their horses forward, but it was too late. Fanny was a full length in front with the final marker in sight. Between her hair and her sweater, she looked like a ball of fire. She laid flat, pressed into Fiona's neck. "We got them, girl," she whispered. She crossed the finish line, wheeled Fiona around to face the crowd, and stood high in her stirrups. "Lymington, Free and Fair!" she shouted. At first, there was silence, then a loud whoop came from the back. Fanny looked over the crowd and saw a tall figure with a dark head of hair. That sound was followed by a high-pitched hooray from the front. It was Aunt Biddy, jumping up and down and laughing. Her joy was so infectious that other people started to cheer as well.

Mr. Woodson strode up to Fanny and sputtered, "What did you do, girl?"

"Well, sir," said Fanny. "I believe I just won the race. May I have my prize?" Mr. Woodson was apoplectic, but he could do nothing but hand her the coin. She thanked him, held up the coin, and bowed to the crowd of boys she had just beaten. They stood there sheepishly, shaking their heads and glowering. She ran over to Sara and Nate, who were both grinning ear to ear. Joshua was beside himself with joy, jumping up and down and shouting.

"You were the best, Fanny, you were the best!"

"I can't believe you didn't tell us," said Sara.

"You would have tried to talk me out of it. Anyway, this is for you all to buy something nice at the mercantile. Save the rest for when you need it. I'll see you at home." She handed Sara the coin, who stared at it with her mouth open. Then

Fanny jumped back on Fiona, leaving them speechless. As she rode out of the fair, she scanned the crowd for Will and was sorely disappointed when she couldn't find him.

FOUR

WILL'S STORY

IT WAS EARLY morning when Will's ship, the *Queen's Courage*, limped into Boston Harbor with storm damage. When Will's superiors sent him and a skeleton crew to a small town called Lymington that was said to have a superior shipyard, Will questioned their wisdom. He did not expect a top-notch operation out here in the backward colonies. Nevertheless, he chose ten men and took to sea.

At the mouth of the Lymington bay, he spotted an amazing sight through his glass. A small sloop, piloted by a girl with long red hair, was up on its keel speeding across the water. Just when he thought it would flip over, she righted it, came about, and guided her craft toward the beach. It was a superb piece of seamanship. *Who was that?* he wondered.

When they arrived at the Lymington shipyard, he was pleasantly surprised. The yard had a full complement of carpenters, shipwrights, and ironworkers, hard at work, and a sturdy drydock, lined with granite and built well out from the shore. His helmsman maneuvered the ship slowly into the channel. Workmen closed off the caisson across the opening and began to add shores to prop up the hull once the water was pumped out. Will watched until the ship was secure and then went off in search of lodging for his crew.

He found a boarding house with enough space, run by an exuberant Portuguese woman with a loud voice and a hearty laugh. Mrs. Isabella Da Silva was delighted to have eleven new lodgers, was not so delighted they were English, but was mollified to have been paid for three weeks in advance. Will didn't think minor repairs would take much longer than that.

He then returned to the shipyard and surveyed his ship with dismay. The hull was now open, and the ribs exposed. The workers were hauling away large pieces of diseased wood. The head shipwright, a tall, thin fellow named Ryan, came over shaking his head.

"I am sorry, sir. When we lifted her out of the water, we found that she was riddled with ship worms." Ship worms were tiny larvae that floated on the surface of the ocean. Will knew that, unchecked, they could sink a ship easily. He put his hand on the hull and saw the bore holes the ship worms had left. *How did this happen?* he wondered.

"She needed to be scraped a long time ago," said Ryan, as if he had heard Will's thoughts. "We will be replacing almost the entire hull. This could take months or even a year. We still don't know how deep the damage goes."

Will gave a heavy sigh, thanked him, and headed back to the boarding house. He asked Mrs. Da Silva if she had a quill, ink, and a piece of parchment.

"That's asking a lot; those things are very dear." She stood with her hands on her hips, waiting.

"I will be happy to pay for the items and a bit more for your trouble." He gave her his most sincere smile, and Mrs. Da Silva unbent a bit. She took him into a small library off the main room and sat him at a small desk. Will could barely get his knees under it but he did not complain, as he was sure he would need more favors from Mrs. Da Silva in the future. She brought him the things he had asked for, plus a cup of tea. Will hoped that was a good sign. He was afraid he was going to be around a lot longer than he wanted. He penned a rather long letter to his superiors detailing the damage and the time frame as it stood now. Mrs. Da Silva directed him to the livery stable where he found a rider to take his message to Boston. That done, he went in search of his crew and found them at the local tavern, drinking ale and chatting in a desultory fashion.

"Look alive!" he shouted, and they all leapt to their feet.

"Aye aye, sir!" They gave the proper response and saluted. Will stalked in front of them with a stern look on his face and then laughed.

"Ah, sit down, you daft idiots. We aren't at sea yet. I have some news you may consider good or bad." The men all fixed him with a worried gaze. "The ship is in dire shape. Ship worms have taken hold and bored through most of the hull. She will be in drydock for some time. The repairs could take months." The men groaned in unison.

"Sir," said Johnson, the first mate. "There is nothing to do here. This is the only tavern, and as far as I can tell there are no available women. What shall we do for months?"

"I have thought long and hard about this very thing. I am giving you all provisional liberty to travel to Boston. There you will report to command. I have sent a letter ahead to my superiors, and I will have a letter for you to take with my recommendation that you be given liberty until the ship is ready to sail. When that day comes, you will return as fast as possible, and we will be underway and back to our original task of sweeping the seas for pirates. I, for one, am looking forward to that day."

The men all crowded around. It was obvious that Will was much beloved by his crew. They thanked him profusely and clapped him on the back until he could stand no more.

"Enough," he shouted. "I am still your commanding officer. Now sit down and drink your ale and someone get me a tankard as well."

Will leaned back in his chair and returned to musing about the redhead. He had never seen a girl like her before. The girls in his English town were, as far as he could tell, prim and prissy, with little thought for anything but fashion; they certainly would never get their hands dirty. Who raised a girl who could sail a sloop as well as or better than any sailor he knew? His parents would not have approved of his interest. Their wish had been that he come back from sea, settle down, and run the estate. But then, on a short boat trip from Cornwall to Devon, they were attacked by pirates and killed. Most pirates had been cleaned out of the coastline of England by then, but there were always the few scoundrels who continued to terrorize smaller villages. Will came home, buried his parents, left the estate in the care of his younger brother, John, and signed on to the *Queen's Courage*, a pirate-hunting warship bound for the colonies to protect the King's interests.

He was yanked from his revery by the gravelly voice of his first mate. "Sir, when may we take our leave?"

"Now, you bunch of raggedy tars. Get out of here! Go pack your kit and be on your way. Tell Mrs. Da Silva I will be there shortly." The men pushed and jostled their way out the door, cheerfully exchanging insults. He pushed back from the table, paid the bill, and stepped out into the dusty sunshine to ponder his next move. Will's thoughts returned to the girl. She would not leave his mind. He knew in an instant what to do. Now that he had time to spare, he would set out to find the redheaded sailor. But first he had to see Mrs. Da Silva, and he knew she would not be pleased.

As he entered the boarding house, he could hear his men busily packing. Then he saw Mrs. Da Silva, glowering at the top of the stairs. Before she could speak, Will held up his hands in supplication. "I am so sorry that the situation has changed, but these things happen in military life. I would like you to keep the full three weeks of payment. I know you will have to do extra work to clean the rooms, and it is only fair." Mrs. Da Silva was marginally disarmed. As she came down the stairs, she asked a bit slyly if he would be going as well.

"Oh, no, I am here for a good long while."

"Well, then, you need a better room. Come with me." She led him to a big room with a dormer window on the top floor that looked right out on the bay. She threw open the window and said with pride, "This is our very best room."

"I can see that," said Will. He looked around, taking in the flowered curtains and the thick coverlet on the wide sleigh bed. "Mrs. Da Silva, this is perfect. I shall be very comfortable here." What Will liked best was the big wing chair by the window. It even had a small table where he could write. He sat in the chair and leaned back with a sigh.

"I will leave you to settle in. Will you be having dinner here?"

"Yes, indeed. I was told at the shipyard that you are a wonderful cook." It was a little lie, but the way her face lit up made it the right thing to do. He stood up politely as she left and then sank back down into the chair as the door closed. His gaze returned to the bay. He could see all the way from the town to the outermost point from his window He scanned the bay to see if the girl was on the water.

He wondered where she could have acquired such skill. *Could she be a pirate or a smuggler?* he mused. *Don't be ridiculous. She is just a girl*, he told himself. Nevertheless, now that he had spare time, he would set out to find out who she was.

It was now late afternoon. The sun was beginning to sink lower in the sky. Will gave his men the letter he had promised, said his goodbyes, and ran down the stairs of the boarding house into the town. There were neat houses of clapboard and a small brick schoolhouse. He could see the lighthouse on the point and in front of it a white church steeple. He took the dirt road past the shipyard out of town and quickly made for the water. He followed the curve of the bay looking for where she had beached her boat. At the top of a hill, he came across a small farm with a barn and a few outbuildings. He took care to avoid it by moving on the edge of the field toward the water. He had no real reason for such stealth, but in the words of Falstaff, caution was indeed preferable to rash bravery. *Oh, shut up, Will*, he said to himself. *No one here would be impressed to hear you quoting Shakespeare. They probably haven't even heard of him.*

He looked across the field, and there she was. He could only see the top of her red head as she was in a deep hole. He once again considered whether she could be a pirate burying booty. *Ah, Will, curb your imagination. You see pirates everywhere. She is a girl who happens to be a phenomenal sailor, that's all.* He eased up to the edge of the hole and looked down. She was covered with dirt and straining at a chain strung round a large stump. Just then, a huge set of paws followed by an even bigger black head appeared, followed by a low growl. *Time to speak up*, he thought, and cleared his throat. Keeping distance from the dog, he asked her if she needed help. She said yes, after a fashion. He jumped into the hole. Helping her was almost as much fun as watching her sail.

And then, next day, at what he chose to think of as her invitation, he went out in the morning to see what Training Day was. He got there just in time to see Fanny destroy the field of riders and speed to the front. *This girl is magnificent*, he thought, and whooped loudly as she crossed the finish line. He was going to need to see her again.

FIVE

WILL APPEARS

AS FANNY STOOD and looked at the mess in the kitchen, she wished she had not told Sara she would do all the chores. She looked out the window. The trees on the edge of the forest were a riot of color. Between the gold of the oaks and the shining red and orange from the other trees, it was like watching a perpetual sunset. Sara was so inspired by the colors, she left at dawn, taking Nate and Joshua with her to collect herbs and barks needed for her dyes. "I will dye cloaks that look like an autumn day. You can have the first one," she told Fanny.

"When will you be back?"

"Who knows?" Nate said. "When Sara has a vision, we just go along with her. For sure we will be back by dark."

Fanny turned in a circle. The bread oven in the stone fireplace needed cleaning. The dishes from the morning meal stood in a basin by the stove. The laundry had been collected in a pile by the front door, and the firebox was empty of wood. Fanny groaned. *I'll start with the animals*, she thought. *I'll get them all fed and the stalls cleaned out, and maybe the dishes will do themselves.*

"I hate kitchen chores," she said aloud. She opened the front door to get her boots and stepped back.

"As do I." A large figure blocked the sunlight.

Oh my, that's him, she thought. *That cheeky fellow from the field with that smile.*

"What–what are you doing here?" Fanny stammered.

"Didn't I say I would be back? William Marston Lowell, Lieutenant of His Majesty's Navy, aboard HMS *Queen's Courage* at your service." He gave a slight bow. "Is this a bad time?" Fanny squinted against the sunlight and took a deep breath.

"Hello. This is not a bad time. Well, it is. I'm in the middle of chores, but it's not, except that I, well, I . . ." Fanny stopped speaking and stood awkwardly. She backed up a few more steps, wishing she had washed the dishes or at least her face. "Did you want to come in?"

"Why, thank you. I was hoping you would ask." He stepped over the threshold and went straight to the fireplace. It was as tall as he was and took up most of the stone north wall of the house. "This is amazing," he said. "You could roast a whole cow on a spit in here."

"Yes, you could, and we have," said Fanny tartly. "This is a fashion of building here in Rhode Island to keep out the north wind in the winter. My father did it himself." Will ran his hand over the closely fitted stones

"And a right fine job it is." He looked around the room again. "Beautiful colors," he said. He touched the scarlet curtains and the cobalt blue tablecloth. "Someone has a gift with dye. You?"

"Oh, no," said Fanny.

"Your mother then?"

"No." she said crossly. "Not that it is any of your business, but I lost my parents to fever last year." She added hastily. "And I do not live here alone. I live with my friends, Nate and Sara, and their son, Joshua. They will be back soon. Anyway, Sara is the expert. I am just learning." Fanny wasn't really scared of being alone with him, but she was nervous about talking.

"I like the effect," he said. "It's cheerful." His eyes fell on two crossed broadswords hanging on the wall. "Beautiful," he said, stepping closer. "These are not ceremonial. They are the real thing."

"I should hope so," said Fanny tartly. "My father made them." She was relieved to have something familiar to talk about. She took one from the wall and threw it to Will, hilt first. "Feel the balance."

"It's perfect," said Will.

"My father was the youngest armorer in Scotland," Fanny said proudly. She took down the other blade.

"Magnificent," said Will, shifting the broadsword from hand to hand.

"Come on," said Fanny and disappeared out the door. By the time Will followed her into the yard, she had tied back her hair and tucked the hem of her skirt into her apron. She spread her legs into a fighting stance.

"You can't really appreciate the workmanship until you have crossed it with another blade. Come on."

Will didn't move. *I can't fight with a woman. I'll hurt her*, he thought.

She waggled her blade at him. "Surely you can handle a broadsword. Didn't you say you were with the King's Navy?"

"Yes, I did." Will was mesmerized. He had never seen a woman with a broadsword, much less one waving it with apparent skill and strength. He didn't know what to do next. With a wicked swipe in the vicinity of his head, Fanny decided for him. He instinctively raised his blade, and the two swords met with a clang.

"There you go," said Fanny with a grin. She moved lightly from side to side then swung again. This time, Will was ready. He parried and followed with a thrust of his own. The swords crashed together again and again as they circled the yard. Dolly came off the porch with a bound to join in the new game. She pounced and nipped joyfully at their feet.

"Where did you learn to handle a sword?" *Clang! Clang!* They went forward and back, trading advantage.

"My father taught all the boys in his village, but when he came here, there was no one to teach." *Clang!* Will sneaked a blow under Fanny's guard, but she twisted at the last second. "Oh, no, you don't!" she shouted.

Will stepped back, panting. He couldn't believe he was sparring with a woman, with broadswords, and he was tired. Fanny, sensing his fatigue, stepped in with an overhead blow to disarm. It would have worked, but at the final instant, Will thrust his sword upward and they stood hilt to hilt, both unwilling to yield. Their muscles quivered, drops of sweat rolled down their cheeks. Their eyes were locked and unblinking. Suddenly, Will was distracted by the thought that he had not seen eyes that shade of green ever before. That momentary lapse was all Fanny needed to flip his sword out of his grip and across the yard. "Ha! Ha!" Fanny shouted triumphantly

"Well, I'm glad that's over," said Will. "I was afraid I was going to have to lop off your head."

"As if you could," said Fanny with a snort.

"You are right. I cannot deny it." Will shook his head. "You are formidable."

Fanny allowed herself a small smile. "Thank you. As I said, my father used to teach all the boys in his village, but when he came here there was no one to teach. It seems boys in Rhode Island don't fight with broadswords," she said scornfully. "So, in order not to lose his skill, he taught Mother and then me." Fanny's eyes sparkled at the memory. "His favorite exercise was to put a sword in each hand and have me and Ma attack from opposite sides. It was great fun." Fanny's eyes shone, and Will was once again drawn in. She sat on the porch steps. "Father also thought that this far from town we should be able to defend ourselves. It seems there are pirates, brigands, and smugglers up and down this coastline."

"I know," said Will. "That is why I am here."

"You are a pirate?" asked Fanny with a laugh.

"No, as I said, I am an officer on HMS *Queen's Courage*. We are sweeping the coastline for pirates."

"I don't think so," said Fanny. "You are standing in my yard, and panting like my dog, Dolly."

"Ah, that's her name." Will rubbed Dolly's ears. "As I said before, we are in drydock in your boatyard. We took a bad hit in that last storm."

"I wondered why I had never seen you before," said Fanny.

"Do the pirates come inland?" Will asked.

"Not so much, but the farm is so close to the bay, Father didn't want to take any chances. Most of the raids have been on the docks in town. They fire a few rounds, clear out a warehouse, and are back on their ship before the militia can get their guns loaded. Bunch of stinking cowards, I say. I wish they would make a try at us here. I'd show them a real fight." Fanny cut the air with her sword.

"I've no doubt," said Will. "For now, could we leave the swordplay and perhaps take a walk?"

Fanny looked at him, momentarily confused. "A walk?"

"Yes. You know, a stroll . . . together. Maybe I could show you my ship? She is a mess and in pieces, but still beautiful."

"Oh, um, alright, but I have to do my chores first."

"I'll help."

"No. That's alright."

Will ignored Fanny's protest and followed her into the house. He looked around, saw the empty firebox, and said, "I'll start at the wood pile. Then I'll join you when you are ready to tend to the animals." By the time Fanny got out to the barn, the firebox was full, he had pulled down hay for Fiona, slopped the hogs, and scattered the chicken feed. *How did he do all that so fast?* she wondered.

"There we go! Shall we have that walk now?" Fanny was so flustered she could barely speak.

"I think, um, well, I don't know, I don't think I can. I may have to help Sara with lunch."

"Another time then," said Will. "I will be back soon. By the way, that horse race you won was fantastic!"

He left, leaving Fanny to ask herself, somewhat dazed, *Who is this fellow?*

SIX

GERALD & GRAHAM CAMPBELL

ONE MORNING THE next week, Will appeared again. Fanny introduced him to Sara but was again so flustered in his presence, she didn't know what to say, so she decided to take him hunting.

"Be back in time for dinner!" Sara called from the doorway, a twinkle in her eye.

"Do you know how to shoot?" Fanny asked.

"Of course, I do. I am military, and I am English. Either one would qualify me as a shooter, an expert, I might add."

Fanny snorted in derision. "We shall see about that."

They tramped through the woods in an uncomfortable silence. But after a while, the sun dappling through the trees and the soft, slightly cool breeze had them both relaxed. Dolly trotted along beside them, and when she alerted, they both took aim and fired. Before the morning was over, they had bagged two brace of pheasants and impressed each other with their shooting skills. They brought them back to the cabin and gave them to Sara. She was thrilled with the bounty.

"This is wonderful. We will roast them with some new squash and potatoes. Go outside and rest. You have earned it. Will, you will stay for the meal."

Sara shooed them out of the cabin with a smile. Fanny and Will sat on the steps and watched as the sky changed with the clouds. This would become a favorite pastime, but for now, it was uncomfortable for Fanny to be sitting so close and so still to this big, odd man. She tried to think of a way to make conversation but could only think of one thing.

"Where are you staying?" *Oh, my,* she thought to herself, *how boring and banal. I do not know how to chat!* Will didn't seem to think so. He perked up as though happy to have something to talk about.

"We found a boarding house run by a woman named Mrs. Da Silva."

"Oh, please give her our regards. She was very kind to my father and his brother when they first arrived in Lymington." Fanny started to relax. Maybe this chatting thing wasn't so hard after all.

"I shall tell her you said so. Maybe she will like me better if I use your name." Fanny socked him in the arm and laughed.

"Don't be daft. She will never like you. You are British."

"And why is that a problem?"

"Her husband's ship was attacked by a British warship, and he was killed. It was a Portuguese fishing vessel, but they mistook it for a pirate ship."

"That explains it. She is happy enough for the boarders, but I got the feeling she wished I would go away. I can't really blame her." Will shifted uncomfortably and abruptly changed the subject. "How did your father end up here? I can't imagine that he was in Scotland, and one day he said, 'Oh, I think I will go to a place I have never heard of on the other side of the world.'" Fanny socked him in the arm once more. "You are going to have to stop doing that, or I will not be able to use my sword arm again."

"Then you are going to have to stop saying stupid things. I will tell you this story, but only if you keep your mouth shut." Will put his hand over his mouth and made an unsuccessful attempt to look contrite. Fanny looked away so he wouldn't see her laughing. She began the story.

"Dad was Clan Campbell and very proud of it. But when the Jacobite uprising began, a good half of his clan went against King George and supported Bonnie Prince Charlie."

"The Stuart pretender to the throne, right?" Will interjected without thinking. Fanny made to sock him again. He winced.

"That is not the belief in this household. Now, you will shut up or I will not tell you this story, and it is a very good one." Will tried on his contrite face once more.

"Oh, stop it," said Fanny. "You look ridiculous!" She stood up on the top step and looked down at Will. "I am going to tell this story the way my dad did, so please imagine I have a thick Scottish brogue, and do not say a word."

"You are very strict, but I shall comply." Fanny went to raise her fist again but put it down when Will once more covered his mouth.

"This is what Dad would say every time he told it: 'The first thing to remember is that we are Campbells and proud of it! My brother, Graham, and I both had trades that we loved. He was a shipbuilder, and I was the youngest armorer in all Scotland. My steel was exceptional for a reason. One day, a Romany Traveler stopped by my forge with a broken axle on one of his wagons. He did most of the work himself and was masterful with the anvil and hammer. I enjoyed watching him work, and it was such an easy job I didn't have the heart to charge him. A few months later he came by with a nice fat hare as a thank you, and we drank a tankard of ale together. He told me his name was Jack Douglas, and this was the first time he had shared a drink with a Highlander. He said that his kind didn't usually mix with ours. From then on, we were friends. He would come and work the forge with me from time to time, and we would share our ways of working. He showed me some Romany forging secrets that I incorporated into my work. My swords got better and better, holding the edge longer, never weakening in battle and very seldom needing to be refurbished. I owe that all to Jack. We called it the perfect blend of Romany magic and Scottish steel.'"

"Wait," said Will. "Your father believed in magic?"

"Of course he did. So do I. Now hush." Will looked befuddled, and she continued with the story.

"'When the Jacobite uprising began, Jack took his family south to the lowlands, but told me where to find him if I ever needed help.

'The uprising went badly from the start. The fighting was hard and long, and we did not have the same resources as the British. Graham came up from the shipyard to fight beside me, which made it a bit easier, but it was still a little bit of hell every day. Then came the terrible day of Culloden. We were all worn out and practically starving because there was no way to get supplies through the British lines. The battle took place in a low marsh covered in mist.

"'What idiot chose this spot to make a stand?' Graham asked. I told him to shut up, that it had been the choice of our prince. He shook his head, said we were in very deep trouble, and he was right. We had been placed in the rear guard to protect the prince, in case the Brits got through our front lines. The battle was a rout from the start. They had a hundred times as many men. The first wave cut down our men in an instant and was followed by a second and a third in quick succession. Our men were dying left and right. The smell of gunpowder and blood made the air unbreathable, and the mist from the marsh meant we couldn't see anything. We were going to stand our ground, but the commander of our group shouted for us to retreat. He was then cut down by yet another barrage. It seemed the Brits were unstoppable. We thrashed our way through the woods, and when we were about to be overrun, we saw a huge, deep thicket. Graham and I used to play go-hide-in-thickets like that when we were children, so we knew how to navigate the brambles. We got to the middle of the thorns, cut out a small space with our dirks, and settled down to wait our chance to escape. We could hear distant shouts of the bloody Brits as they ran down our clansmen and murdered them as they lay wounded. That day maybe 3,000 or more Scotsmen lost their lives. The rest of us were now being hunted like dogs. When the dark came, Graham and I picked out way through the British lines and headed south. I told Graham we would look for Jack and his caravan, and they would get us to the coast. We came upon them right where Jack said they would be, near a village called Yetholm that was a stop for many Travelers. We rounded the back of the wagon and came upon the tribe sitting around the fire, sharing a stewpot. We were a right mess, but Jack recognized me and invited us to sit. 'Come sit by the yog,' he said. 'We are about to share some rumbledethumps.'"

Will stopped Fanny then with a wave of his hand. "I can't be quiet any longer. What in the name of tarnation are you talking about? Is this some Romany language?" Fanny laughed.

"I wondered when you would finally capitulate. I wasn't being fair, but it was fun to watch your brain try to work it out. *Yog* is the firepit. *Rumbledethumps* is a stew of potatoes, cabbage, and onions. And, by the way, these were not just Romany. These were Romany Lowland Travelers. There is a big difference. Shall I go on?"

"Yes, please," said Will, "but in English as often as possible."

Fanny continued speaking in Graham's voice.

"'We sat by the fire with the whole family, about thirty people of all ages. Jack introduced his wife, Rowen. She eyed us up and down and then shepherded us into the biggest wagon. Two of her sons hauled in a big tub of water.

'Now, off with your clothes and have a wash,' she commanded.

'A wash,' said Graham. 'But it's winter!'

'Yes, it is, and you smell like fetid bog. We wash every day no matter the season, and as long as you are with us, you will as well. Now, I am sorry to say we will have to burn your tartans. No one can know you are from a Highland clan, or it will be death to us all. Now wash.' She swept out of the room followed by her grinning sons.

'Better do as she says,' said the son called Dugan. 'Ma is not to be messed with when she gives an order.' We stripped down and washed as best we could. Luckily, the wagon was warm, and Rowen had left a pile of heavy wool blankets to wrap up in. She soon returned with three daughters and a big bowl of something that looked foul. 'You will not like this,' she said. 'It is a mixture of wood ash, vinegar, and crushed black walnut hulls to dye your hair. Just be glad we aren't Egyptians. They used lye and burnt their scalps. This won't hurt, it just smells bad.'"

"And it did. We sat there naked and wrapped in blankets with black paste on our heads and worried about what would come next. And there it was. More daughters—there seemed be an endless supply of them—appeared with another bowl of paste, this time brown. They smeared it on our faces, arms, chest, and legs and left us once again. We looked at each other for a moment and then howled with laughter. I think we were so tired that we became a bit unhinged.

"After a while, Rowen returned with a pile of clothes. 'I think these will fit,' she said. 'Wash off all of that coloring thoroughly and get dressed. We have heard news of patrols in the area and want to be prepared.'

"Rowen was about to leave when Graham thought to ask a question. 'Rowen, how many children do you have?'

"Twelve of my own and another eight that have been taken in following disasters. We look after our own. No one gets left to fend for themselves. And we also look after our friends. Jack thinks a lot of you, Gerald. That is why we are willing to take the risk to hide you.'

"Graham and I did as we were told, washed clean, then looked at each other with astonishment. We both had black hair and dark brown skin. We got dressed and went out. Jack and Rowen regarded us with a critical eye.

"'Will they pass?' asked Jack.

"'I think so. The blue eyes shouldn't be a problem. We have several of those in our own family.' Rowen looked pleased. Just then a lookout signaled from the top of a hill.

"'They are here. Everyone, sit down and start passing the stewpot. Gerald, you sit here by me. Graham, you go over there and put your arm around Rosalie. Rowen directed us like an army commander, and when the patrol galloped into the camp, all was in place. Jack stood up and faced the leader of the small platoon.

"'What can we do for you gentlemen?'

"'We are hunting down Jacobite escapees. Have you seen anyone?'

"'Just our own family here by the fire.'

"'Well, stay where you are. We are going to have to search your wagons, in case you are lying.'

"'Mind your manners, young man. Do you know who you are speaking to? No? I will tell you. I am direct line from the Faa family. I guess you don't know who they are, either. The Faa are Traveler royalty. Our king, you might say, so treat us politely.'

"Jack was in fine form, gesticulating and orating in front of the fire, distracting the soldiers from all of us huddled around the fire. 'If you would like to search our wagons, do so, but be respectful and tidy.' You could almost hear the soldier about to say yes, sir, but he caught himself and angrily ordered his men to search. 'Why would we hide them?' Jack asked loudly. 'They serve a king no better than yours, and we don't like any of you!'"

"Everyone around the fire laughed, but Rowen.

"'Shut your yob, Jack. Do you want to get us killed?'

"'Sorry, Rowen, they are just such easy stupid targets. I forgot myself.'

"'Stupid easy targets with guns, you idiot. Now, everyone, keep quiet or you will answer to me.' Rowen stood by Jack as the patrol departed without a backward glance.

"'Well, that was lucky,' I said.

"'Not luck, Gerald, Traveler magic.' Jack winked as he spoke. I didn't doubt him for a second, because our heads were not on pikes.

"The caravan packed up and headed for coast. We thanked Jack profusely, and he put us on a Portuguese ship bound for the Americas. The first mate, Raoul Da Silva, was a friend of his and guaranteed we would be well treated. I was never able to repay the kindness of Jack and his family, and I often wonder where they are now.

"The sea crossing was easy. We became part of the crew, and no one seemed to pay attention when the dye washed out of our hair and off our skin. By the time the ship made port in Lymington, we were back to our redhaired Scottish selves."

Fanny sat down on the step. "At this point, Da would always stop, Ma would pour him an ale and say, 'Go on, Gerald, you are almost at the good part, where you meet me.' Da would kiss her and go on with the story."

"On shore, Raoul took us to the boarding house his young wife, Isabella, ran with her parents. They took Graham's watch as payment and promised to give it back as soon as we made some money.

"The next day, Graham got a job at the shipyard and eventually ended up being the head shipwright. I went to work for the town blacksmith as a bellows man. As soon as he realized I had skill with steel, he promoted me to the anvil." Fanny dropped the accent and continued in her own voice.

"The story ends, or begins, with them marrying the two prettiest girls in town, sisters Elspeth and Belinda Northup, my mother and Aunt Biddie. They met at Training Day. Mother watched Da win the race on a borrowed horse, gave him a pie, and that was that. He bought this farm and built this house. Graham built a house in town, and that is the whole story!"

Fanny ended with a flourish and a bow.

"What do you think of that?"

"You tell a wonderful story. How is it you have never given me a pie?"

"I will when you do something to deserve it. Have you won a Training Day race?"

"No, but give me time." He would have said more, but Sara came to the door.

"If you want dinner, I am going to need a bit of help. Will, please draw a bucket from the well, and, Fanny, come roll out the dough for the jam tarts.

Will watched as Fanny went into the house. *That is an exceptional woman*, he thought for the hundredth time, and headed toward the well.

After dinner, Fanny and Will sat on the porch steps. Fanny rested her chin on her knees.

"This was my parents' favorite time of day. After all the chores were done, they would sit and watch the sky go from blue to pink to orange to red and then the beautiful gray twilight. Da said it was the world going for a rest to gird her loins for another day."

Will smiled. "Your father was quite a poet, wasn't he?"

"Yes, he was. He had a gentle spirit, but he could still give a smack with the flat of his blade or worse if anyone disrespected him or his family."

"I think you have an amazing family. I am sorry I will never get to meet your parents."

"I am too. I hate to say this, but they would have liked you!" Will caught her eye in a sideways glance.

"I think you just paid me a compliment, Miss Campbell."

"Did I? Must have been an accident." Fanny smiled to herself as she looked away. They both watched the remnants of the sunset in silence.

SEVEN

NATE & SARA

THE FIRST SNOW hadn't really stayed. A bit of it clung to the bare branches and tipped the ends of the evergreens. Little piles at the bottom of the steps and at the corners of the house were still there for snowball fights. It had made the air crisp and invigorating. Fanny burst into the kitchen with Will at her heels, gasping for air. "Ha," she said leaning on the wooden table. "I win again. Sara, Will is staying for supper, alright?"

"What a surprise," said Sara, hiding a smile.

"Is it alright, Sara?" Will asked. "I don't want to be a bother."

"Another place at the table is a blessing, never a bother," said Sara. Her serene brown face shone in the heat as she easily hefted the iron pot of stew from its place over the fire. "Joshua, lay out the bowls." Joshua pulled a chair over to the hutch, climbed up, and lifted the bowls out one by one. Fanny pulled the hot biscuits from their pan, placed them in a large wooden bowl, and covered them with a cotton towel.

"May I help?" Will asked.

"Have you recovered sufficiently?" Fanny retorted.

"You can get the milk pitcher from the cellar," said Sara. Will looked around a hatch.

"Where would that be, Sara?"

"Under the house, eejit. Where else?" Fanny said as she flicked her towel at Will.

"I'll show you, Will," Joshua yelled as he pushed Will out the back door. Fanny laughed.

"Must you devil that poor boy, Fanny? I'm worried for his health the way you run him ragged."

"Well," said Fanny, "at least he can keep up."

"How long do you think he will be staying?" Sara asked.

"I don't know. They just found more rotted timbers in the ship's hold, so Will thinks maybe until spring." Fanny was quiet for a minute. "Sara, do you think he likes me?"

"Of course, he does. Why else would he put up with your nonsense?"

"No, I mean really likes me, like you and Nate. That kind of liking."

"Well, child, we will just have to wait and see, but I think he'd be a fool not to. Do you like him that way?"

Fanny sat on the stool by the fire and pulled her knees up to her chest. "I think so. I don't know. I have so many feelings inside me I feel like a bloated cow."

"Oh, my, that is a very romantic comparison." Sara laughed as she began to ladle the stew into the bowls. "I can just say this: The first time I saw Nate, my breath stopped and I almost fainted. Then I threw an apple at him for surprising me. We were both slaves on the same plantation, but this was the first time we met. And of course, you know the rest."

"Oh Sara, I just can't imagine how terrible it was being a slave."

Sara looked down at her workworn hands and gave a faint smile. "Yes, it was terrible. More terrible than you could ever imagine, and I don't want you to. Nate made it all more bearable. We were married in secret by a shaman in the woods and couldn't let the master know we were together. But we are here now, and that is all in the past." Fanny put her arms around Sara just as Nate walked in. He touched Sara's hand, then sat heavily in his chair at the end of the table, looking despondent.

"How did it go?" Sara asked gently.

"Well, I don't know," replied Nate, reaching into his pocket. "How does this look?" He pulled out a bag of coins and laid it on the table. It landed with a loud thump.

"You did it!" Fanny shouted. "You sold them all."

"That I did. Every single cow and for the price we wanted." Nate allowed himself to smile and then reached into his pocket again. "I know the money is important for the farm, but here is the real present." He laid a handful of taffy, twisted in waxed paper, next to the bag of coins.

"Oh," said Fanny, opening the twist and popping one in her mouth. "Heaven!" Joshua burst in the door with a shout.

"Daddy!" Joshua landed in his father's lap with a single leap. "You brought candies! Hooray!"

"Only one now, child. We still have stew to eat," Sara said as she laid the bowls on the table. They were filled with a rich, brown stew made from yams, corn, and ham. Will entered with a large enamel pitcher and put it in the middle of the table.

"Everybody is smiling so widely. Are we celebrating something?" he asked.

"Nate sold the herd," Fanny replied. "And now we can buy another bull, some new seed, and maybe . . ."

"More chickens," Joshua shouted. "I need more chickens."

"Yes, you shall have more chickens." Fanny smiled. "Today is a great day for this family. Will, sit here next to Joshua. I am going to tell you my favorite story. I like this one best because it has a happy ending and a lot of them don't."

"Eat your dinner, Miss Fanny," said Nate.

Fanny laughed. "Just so you know, Will, he only calls me 'Miss Fanny' when he thinks I'm being too bold."

"Not too bold, Miss Fanny, only too loud."

"Nate, dear," Sara interrupted. "She will tell the story, so you might as well let her." Fanny grinned.

"So, you always get your way, is that it?" asked Will. Fanny grinned again, enjoying herself hugely.

"I believe what I am is persistent in the pursuit of my chosen goals."

"Ah, persistent," murmured Will. "A fancy word for stubborn."

Fanny tossed a biscuit in his direction. "Do you want to hear my story or not, ya dobber?"

He caught the biscuit with one hand, split it open with a single move, and dropped it in his bowl. "Indeed, I do. It is your favorite one, after all. But first, what did you just call me?"

"*Dobber* is a fine Scottish word for idiot," said Fanny primly. "Shall I begin?"

Nate filled the cups with milk, Sara passed the biscuits, and Fanny leaned back in her chair and began. "It started with Fiona, my horse. From the time I could walk, Daddy said she was mine. We were the same age, born almost on the same day. Daddy said we were linked for life. Anyway, we were now ten, and Fiona was very sick. Daddy couldn't figure out what was wrong. She wouldn't eat or drink, and her mouth was all foamy. Daddy even spent money to have the horse doctor come and look at her. He told Daddy to save his money; there was nothing to be done. That night, she lay down and wouldn't get up. I stayed in her stall and fell asleep with my arm around her neck." Fanny's eyes filled with tears as she spoke. "Daddy carried me up to my bed sometime in the night, and Mamma covered me with a quilt with all my clothes on. When I heard Jimmy, the rooster, crowing at dawn, I leapt out of bed and ran for the barn. Mamma followed me, and Daddy was already on his way. When he opened the barn door, there was this man, black as coal, standing in Fiona's stall, wearing rags and no shoes."

"Sara," Nate leaned over and whispered, "Am I black as coal?"

"Yes, my love, you surely are."

"Do not interrupt me!" Fanny said, as she tried not to laugh. "This is the best part. May I continue? Standing right behind this very strange man was Fiona. She was drinking from her water bag, right as rain."

"'I'm sorry, sir,' the man said. 'I passed the night in your barn. I will be moving on.'

"I ran past him and hugged Fiona's neck. As the man turned to go, my father said, 'Wait, how is it that our horse, who seemed dying last night, is up and about today, without a care?'

"'Oh, you see, sir, she was severe gastric, is all. I gave her some brewed willow bark and herbs I carry and rubbed her belly for a bit, and she came just fine.'

"'Where did you learn horse healing, son?' my father asked. The man paused and took a deep breath.

"'In Virginia, sir.'

"'I see,' said Daddy. 'I take it you are escaped!'

"The man drew himself up with a sigh. 'Yes, sir, I most certainly am.'

"'Good, well done!' said Daddy. 'Did you have a place you were headed?'

"'No sir,' said the man.

"'Better still,' said Daddy. 'I would be obliged if you would stay here and help look after the animals. For that, I will pay you with room and board. Then, when we bring in the crop, you will be paid a fair percentage for helping me in the field. Would that suit you?'

"'Yes, sir, it would.'

"'What is your name, son?'

"'Nathanial, sir, but my friends call me Nate.'

"'Nate it is, then. Mother, can we please set another place for breakfast? We have company.'

"Mamma put her arm around Nate's shoulders and guided him toward the house. 'We will be more than happy to share our table with you, young man. Fanny, show him where to wash up and give him a clean towel.'

"And that is how we all came to be sitting here around this table," said Fanny proudly.

"Will, may I serve you more stew?" asked Sara.

"Yes, please. It is exceedingly delicious." Sara got up from the table and dished out from the iron pot.

"I like that story a lot," said Will. "I'm sorry I never got to meet your parents."

"You would have gotten on uncommonly well," said Fanny.

"I know." Will smiled. "I see both your parents all around this table."

"Daddy, tell him about me and Mamma and the secret Virginia trip." Joshua bounced up and down with excitement.

"Not tonight, son. We will save that story so Will has a reason to come back."

Will winked at Fanny, making her duck her head, cheeks flaming. "Oh, I have a reason," he said. "The story will just be another one."

EIGHT

INTO TOWN

LATE FALL HAD turned the bay a dark gray but had not diminished at all the pleasure Fanny and Will took in sailing. Will now felt almost like part of the family. He had been showing up to help with chores on almost a daily basis. Sometimes he and Fanny would hunt or fish. Today, they were sailing for fun. The boat scudded over the choppy water, flying directly toward shore. Dolly stood the bow like a figurehead, her fur flattened by the breeze. "Shall we slow?" Will yelled above the wind. Fanny shook her head and snorted as she hauled on the tiller, keeping the boat in a straight line. Will laughed and tightened his grip on the boom line. Fanny's hair blew out behind her. To Will, it looked like a shining copper flag.

Just then, Fanny maneuvered the boat halfway up the sand with a bump.

"Look alive," she said to Will, who, fixed on Fanny's hair, almost lost his grip. She flung her skirts over her arm and jumped to the sand from the bow. "Will you be giving me a hand here?" she asked over her shoulder.

"It doesn't look as though you need one." Will made his way forward. "But just so no one takes me for less than a gentleman, I am at your service." As he jumped on the sand, Will lost his balance. His arms windmilled hopelessly, the sand slipped from beneath his feet, and he landed on his back like a turtle. Just to add to his predicament, Dolly jumped out of the boat onto his chest and took off up the hill. Fanny shook her head. Will's breath punched out of his mouth like a bark.

"Are you imitating Dolly? Joshua always tells me you are funny. Is this what he is talking about?"

"It's your fault, you know," said Will. "You distract me. And I think Dolly hates me." He attempted a rise and fell back yet again. Fanny's grin became a guffaw.

"My fault?" she managed to get out. "All I'm trying to do is beach my boat, which would go a lot faster if a certain clumsy oaf would quit horsing around and get his carcass out of the water."

"Then take pity on me and give me a hand. I promise I will coil all the lines."

"Ah, yes," said Fanny, "but will you do it properly?"

"Well, I am a naval officer, so I have had a bit of practical experience. Come on, Fanny, have a heart. My britches are full of sand." Relenting, Fanny grabbed Will's hand and hauled him upright. He rose from the shore break with bits of kelp hanging from his buttons. Just as he took a step onto dry land, a small wavelet hit him from behind. He stumbled backward, grabbing Fanny's waist as he fell. Try as she might to stay upright, Fanny landed beside him, face first in the bay. She instantly rose from the water like a vengeful sea dragon, eyes flashing, hair whipping back with a sharp spray of water.

"You did that on purpose!"

"I never," Will choked.

"What did you say?"

"I never . . ." Will couldn't continue.

"Are you laughing at me?"

"I am."

"Well, stop it right now!"

Will doubled over, his nose almost touching the water. "That is by far the funniest thing I have seen since the day you fell on your face in the pigsty."

"And now that you mention it, that was your fault too!" Fanny spun around to stalk from the water, got her petticoats wrapped around her ankles, and sat down with a splash. Will laughed so hard he fell over sideways, knocking Fanny to her back. And that was where Joshua found them, lying on their backs in the bay laughing like loons. "Why are you in the water?" he asked.

"Why not," said Will. "Want to join us?"

"No." Joshua stepped back quickly. "Mamma said I was to fetch you both right quick. Aren't you cold?"

"Yes, we are," said Fanny.

"Freezing," said Will, and they both howled with laughter all over again.

Grown-ups are very strange, Joshua thought. He moved to the edge of the water and tugged at Fanny's dripping sleeve. "You have to come now. Mamma says Aunt Biddy has gone missing." Fanny was out of the water in a flash.

"Will, you square away the boat, please. I'm going to saddle Fiona. I'll meet you at the stable." She was up the hill and gone before Will could ask any of his thousand questions.

"You had better hurry up," said Joshua. "She can saddle Fiona in a wink."

"Joshua, will you ask your mother to bring some dry clothes to the stable for Fanny? I have dry britches in my pack. We can't go into town like drowned rats. We are going into town, aren't we?"

"Can't say," said Joshua, and disappeared up the hill.

Things change very quickly around here, Will said to himself. *I shall have to pay closer attention. And who in tarnation is Aunt Biddy?*

When Will reached the stable, Fanny was in the saddle.

"You can ride behind me."

"Thank you," said Will. "I'd prefer that to running alongside. Do I have time to change my britches?"

"No, they'll dry as we ride. Climb on."

Will swung up easily behind Fanny. "Where are we going? And who is Aunt Biddy?"

Fanny guided Fiona down the lane at a brisk pace. Dolly ran alongside them. Will gripped the saddle behind his back. "Oh, just hold on to me, will you?" said Fanny. "I won't break, and if you fall off, I won't stop to pick you up." Will wrapped his arms around Fanny's waist. She could feel the heat from his hands through her damp singlet. She grasped the reins tighter. Will smelled her sea-clean hair as it blew over his face. It was hard to concentrate. He felt Fanny's muscles move as she kicked Fiona into a gallop. He slipped sideways and righted himself.

"Who is Aunt Biddy?" he shouted over her shoulder.

"I told you about her before. Don't you remember anything?" Worry had made Fannys tone sharp. "My mother's sister. She has lived with her other sister, my Aunt Maude, since her husband died."

"And why are we looking for her?" Fanny's hair slapped across Will's face. He moved it aside. As Fanny felt his hand in her hair, a shiver went across her shoulders.

"Are you cold?" Will asked. "I'll give you my jacket."

"I'm in wet clothes, thanks to you," she replied tartly. "And I don't want your jacket. I'm fine." She hunkered over Fiona's neck and didn't speak again until she slipped from the horse and tied her to a post in front of the mercantile. "Uncle Graham was killed in an accident at the boatyard a few years back, and sometimes Aunt Biddy goes looking for him." She shot a hard look behind her. "It's not like she's crazy or anything. She just misses him and sometimes forgets." Fanny glared in Will's direction, daring him to disagree. "I talk to my parents. Do you think that's crazy?"

Will touched Fanny's hand. "Not one bit. Let's find your Aunt Biddy and bring her home." Fanny turned and strode down the dusty street, not wanting Will to see that her eyes were wet. Will trailed in her wake like a pilot fish. She swept her head from side to side, peering across the low wooden buildings and narrow alleys. Lymington had grown from a one-road village into a small town in the past few years. More and more settlers were arriving from England and Ireland, Portugal, and even some from France.

"I haven't been in town in a while," Fanny said as she stopped in the middle of the street. "Everything looks different."

"How about you go up to the top of the street and I'll go down?" said Will. "We can cover more ground that way."

"Good plan! Aunt Biddy is very tiny with curly hair and probably a lace cap on top," said Fanny, and took off up the street and yelled over her shoulder, "Look in the boatyard. She used to take him his supper there. That's where we found her last time."

'Right," said Will, and started toward the bay. "Fanny," he called out, "I talk to my father all the time."

"Really, truly?" She turned back. "You aren't just saying that so I won't look a fool?" They came together again in the middle of the street.

"Not likely." said Will. "Both my parents are gone, and when I am on watch, I talk to them all night. I miss them fierce. It was because of my pa I took to the sea. He taught me to sail as soon as I could see over the gunwales."

"My pa too," said Fanny. "He was a brilliant sailor." Her hands flew to her mouth. "Oh, my God! I'm standing here jawing and forgot Aunt Biddy. Meet me at the mercantile in an hour."

Fanny ran off, skirts flying, leaving Will, his mouth open, about to speak. Fanny ran up and down the streets. She poked her head into shops, the butcher, the mercantile, and asked if anyone had seen Biddy. The answer was always no. Fanny was starting to feel frantic. This wasn't that big a town. Where could she be? She paused in front of the tavern. She didn't think Aunt Biddy would ever go in there, but she was running out of options.

Fanny pushed open the low door. Dolly came with her and then sat to the side, watching the room. Fanny couldn't imagine why Aunt Biddy would be in the tavern, but she had looked everywhere else. The sod walls were rough and damp and made the room smell like a plowed field. Fanny didn't mind that, but mixed with stale ale, it was unpleasant at best. In the dim light from the hearth fire, Fanny scanned the room. Across one wall was a bar built from old ship planks. The ceiling was hung with lobster traps, glass floats, and odd bits of hemp. Several men leaned on the bar with tankards of ale. Fanny suddenly realized how she must look, with her wild hair and her damp clothes. No wonder they were staring. Fanny took another step into the room and spotted Aunt Biddy at a small table in the corner. She was so tiny she looked like a child with grey curls peeking out from her white lace cap and a dreamy smile on her lips. A man with a leather apron came from behind the bar.

"She's been sitting there all day," he said. "Is she yours?"

"Yes," said Fanny. "Has she said anything at all?"

"Sure, she asked for a cup of tea and told me to tell Graham she was here. I know Graham from the boatyard passed a while back, but I had never met his missus, so I wasn't sure if it was her."

"What did you do?"

"Well, I gave her a cuppa, didn't I? And I said as soon as that fellow showed up, I'd send him right over. A' course that was hours ago. Just now when I asked her did she want anything, she just smiled and nods like this." He bobbed his head. "Truth be told, I was getting a bit worried."

"Thank you," said Fanny. "I'll take her home now." Fanny walked toward the table and a burst of laughter came from the bar. "Hi, Aunt Biddy," she said with a big smile. "Time to go home."

"Oh, Fanny, dear, I was just waiting on Graham. It's time for his tea, you know."

"Yes, Auntie, I do know. That's why I came to fetch you. He's waiting at home." Fanny helped Aunt Biddy to her feet. A drunken man peeled off from the group at the bar.

"Hey there, missy. Why don't you dump the old crone and join us for a splash?" He waved his tankard around. Some of it came over the side and down his arm. He didn't notice.

"No, thank you," said Fanny. She took Aunt Biddy by the arm and gently pulled her toward the door.

"Ah, come on," said the drunk. "It won't hurt to have one drink. You're already a mess." The men at the bar laughed raucously.

"Right you are, Seth. She's a sloppy one, she is. Looks like she crawled out of a keg, don't she?" Fanny ignored them and kept moving. When they were almost to the door, Aunt Biddy stopped by the man in the leather apron.

"Thank you for the tea, young man. May I pay you now?"

"Nah, consider it a gift." he said.

"Well," said Aunt Biddy, "I will be sure to mention to my husband, Graham, that there is a gentleman right down the street."

The men at the bar had sidled a bit closer by now. "Miss," said the barkeep, "I think you should move on quick. That gang from the docks has been drinking all day, and they weren't a pretty bunch to begin with." He held the door open, and Fanny led Aunt Biddy out onto the porch. Dolly, growling low in her throat, followed.

"Hey, wait." The loud drunk named Seth lurched past the barkeep. He was tall, skinny, and reeked of ale. "What's the matter, little missy? Too good to have a drink with us, are you?" He loomed over Fanny, who had bent to help her tiny aunt down the stairs. She stood to her full height, looking the man right in the eye.

"Go back to your friends, sir. Anything else will be a mistake."

"Oh, will it?" he said with a leer. He made a grab at her, and Fanny slapped his hand away. Dolly planted her feet apart, preparing to jump, the low growl getting louder. Seth was so drunk he didn't even notice.

"I'm warning you." Fanny's eyes narrowed.

"She's warning me, lads," he said, and quick as a snake he grabbed her by the hair. The barkeep started toward them, shouting.

"Leave her be, Seth."

Just as fast, Fanny grabbed the drunk's wrist and bent it toward her until he released her hair with a roar. Before he could move, she punched him in the head on the right, then the left for good measure. He crumpled in a heap at her feet, moaning. Dolly put both paws on his chest and held him down, her bared teeth close to his face.

"I told you it would be a mistake," she said. "Come on, Aunt Biddy." Seth's friends gaped from the bar.

Aunt Biddy smiled and nodded. "Thank you again, sir," she said.

"No problem," said the barkeep with a smile. "It was worth it to see Seth Barker put in his place. And wait one minute. Are you Gerald Campbell's little girl?"

"Yes, I am," Fanny smiled.

"Well, didn't you grow up just fine. I haven't seen you since you were a little bit. Your da was a grand fellow. Didn't spend much time in my place, mind you, but always a kind word or a how-de-doo. And the first one to put his hand out to help. I was real sorry to hear the fever got him and your ma. Kevin O'Herlihy here. You ever need a hand, you remember my name."

"Thank you," said Fanny with a touch to his arm. As she turned to go, Dolly gave a final growl and put herself at Fanny's heel. Seth, being the drunken idiot that he was, lurched to his feet and made as if to hit Fanny from behind. Instead, he flew down the stairs and landed on his face in the dirt.

"I believe the lady is not interested," said Will. "You best keep yourself in check or she might hurt you again. Ladies, may I escort you home?" He offered his arm to Aunt Biddy.

"Thank you, young man," she said, oblivious to the chaos around her. "You have very nice manners."

Fanny grinned. "Thank you, Will. I probably couldn't have taken them all."

"Oh, I don't know. You were doing fine from where I stood. I just stepped in so as to meet this lovely lady."

"Fanny, where are your manners?" Aunt Biddy chirped.

"So sorry, Aunt Biddy. May I present William Marston Lowell?"

"Oh, good. That sounds like a fine Scottish name. My Graham is Scottish, you know." Aunt Biddy clapped her hands as she spoke.

"Ah, well," said Will. "I'm sorry I am not Scottish but rather English."

"No matter," said Aunt Biddy. "We are all cousins anyway, my husband, Graham, always says. Even those bloody British. You must come have tea with us. He will enjoy meeting you." Fanny and Will exchanged glances.

"I would be honored," said Will.

The trio walked up a path to a white clapboard house. Dolly followed, her tail waving proudly like a flag. The door banged open. Aunt Maude, as tall and spare as Aunt Biddy was short and round, flew down the steps.

"There you are. Where have you been? I was so worried."

"Maude, dear," said Aunt Biddy, "Could you set the tea for Graham and these lovely children? I think I need to lie down for a spell." With that, Aunt Biddy toddled into the house, closing the door behind her.

"Well, I never!" Aunt Maude sputtered. "Not even a by-your-leave. Where was she?"

"In the tavern."

Aunt Maude turned to Fanny in shock. "The tavern? What on earth was she doing there?"

"Perhaps she went for a pint," said Fanny. "That's a joke, Aunt Maude."

"Well, I never. I'll have to keep closer watch,"

"Or go to the tavern with her," said Will. Fanny elbowed him sharply.

"And who are you with your cheeky tongue, sir?"

"Aunt Maude," Fanny jumped in, "this is my friend William Lowell, officer on the *Queen's Courage*."

"It is lovely to meet you, Miss Maude, and may I please apologize for my cheeky tongue? I had no call." He scraped a low bow. Aunt Maude looked him up and down.

"Well, I never, I'm sure," she said, and went into the house.

"Not much of a talker, is she?" said Will.

"Oh, I don't know, you may charm her into being a real chatterbox."

Aunt Maude stuck her head out the door. "You two come in the house before the tea goes cold."

"See," said Fanny. "It's working already."

The door slammed, then opened again. "And leave that dog on the porch. She always sticks her nose in the biscuits."

NINE

TEA WITH BIDDY & MAUDE

THE TINY HOUSE was spotless with a lace doily on every surface. Will picked one up. "This is beautiful work. Whose is it?"

"Mine," said Aunt Maude. "Don't stain them with your dirty hands."

"I shall wash up directly," said Will. "You know, this is as fine as any tatting out of France." Will ducked out the door, leaving Aunt Maude pink-cheeked and frowning.

"Well, Fanny Campbell, what is going on? Popping into town with a strange man. What will people think?"

"Aunt Maude, he is not strange. Nate and Sara like him, and he has been helping us at the farm for weeks now."

"But who is he? Who are his people?"

"May I answer that?" Will stepped through the door and stood at attention. "Ma'am, I am Lieutenant William Marston Lowell of Her Majesty's vessel the *Queen's Courage*, which is in drydock in your boatyard at this moment. I hail from Plymouth, Devon. I have one brother, and we are orphans. My father was a master shipbuilder. My father took my mother on a short testing run of a new ship. Just outside the harbor they were attacked and sunk by pirates. Now, aboard the *Queen's Courage*, I hunt the scurvy devils and give them their just reward."

"You don't say! Sit down, young man. Tell me how you came to our town." Will sat on the edge of the wooden bench. Fanny stood back, fascinated. She had never seen Aunt Maude as taken with anyone before.

"Well, ma'am, we had a bit of bad luck that turned out well. Our ship was stove in on the reef outside the bay. The good part came when the hole revealed an undetected rotting throughout the hull. We have been waiting for the lumber needed to finish the job. In the meantime, I have had the pleasure of spending time with the rest of your family. And now I am grateful for the same pleasure here in your fine company." Fanny rolled her eyes. Aunt Maude smiled.

"Please sit, sir. I want to hear how goes your hunt for pirates." Aunt Maude glided out of the room with a backward smile.

Fanny almost gasped aloud. "How did you do that?" she asked. "Aunt Maude doesn't like anyone, and she never smiles."

"Natural charm?" Will asked.

"More like hot wind and beans," said Fanny.

"Hello, hello. What have we here? A party?" Aunt Biddy bounced into the room, nicely refreshed from her nap.

"Aunt Maude invited us to stay for tea, Auntie."

"Well, how nice. And who is your friend?" Fanny winced.

"William Lowell, ma'am. A pleasure to meet you." Will stepped in smoothly, taking Aunt Biddy's hand. "May I offer you a seat?" He guided her into the wingback chair at the corner of the room. Aunt Maude entered with a laden tea tray.

"I'll take that, Aunt," said Fanny.

"Thank you, dear. Biddy, William here was just about to tell us about his encounters with pirates. His ship hunts them."

"Oh, my. Isn't that dangerous?" Aunt Biddy's eyes sparkled. "Graham would have loved that. He had no patience for fellows that disobeyed the law, no, indeed."

Fanny laid out the tea cups. "Shall I pour, Aunt Maude?"

"Please, dear. Go on, Mr. Lowell."

Will took the delicate china cup from Fanny and had a small sip. "I'll tell you of our last encounter. It was a good one, though the ship got away. We were sailing upwind of the Channel Islands, just south of Virginia. It was a foggy day with not much breeze. Without warning, out of the gray, a ship appeared off our starboard bow. As soon as she spotted us, she raised a black flag with a bloody rose in the center and opened her gun ports. We did the same and fired away.

"All of a sudden, the wind died, and there we were, two great ships, prepared for battle and becalmed. We fired again, but the distance was too great, and with nothing to bring us around, we had no choice but to keep up a barrage and hope for wind. Cannon balls flew, but none landed. It was a strange standoff. Finally, they stopped, as did we, and we just looked at each other across the water. Then, their captain came up to the fo'c's'le and lifted a wine glass in our direction. He had the crew haul out some planks. They covered the planks with what looked like white linen and set this 'table' with silver. I looked through the spyglass in amazement. The pirate captain then called his men down from the mast and the rigging, and the entire crew proceeded to eat dinner on deck. It looked like they were eating beef. When the meal was done, the whole ship turned and raised a glass in toast in our direction. Our captain was outraged, but there was nothing to be done.

"When it was dark, we heard music coming from the pirate vessel and the sound of laughter. It went on most of the night. I was on duty at dawn when the calm ended and the wind freshened. We sprang into action, but the pirate ship caught the first wind and disappeared as though it had never been there at all. What do you think of that?"

Aunt Maude and Aunt Biddy were enthralled, but Fanny laughed.

"Did you make that up, Will? A bloody rose? Really!"

"On my honor as an officer, that is the truth." Will smiled at Fanny, and her knees trembled.

"My, my," said Aunt Biddy. "I didn't know pirates drank from glasses. It seems so civilized." Aunt Maude held out the plate. "Would you eat some more cake, William?"

TEN

A MAGIC CHESTNUT TREE

THE DAY BEFORE Christmas, Fanny and her whole extended family, including Will, went into the forest to mark the perfect tree. Joshua ran ahead, kicking at the snow. Nate and Sara walked arm in arm, and Will and Fanny lobbed snowballs at each other. They would wait to cut the tree tomorrow, so it would be fresh. That night, they sat in front of the fire and made decorations out of twists of colored paper, bark, fabric, and pine cones. Fanny couldn't remember feeling so content and happy.

"Fanny, what are you thinking with that silly smile on your face?" Will teased.

"I'm thinking to rub your face in the snow the next time we go outside so you will think twice about calling me silly."

Fanny threw a pine cone at his head. He ducked, and it hit Nate instead. "Nate, I am so sorry! I really wasn't aiming at you. Honestly, I wasn't. I was aiming at the nincompoop in front of you, but the big coward ducked."

"Mamma, is *nincompoop* a bad word?" Joshua was curious as he had never heard it before.

"See what you have done, Fanny?" said Sara, hiding a smile.

"Now we will have to explain what it means and why he should never use it!"

"May I explain?" asked Will.

"Certainly, you may," said Sara. Will stood up as if to make a speech.

"Well, you see, Joshua, *nincompoop* is actually something you call someone when you really like them and want to pretend you don't." Fanny jumped up in a fury.

"William Lowell, now I will wipe that smile off your face."

"Fanny, sit down," said Sara sharply. "Will is our guest, and I don't want him bleeding all over the Christmas presents."

"Fine," said Fanny, "but don't think this is forgotten."

"I surrender," said Will. "I should probably be getting back to town." He turned to Nate. "I will come back in the morning to help cut the tree."

"Will, why don't you stay the night with us?" Sara said. "We can put a pallet next to the fire."

"Can I sleep next to the fire with Will?" Joshua was practically shivering with excitement.

"If that is good with Will, yes, you can."

"I would be honored to share the fire with you, Joshua. Do you snore?"

"Of course not. Dolly snores; I don't."

"Well then, it's settled. Fanny, will you pull out some quilts for our two gentlemen?" Sara and Nate were both trying not to laugh.

"Happy to." Fanny flicked Will's ear and grinned as she passed.

Christmas Day dawned bright, the light bounced off the snow and made Fanny squint. She put a large basket with a leather strap on her shoulder and started down the slope toward the enormous old chestnut tree. It stood on its own little hill overlooking the bay. Joshua ran out onto the porch without a coat.

"Fanny, can I come with you? I am a very good climber."

"Yes, you are, but your mamma needs your help inside. Nate and Will are coming back with the tree very soon." Joshua went back in the house, and, as Fanny had predicted, Will and Nate rounded the stable, hauling the large pine tree they had picked on a rope behind them.

"Isn't she a beauty?" Nate grinned as he dragged the tree up the steps. Will assisted by carrying the trunk.

"Oh, she surely is." Fanny put her face close to the branches and breathed in deeply. "I love this pine smell so much. I don't know why we can't have a tree inside all year round."

"You know," said Will, "We could plant a seedling in a

bucket and move it inside when it takes hold. That way you can have Christmas, as you said, 'all year 'round.'"

"Sometimes you have some very good ideas, Will Lowell."

"You might be surprised," said Will.

"And just what do you mean by that?"

"Oh nothing, but it is Christmas, you know. Anything can happen."

"Oh, pish! Now, come down and help me harvest some chestnuts. Race you to the tree!" Fanny took off like a shot, Will close at her heels. When they crashed into the tree, Fanny whooped, "I won again!"

"No," said Will, "I won." And he took her face in his hands and kissed her softly on the lips. Fanny drew back a fist, then thought better of it and kissed him back, hard. Then she backed up a step, face flushing, and began to scoop the prickly chestnuts into the basket. Will looked at her half-smiling, leaning against the tree.

"I love this tree," he said. "Bet I can beat you to the top." Fanny hoisted herself easily onto the first branch. "I don't think so." She kept scrambling up the branches. But Will swung past her in a flash, then hung upside down from an upper branch and leaned in to kiss her again. She was so surprised she almost fell out of the tree, but he caught her and pulled her up to his branch. He wrapped his arm around her and said, "That was fun, wasn't it?"

Fanny squirmed from his grasp, jumped down to the ground and picked up the basket. "Will you help me or not?"

she said. They filled the basket in silence, Will sneaking sidelong looks at Fanny, who gave away nothing. But as they started back to the house, she slipped her hand into his, and they walked back to the house linked together.

ELEVEN

BEST CHRISTMAS EVER

THE ROOM WAS quiet, bathed in the light of the fire and the candles burning in the windows. The family was seated around the table, staring at their empty earthenware plates.

"I think I might explode," said Joshua.

"That is a possibility," said Will. He stood up, cleared his throat, and began to pontificate. "It is a scientific fact that if you eat too much turkey with chestnut stuffing, plus potatoes, yams, corn with cream, and finally three kinds of pie, your body will be filled right up to your nose. Your stomach will grumble and grumble and then finally *BOOM!*" Joshua looked about to cry.

"Stop teasing him," Fanny said. "Besides, that only happens if you are English, so Joshua, you are safe."

"Will, I hope you don't explode," Joshua said softly.

"I promise I won't. I was very careful and only ate two kinds of pie." Will sat back down and gave Joshua a hug.

"Daddy, is it time for the story?"

"I guess it is, son," said Nate. "Let's all sit by the fire."

"Nate, may I tell the first part?" asked Fanny.

"Of course. It is as much your story as it is ours."

"One morning, Mamma pulled Daddy into the house, and said, 'Gerald, I am worried about Nate. He has been so quiet the past few days. Something is wrong, I know it.'

"'I have seen it too, Elspeth. What do you think we should do?'

"'He is down by the bay right now. Go and talk to him. He trusts you. He will tell you. I know he will.'

"Daddy walked through the meadow. It was covered with summer flowers. The bees were busy gathering pollen, and the lazy hum they made was hypnotic. He came up next to Nate sitting on a hillock overlooking the bay and sat down. They sat in silence for a few minutes. Finally, Daddy said, 'My friend, we know you are troubled. We do not want to intrude, but we want you to know that we will help in any way that we can.'

"Nate didn't turn his head. He just kept staring at the bay. Then, he spoke so softly Daddy almost didn't hear him say, 'Today is my wedding anniversary.'

"Gerald caught his breath. 'I didn't know you were married. I am so sorry. Is she still . . . there?'

"'Yes. We made a decision that I would try to escape and come back for her. I was a field hand, so it was easier for me to slip away. She is a house slave and watched much more carefully. I have been pondering how to get back for her. It seems impossible.'

"'What is her name?'

"'Sara.'

"'Very well. We will just have to go south and get Sara back. Come to the house. We have a lot of pondering to do.'

"A few days later, the house was full of busy energy. Mamma was creating a document of ownership. She wrote it out in very official language: *The slave known as Nathaniel is the legal property of Gerald Campbell of New York.*

"I asked her, 'Mamma, why does it say New York? We live in Rhode Island.'

"'Because we don't want them to know where we live.'

"I understood instantly, but I asked, 'In case the bad people come looking for Nate and Sara, right?'

"'Exactly,' said Gerald. 'And look at what your mother is doing now.'

"Mamma had fashioned a seal out of one of Daddy's uniform buttons. She stamped it on the paper and edged it in gold paint she had made from pyrite and paste. She did the same to another paper in Sara's name and then stepped back to look at her work.

"'I think this will pass, don't you?'

"'They look absolutely real, my clever wife! Hopefully we won't need them.'

"Gerald and Nate had collected supplies for the trip and began to pack the horse and wagon Mamma insisted they borrow from Graham and Biddy, saying, 'That way you won't have to sleep on the ground, plus Nate and Sara will have a place to hide, if need be.'

"'It's a long trip, Elspeth. We will likely be gone more than two months,' said Daddy.

"'Don't worry, dear. Fanny and I will be just fine. The crops are in, we have plenty in the storeroom and a musket by the door.'

"I had made a gift for Sara, which I gave to Nate. 'Look Nate, it's our house. See, I made it all by myself, out of scraps of fabric stitched together. This is for Sara, so she will know what her new home looks like.' It was a little cloth house, almost like a handkerchief.

"Nate folded it carefully and put it in his pocket. He hugged me tight and said to all of us, 'I don't know how I will ever repay you for your kindness, but you can be sure I will.'

"Mamma said, 'Hush, Nate. You just concentrate on Sara and in no time at all, there she will be, right by your side.'

"And the next day at first light, they left. As we watched from the doorway, I asked Mamma if she was worried. She replied, 'Heavens no, child! Your father survived warfare, treachery, betrayal, and a death-defying sea voyage to get here. He is not going to let some poncy southern slave owner get the best of him.'"

Will laughed, "I would have loved your mother."

Fanny grabbed his hand. "Yes, you would have. Now shush! Nate, this is your part of the story to tell." Fanny sat back with a sigh, still holding Will's hand.

At this point, Nate took over the story. "The trip to Virginia went smooth. We slept rough, used fire sparingly, and kept off the main roads. Mrs. Campbell had packed homemade brown bread, cheese, dried meat, and fruit, so we were well fed and didn't have to stop. When there were people around, I rode in the back and kept my head down. Only once, near the border with Virginia, did anyone show any interest. A man on a horse in very fine clothes rode past us, but then came back and said, 'Sir, do you have any interest in selling your slave? I have need of a new one.'

"Gerald bit his tongue and then turned and smiled, saying, 'Oh, no, this boy is one of my finest workers. I could never sell him.'

"'Understood,' said the man and rode off.

"'Jackass,' Gerald muttered under his breath.

"'We are almost there, sir,' I said to Gerald.

"'Alright, get in the back and keep your hat low on your head. We don't want anyone recognizing you.'

"I can't believe I remembered the way so well. I really wanted to forget all about it, but I thought of Sara, and I couldn't. I remembered the location of a small stream, and we stopped there so that Gerald could wash the travel dust from his face and dress in what Elspeth called his gentry costume—shiny boots, a long waistcoat, and a cravat for good measure. He looked monied for sure.

"The plan was that Gerald would pretend to be a buyer from the north. He was going to make a big slave purchase, but he wanted to check on how they were trained. He presented himself at the door of Belvoir Plantation and handed a card to the immaculate butler. The ruse worked, and he was escorted into a great salon.

"'This is Master Jebediah Wiggins,' the butler announced and backed out of the room. A mean-eyed man as wide as he was tall stood at the window in tight, green velvet pants. Gerald hated him on sight. He said later that the man looked like a moldy sausage. I stayed hidden in the wagon. I remembered that blackguard really well.

"'I understand you have a letter of introduction,' said Wiggins with a pronounced southern accent.

"'Indeed, I do,' Gerald replied with an equally thick Scottish brogue. He had lost most of his accent years ago, but thought it was appropriate for this highly annoying, pompous little man. He handed him the parchment Sara had prepared. 'I represent the Percys of Philadelphia. I am sure you have heard of them.'

"'Oh, yes, of course. They are most respected here in the colonies.' There was no such family, but Gerald was having a great time watching Wiggins lie.

"'Then I am sure you have heard of their new property, Percy's Haven, that has just finished construction. It is three stories with sixteen bedrooms and a ballroom. It will need a full complement of house slaves at once. I am prepared to make payment in gold as soon as I am satisfied with the merchandise.' Wiggins's eyes gleamed at the mention of gold.

"'Henry, line up all the house staff in the great salon at once,' he shouted to his butler. 'I am delighted to show you my property. I am sure you will be pleased.' They entered the great salon, and Gerald saw twenty or more people against the wall. He was horrified but kept to the act.

"'Have them say their names, please.'

"They kept their heads down and quietly said their names: Priscilla, Julia, Mary, Jim, George, Betty, Amanda, Sara. There she was. Gerald kept his face impassive, but he was trembling inside. Sara was a small, beautiful woman with lovely eyes that she kept cast down. Eliza, Nancy, Stephan. The list seemed to go on forever, but when it ended, he began the next part of his act.

"'Girl, you!' he said rudely, pointing at Sara, 'Come help me off with my jacket.'

"As she pulled on his sleeve, he whispered, 'Nate is here.' He threw his jacket at her and made sure she dropped it. 'You clumsy wench. Take this outside and brush it off.' He manhandled her out the door by her collar. On the porch he yelled, 'I'll teach you to ruin my clothes,' and he whispered, 'Cry out, then hold your cheek.' He slapped his hands together and Sara gave a cry. 'Where do you sleep?' he whispered again.

"'Under the stairs with the other girls.'

"'Can you sneak out?'

"'I will find a way.'

"'We will be waiting at the end of the lane. Now cry.' He clapped his hands together again and dragged her back in the house by her arm. 'Help me on with my coat, wench. And stop that blasted crying.'"

"'Yes, sir.' Sara did as he asked and dropped a curtsy, lowering her eyes to the floor. She didn't want to take a chance Wiggins might notice her tears were tears of joy.

"Gerald looked the other slaves up and down and said to the master, 'I will come back in two days' time and make my selection. Have eight house servants and six field hands ready for inspection.'"

"That night, we waited and waited in a thicket at the end of the lane. Just as I was about to collapse in despair, a shadow flitted down the side of the lane, appearing only in small slivers of light from the moon. When she reached the wagon, she collapsed in my arms.

"'No time,' whispered Gerald. 'Into the wagon with you.' He covered us with the horse blanket and headed out at a fast clip. He drove north all through the night and the next day as well. He wanted to get us as far away as possible before he stopped. Finally, he and the horse were near collapse, and we stopped to rest. He slept for a few hours while we huddled together and watched over him.

"'I can't believe you are real,' Sara said, stroking my face. 'Will we finally be safe?'

"'Oh yes, more than safe. We will be home.' I took out the little cloth picture Fanny had made and told her all about the farm and the family and how they were now our family. She couldn't believe there were people like that in the world. Our previous experience had been much different . . . much, much different.

"In Baltimore, I left Gerald and Sara outside town and went to the docks. I had heard whispers of free Black dock workers that were helping escaped slaves to get north. The very first man I encountered was as dark as me, with huge, scarred hands. I took a chance and asked if he could help. He asked what my story was, and I told him everything. He said Gerald must stay in town so as not to endanger others escaping. I told him Gerald wasn't like that. He said, 'I know, but a white man in our village would draw attention, and we try not to attract any . . . ever. You can meet up with him in the morning.'

"He told me his name was Joe, called me 'brother' and promised to help. That night, Sara and I rested in a little cabin in a small black village, right on the water. A cozy fire, delicious food, and such kindness from Joe's family. We slept together in a real bed for the first time, wrapped in each other's arms. I didn't even know such a place existed for Black people.

"In the morning, we met Gerald at the crossroads outside the village. He had spent the night in the wagon, not wanting to be questioned by anyone. Joe and his friends set us off on the secret tracks north. As we got farther and farther from Virginia, we all began to relax. Gerald started making bad jokes, and Sara actually laughed. We were able to stop from time to time with more of Joe's friends and then continued on, refreshed. As we crossed the border into Rhode Island, we rode in the front of the wagon with Gerald. The air was fresh, and the coastline was beautiful and new for Sara. The farmhouse showed up on the rise in the distance, a puff of smoke rising from the chimney, the blue bay behind it. 'Look Sara, we made it, we are home,' Gerald shouted.

"'Gerald, sir, why are you so kind?' she asked.

"'Because we are family.' And Sara wept."

"I did," said Sara. "I think I may not have stopped weeping for several days. Gerald and Nate started building us our own little cabin. Fanny and Elspeth delighted in showing me everything—the animals, the boat, the garden—and just like that, our lives changed forever."

"Wait! That's not the end," said Joshua. The best part is that the next year, I arrived!"

"You are so right, Joshua. That is the best story ever, and you are the best part" said Will, with a tear in his eye.

"Are you crying, Mr. Lowell?" Fanny couldn't help teasing him.

"Yes, I am and mighty proud of it. If a man can't cry at a beautiful story, he isn't much of a man, I say."

"Well said, young fellow." Nate clapped him on the back, while Fanny was, for one of the first times in her life, speechless.

TWELVE

THE PROPOSAL

AS THE MONTHS went on, Will made himself indispensable around the farm. He helped with planting, taking care of the animals, and chores around the house. He even started going into the woods with Fanny and Sara. He learned the names of plants and herbs for eating and for making colors to dye Sara's beautiful woven fabrics. And on market day, he would go into town as part of the family and help sell their wares. Joshua idolized him. Fanny and Will made everything into a contest, with Joshua as the judge. Who could milk the fastest? Who could collect the most eggs? Who could carry the most water or chop the most wood? Then they would have foot races and sword fights to round out the day. Nate and Sara shook their heads in wonder.

"They are having too much fun." said Sara. "How is it that no one is getting hurt?"

"I know," Nate replied, "but I went by the yard in town and the repairs on Will's ship are almost finished. So we have to let them play while they can. Where are they now?"

"Out on the bay, playing pirate, I think!" Nate wrapped his arm around Sara, and they both laughed.

The boat was running at a high speed in front of a fresh wind. Will was at the tiller and Fanny handled the sheets. The spray soaked them, but as usual, they didn't care. A wave crashed against the hull, causing the single-masted skiff to heel over at a precarious angle. "Brace!" Will shouted. The boat hovered impossibly on its side, then righted itself with a bone-rattling smack.

"Prepare the hooks! Heave away!" Fanny shouted, and Will let the braided rope snake across the bow and into the water. A furry black streak dove after the hooks and disappeared under the water. "No, no! Bad dog! Dolly, get back in this boat, you silly girl!"

In the stern, Will hauled in the sheet and cleated it with an expert twist of the wrist. A dripping head appeared over the gunwale with a three-pronged hook in its mouth.

"Dolly, how many times have I told you this is not a game! We haul in the hook, not you. Fighting pirates is serious business, and you are a terrible first mate."

"I thought I was first mate," grumbled Will.

"You are. She has just been reduced in rank. No dried squirrel for you, Seaman Dolly. Come on, you big dummy, get on the boat." The black lab heaved herself over and lay the hook at Will's feet.

"Pleased with yourself, aren't you, you rascal!" Dolly grinned and rolled over as Will rubbed her belly. "I like these pirate games," said Will.

"So do I," said Fanny, "but they aren't really games. My father said that pirates are among the best sailors and fighters in the world, and we must hone our skills razor sharp if we are to prevail."

"Your father was completely right. I think I will be better prepared when I return to sea, just from our practicing together."

"I suppose we should go back. It's almost supper," said Fanny, sighing.

They sat quietly in the stern together and Fanny put her head on Will's shoulder. He wrapped his arm around her and guided the boat toward shore. "I would be happy if that ship of yours were never finished."

"Me too," said Will. "We could always burn it." They exchanged looks and burst out laughing as the boat caught a small surge toward shore.

Spring was finally poking her head out a bit. The trees were budding, the meadows were showing a riot of color, and the sky that had been a dull gray for months was finally blue again. The ground was still too hard for early planting, but all the seeds were sorted and ready. Fanny and Will darted into the woods, hiding behind trees and throwing pine cones at each other. They only stopped playing long enough to check the traps they had set earlier. They traipsed out of the woods, slapping aside the branches, both breathless, and now they sat companionably on the steps of the porch, watching the sunlight fade away. A rider appeared in the distance. "I'll get the musket," said Fanny and went inside. The rider pulled up to the steps.

"Message for William Lowell."

"That's me," said Will. "Thank you." The rider handed him a letter and galloped off. Will glanced at the letter and shoved it in his pocket as Fanny came onto the porch carrying the musket.

"Is everything alright?" she asked.

"Of course, it is! I just have one thing to say, Fanny Campbell. You meet me at our tree right this minute or suffer the consequences." And he took off running down the hill. Fanny stood still for a moment, confused, but then propped the musket against the house and sped after him. Will reached the tree and disappeared into the branches. Fanny hiked up her skirts and scrambled after him. She pulled herself up on a high branch beside him.

"Will, what in the name of heaven are we doing up here?" she panted.

He took her hand as they sat easily together on the tree branch. "Fanny, I have been called back in ten days' time."

Fanny's face fell. "Oh no, Will."

He crushed her to his chest, and she hugged him back hard.

"I will be back in six months and at that time I can resign my commission, but I wanted to know . . . will you wait for me?"

"There you go being an eejit again." Fanny's voice was muffled against Will's jacket. "Of course, I will wait for you."

"And when I return, will you marry me?"

"Will, I would like nothing more but . . . I have a thought." Fanny's head popped up from Will's chest. "Could we marry before you leave?"

Will pulled back and looked directly into Fanny's eyes.

"I would like nothing more," he said, repeating Fanny's words. "But is there time?"

"Yes, we will make the time . . . but I want a proper proposal first."

"Yes, my lady." Will grinned and placed himself on one knee, awkwardly balanced on the tree branch.

"What are you doing? You will kill yourself; get on the ground," Fanny sputtered.

"Fanny Campbell, will you marry me?"

"Sit down! Are you insane?"

"No questions, just an answer. Will you marry me? You have to answer before I fall off this branch."

"Don't be daft! Of course, I will. Now sit down before you kill yourself!" Will sat back down and took Fanny's hand in his.

She punched him in the arm. "It took you long enough to ask." Fanny's eyes filled with tears, and she threw herself against his chest again. They were still for a long moment, and then she shook her head hard and said, "Back to the house, quickly now. We have to post banns, and Sara has to make Mother's wedding dress fit. Oh, lordy, ten days is not a lot of time to make a wedding. We have to get started now!" She and Will both jumped lightly from the tree. Will wrapped his arms around her.

"Do you remember telling me you believe in magic?"

Fanny nodded, not sure of his intent. "Well, now I believe in magic too, and this is our magic tree."

As the light from the disappearing sun lit their faces, they kissed and kissed and kissed again, leaning against the gnarled trunk of their magic chestnut tree.

THIRTEEN

WEDDING DAY, EARLY MORNING

FANNY THREW ON her petticoats and laced up her boots. Today was the last day she would sleep alone in the tiny loft above the kitchen. She edged down the ladder in the dark. There was a soft glow from the embers Sara never let die out. Tomorrow Fanny would have to remember that herself. After all, she was a grown woman now, so Nate, Joshua, and Sara would move back into their little house. They had moved into the cabin when her parents died so that she wouldn't be lonely. It was an arrangement they had all liked very much, but tomorrow she would wake up a married woman. She lifted the iron kettle that lived on top of the stove and poured some warm water into the chipped basin. *Maybe I'll get a new basin as a wedding gift*, she thought, and stifled a laugh. *I'm not even sure anyone is coming.* She splashed her face and dried it with the rough linen towel she had woven herself. Not that she cared about sewing or weaving, but her mother had insisted, and Sara would not let her slack off after her parents were gone. This one towel was the result. Fanny glanced at the curtain that closed off the back of the cabin. Nate and Sara had slept there for years, but tonight they were going to stay with Aunt Biddy and Aunt Maude. "When you come back a bride, you will want some privacy," Sara said. Fanny didn't see the point and said so, but she agreed when Sara gave her a stern look and said, "You don't have to understand, just know that we are right." She caught Nate and Sara sharing a smile. *What was that about?* Fanny wondered. They looked fair pleased with themselves. She slipped out the front door and stood on the porch listening. Even the doves were still asleep. She couldn't believe she was up before Sara. This was truly a unique day.

She jumped from the porch and fairly flew down the lane. When she was younger, she used to see how far she could get with her eyes closed. Today, it was no challenge at all. She skipped over hummocks, skirted rocks, and opened her eyes only when she touched the painted wooden fence. She remembered the day her father had built it. She had turned eleven the month before, and everyone was waiting for her little brother to be born. Fanny had never been so excited. Her mother lay in the bed, smiling while Sara wiped her face. Mrs. Fallon, the midwife, kept her hand on her mother's rounded belly.

"Here, Fanny, you do it." Sara handed her the cloth, and Fanny laid it on her mother's forehead.

"That is lovely, daughter, thank you." Suddenly her mother's face went all still, and a low sound came from her mouth, a sound Fanny had never heard before.

"Do you hurt, Mamma?"

She didn't answer for a long moment. "Only a little, child. It's your brother getting ready to come out and say hello. It will be done before you know it." She lay back and closed her eyes. Fanny sat holding her mother's hand for a long while. The room was dark and warm, and she began to doze. All of a sudden, there was loud screaming, and people were rushing around. Fanny was afraid, but Sara led her to the porch.

"Nate, take Fanny to feed the critters. We have work to do here." Nate took her by the hand they walked toward the barn.

"It won't be long now, child. You do your chores, and before you know it, you will have a brother to help you." But that wasn't what happened. When Sara came out to get her, Fanny's chores had been finished a long time, and the sun was going down.

"Dear girl, I want you to look in and hug your mother, then leave her be. She is very tired."

"What about my brother?" Sara put her hand on Fanny's cheek, her eyes sad and full of tears.

"He stopped here for just a minute and went straight up to heaven. God has some other plans for him."

The next morning, her father built that wooden fence. Fanny always made sure it stayed painted just the way he had painted it. She pushed through the gate and sat in a pile of leaves, her fingertips just touching the carved stones on either side.

"Mother, Father, guess what? Today, I will be married. I so wish you were here. I'm wearing your dress, Mamma. And, yes, I promise to cover my hair, at least for today. Sara has made me a lovely lace cap and covered it with flowers. Daddy, Nate will give me away in your place. Pastor Wilcox will ask, 'Who gives this woman?' and Nate will say, 'I do, in the name of Mr. Gerald Campbell.' Isn't that nice? It was Nate's idea to say your name. Pastor Wilcox tried to be difficult, what with Nate being a Negro; he said it wasn't proper. But I told him that Nate was a free man and a member of my family, and if he didn't want to perform the ceremony, I would find someone else. Maybe that itinerate preacher over in Lynn. He turned all red and sputtered for a while, but in the end, he said, 'You are as stubborn as your father,' and agreed to it.

"I thought that was a rather nice compliment. I so wish you could meet Will. He says I'm stubborn too, but he wants me that way. You would both like him so much. He is handsome and strong and good, but he is also wicked funny and smart, not to mention the youngest officer on his ship. I remember something you said, Father: 'It isn't so much what a man says, as the action he takes.' That's why I know you would approve of Will. He always does the honest and true thing. Mamma, you told me not to worry about being different, that every iron pot has a lid to match, and I would find mine. Well, I did, and you know what? He doesn't care that I am strong or that I love to sail. He races me and laughs when I beat him. He said he is going to keep racing me until we are old and gray, and I finally let him win. What do you think of that?" Fanny stood up and brushed the dried leaves from her skirt.

"One other thing—we decided that our first boy will be called Jared." She looked at the small stone between her parents. It read "Jared, Beloved Son." "It makes me happy to imagine you are all in heaven together. Please look down on us today. We want you with us." The dawn was streaking pink, and as Fanny looked up, a star shot across the morning sky. She clapped her hands and laughed. "Oh, thank you, I'm so glad you approve," she shouted. She put her hand to her check and was surprised to find it wet. She hadn't known she was crying. "After the wedding, Will and I will come back here together, and you can meet him properly. I love you."

Fanny walked back toward the house and began to scatter feed for the chickens. When Sara appeared in the door, Fanny tossed a grain bucket her way. "Today isn't a day to be a slugabed you know. There is work to be done."

"I'm sure there is," said Sara, "but the first thing you will do is come in and eat a decent breakfast."

"But I still need to brush Dolly and wash the wagon."

"Fanny, slow down, and leave something for the rest of us to do." Fanny opened her mouth to object, but Sara was firm.

"No buts. I will not have the bride collapsing from hunger in the middle of the ceremony."

"Sara, have I ever in my whole life collapsed?"

"No, but you've never gotten married, either. Sit down and eat."

Fanny flopped down at the table and absently twisted her hair. "Where are Nate and Joshua?" she asked.

"I sent them down by the creek to collect vines for the bridal bower. You aren't the only one fidgety this morning. Everybody beat the rooster by a good hour. The chores are all done." Sara put a bowl of porridge in front of Fanny. "Now eat every bit of this so you can keep your spark all day long."

Fanny poured milk into the bowl and topped it with a spoonful of black molasses. "I'm not really hungry." She added another spoonful. "I'm only eating so you won't worry."

"Fine," said Sara.

Fanny ate a bite of porridge. "Do you think anyone from town will come?"

"They had better," said Sara. "I made enough food for the whole pack of them and all their distant relations."

Fanny ate more and frowned. "Yes, but will they come?"

"Of course, they will, child. The ones who disapprove will come to stand there and proclaim, 'Tsk tsk, isn't it a shame they are not in a church.' Some will come for the free supper. And the ones that matter will come to share the joy of your wedding. Your Aunt Biddy has spent the last two days on the wedding cake, you know. I hear it's so big that Blacksmith John is hauling it up in his wagon. He is also bringing some long planks for the tables outside."

"What if there's not enough food?" Fanny said with her mouth full.

"I like that!" said Sara. "First, you think no one will come and now you worry we won't have enough food. The Jensens have a huge kettle of mutton stew on the fire; Mrs. Peeple has done her applesauce; and I know for a fact that Mary Robertson is bringing her oat and corn pudding. We have four turkeys already stuffed and roasted, you and I have baked enough bread to build a house, and I believe Will's friends from the shipyard are bringing a side of beef they bought from the butcher. I think that will be enough." Sara looked at Fanny's empty bowl. "I am so blessed that you ate all that porridge just for me. Now, clear off the table and let's get started on the partridge stew." Fanny laid her bowl in the kitchen basin and took down a large brace of birds from the hook behind the door.

"How many shall we do?" she asked.

"Seven," said Sara, "for luck, and we will stuff them in eleven pumpkins." Fanny began plucking the birds and Sara sliced the tops off the pumpkins. She scooped out the orange flesh with a flat wooden spoon, separating out the seeds as she went along. "We will roast these with pepper and salt in case anyone gets hungry before supper," she said. Fanny skewered the clean birds on a long iron pole and hung them above the fire. She cut up carrots, parsnips, and potatoes and stuffed them in Sara's empty pumpkins. Sara added maple syrup, butter, and currants.

They worked quickly and efficiently. Sara hummed and tapped her foot. Every once in a while, Fanny would forget what she was doing and stare out the window with a half-smile on her face. And so passed the morning. When the pumpkins were all assembled, they put the tops back on and laid them directly on the hot coals.

Sara stood back from the fire and rubbed her hands together. "Now, when the birds are roasted, we will take the meat off the bone, put it in the pumpkins and we are done." She looked sideways at Fanny and smiled. "Then we start on your hair." Fanny groaned.

Outside, Will walked briskly up the lane and was stopped by Nate and Joshua with a wagonload of vines and flowers. "You aren't supposed to be here, young fellow," said Nate. "Sara will run you off with a broom if she sees you."

"I know," said Will. "Fanny told me. Bad luck to see the bride and all that, but I was going crazy just sitting there at the inn. Isn't there something I can do to help?"

Nate tipped his head to one side. "What do you think, Joshua, should we let him help?"

"Oh, yes, please, Daddy. Will is funny. Sometimes he makes me laugh so much my eyes cry all by themselves."

"Well, this I must see. Hop on. We have work to do."

Will smiled. As they rolled up to the chestnut tree, a bower of bent saplings stood out against the bright blue sky and the darker blue of the ocean. "Good day for a wedding," said Nate.

"Yes, sir, it is," Will replied. "And a good spot too. I know the people in town think it's strange that we are marrying outside, but this is the exact spot where I proposed, and Fanny would have it no other way. What a grand girl she is!" Will's eyes began to shine and then water. He jumped down from the wagon. "What do we do with these vines?"

"I know," said Joshua. "Mamma said to start at the top and weave them all through like a piece of wool."

"Then that is just what we will do," said Nate, "because your Mamma is always right. Will, take that end and we will haul them up together."

"What about me, Daddy?"

"You stand on the wagon and make sure we have the ends in place. If it's not right, you know your mother will have us do it again." They worked the vines into the bower, and soon it was a green arch accented by wild white flowers.

"Will, are you to wear your uniform?" Joshua asked shyly. "I would like to see you in it sometime."

"No," said Will. "Fanny and I talked about it, but we decided that it wasn't what we wanted. After all, I won't be wearing it much longer. I am going to resign my commission at the end of this tour and come back and be a farmer, just like you!"

Joshua jumped up and down with excitement. "Really? For true? You will come and live with us forever?"

Will smiled and shouted back. "For true! Our Fanny wouldn't have it any other way and neither would I. Playing and working with you is much better than being cold and wet all the time, eating bad food, and chasing nasty pirates."

Nate got them all back to work on the wagon, but from time to time, Will would stare out to sea, causing Nate to flick him with a vine. Will would then jump around and yell as though it really hurt, and Joshua would laugh until his eyes cried all by themselves. And so went the morning.

FOURTEEN

WEDDING DAY, LATE MORNING

THE LATE MORNING light filled the cabin with a soft glow. Fanny stood by the window, shifting from foot to foot. "Hold still," said Sara, her mouth full of pins. Fanny smoothed the soft white cloth of the billowing skirt. She ran the tips of her fingers over the tiny, embroidered flowers at her waist.

"Mamma did all this?" she asked.

"Oh, yes," said Sarah. "She said it took her months to finish the roses on the hem." Fanny bent over to look. "Hold still now, or I'll poke you right in the back of your head with this needle and then you'll have to get married with blood all down the back of your Mamma's wedding dress."

"Sara, that's awful." Fanny tried not to laugh at the thought.

"Then you had best not move." Sara took two deft stitches. "There, all done. Now you can look." Sara held up a polished tin mirror. "What do you think?" Fanny turned her head this way and that. Her long curls were caught up at the nape of her neck. The veil sweeping from the satin cap slid over her shoulders. She took in a quavering breath.

"Sara, I look like Mamma, don't I?"

"Yes, child, exactly like her. Just as beautiful and just as dear." Sara's eyes shone with happy tears. "What a grand day this is! Your mamma and daddy are looking down on you, so proud and happy. You know that, don't you, dear one?"

"I do," said Fanny. She looked into the mirror again and broke into a grin. "And I know just what they are saying. 'Finally, thank God.'"

"Your parents had every faith in you. They weren't worried for a second," said Sara.

"Well, Aunt Biddy and Aunt Maude surely were. Do you know what happened last night? We were all in their parlor having tea. Will was being so charming, and everything was going like a top. Aunt Maude picked up the teapot to pour and just then Aunt Biddy stood up." Fanny clasped her hands to her bosom and made her eyes very wide. "'Oh, Fanny, dear,' she said in a high voice. 'I am so happy. I was afraid you would never marry and would end up a spinster lady, just like Maudie.' Aunt Maude poured tea all over Will's knee. He never yelled or anything. Just ran straight to the backyard. I ran after him, but he wouldn't let me help. He stood on one leg and plunged his knee straight into the horse trough. I asked if he was alright. He said he was, pulled his sopping leg out of the water, and emptied his shoe. Then he said if I didn't stop laughing, he would take back his proposal. I dared him to, but Aunt Maude came out just then and was so upset, we had to stop playing and promise her that everything was fine, and Will would be able to walk for the wedding."

Outside the window came the sound of creaking wheels and harness bells. Fanny's head snapped around.

"Is it time already?"

"It sounds like it is."

"I'm not ready, Sara. I mean, I'm ready to marry Will; I'm just not ready to go down the hill and stand in front of all those people. Couldn't we just have a big party? Will and I will make our promises tomorrow. Somewhere else. Alone."

Sara hid her smile.

"Take a deep breath, dear. Everything is going to be fine."

Joshua came through the door just then and whooped.

"Fanny, you look like an angel or maybe a princess, but I never saw one, so I'm not sure. What do you think, Daddy?" Behind him, Nate paused.

"Well, son, so far as I know, angels are supposed to have wings, and since our Fanny is wingless, I'm thinking princess."

"Stop it, you two," Fanny's cheeks stained deep red.

"Will rode Fiona down the hill already and a whole heap of people are there." Joshua kept up a stream of chatter as he took Fanny by the hand and dragged her out the door. "Look what we did to the wagon! Me and Daddy, we did that, and Will, he helped some, but mostly he just kept staring up the hill. Look at the flowers, Fanny. See how they are all woven together in a braid? That was my idea, wasn't it, Daddy?"

"Yes, it was, son, and a clever idea too." The wagon was now a rolling garden. Flowers crept in and out of the spokes and up onto the high seat in the front. Garlands of white buds hung from the harness, and every piece of leather that could be wrapped was in brightly colored ribbon. A bench nailed to the wagon bed was painted white and heaped with blue and white pillows. "The blue is for the ocean," crowed Joshua, "and the white is for, I forget. What is white for, Daddy?"

"It's for love, son. Love is the purest and most important thing of all." Fanny took Joshua up in her arms.

"Thank you, little brother. This is all too beautiful." She buried her head in his neck.

"Hey, you're squishing me." Joshua squirmed free. "Let's hurry up and do the wedding, so we can eat." Fanny looked at Sara and flashed a tiny smile.

"I don't know what I was thinking. Let's do the wedding, so we can eat." Nate handed Fanny carefully up onto the bench and then settled Sara next to her. Then he and Joshua climbed onto the high seat.

"Can I take the reins, Daddy?"

"Not today, son. This one is mine." Nate picked up the reins, the harness bells rang out, and they started down the hill.

FIFTEEN

THE WEDDING & BEYOND

THE AFTERNOON SUN gave the sky a burnished look. Will wondered if it would ever be this blue again. He let his eyes wander out to sea. There was not a ripple on the bay, only a mirror-bright shine off the water. A gull dipped down and swooped aloft with a fish in its mouth. Will felt as though he were the only one on the hill.

A cheer went up from the waiting crowd, jolting him back to reality. His eyes swept the hillside. He saw John Steadman, the blacksmith, grinning from ear to ear, dressed in a clean white shirt. He saw his entire crew in their dress uniforms. They had arrived the night before, just in time for the wedding. He saw Aunt Biddy in a new lace cap, dabbing her eyes with a tiny linen square. Aunt Maude stood as stiff as a board, looking straight ahead, but Will could see a tiny smile at the corner of her mouth. He heard the harness bells, then saw the gaily decorated wagon as it crested the hill. Nate pulled the horse to a stop at the flower-laden bower. Will's heart skipped at his first sight of Fanny in her wedding finery. She stood up slowly. The white dress hugged her waist and fell in shining folds to the ground. The veil moved gently in the breeze, as though she were followed by her own spring cloud. *My God*, Will thought. *How is it she is more beautiful than ever, and yet, she is still my Fanny?* Nate stopped next to the chestnut tree, jumped from the front seat, and held his hand out to Fanny.

"My lady," he said, guiding her down the step.

Joshua did the same with his mother. "My lady," he said. Sara bowed gracefully, took Joshua's arm, and walked to her place as Fanny's matron of honor. Fanny clutched Nate's arm with both hands as he led her to Will's side. Before, she was afraid no one would come. Now, the hill was covered with people, and it scared her even more. It looked like the whole town was there, dressed in their Sunday best. *Stop it*, Fanny said to herself. *You are a Campbell. We are not afraid. We are never afraid.* She shut her eyes briefly. When she opened them, her first sight was of Will. He dropped his eye in a slow wink and then cocked his eyebrow. Fanny stifled a laugh.

"Oh, God," Pastor Wilcox's voice rang out as he lifted his hand, closed his eyes, and began to pray. "Look kindly on this gathering as we stand here in the open, under your sky, in this, your largest church. Shower your blessings on us all."

"But no rain, eh, Pastor?" Pastor Wilcox ignored the shout from the back, and the ripple of laugher that skittered through the crowd.

Keeping his eyes closed, he added, "And thank you for keeping all storms far out to sea." He continued to pray for all manner of things, good crops, clean hearts, and healthy cows. Fanny knew that if she caught Will's eye again, they would disgrace themselves with gales of laughter, so she lowered her head and looked at the tips of her white cloth slippers. She noticed that the embroidery she had struggled to complete on one toe still had a loose thread. *Well, I won't have to do that ever again*, she thought gratefully. Pastor Wilcox finished praying with a loud amen and opened his prayer book to begin the wedding.

"You, there!" Fanny's heart sank. She recognized Mrs. Wilcox, the pastor's wife, by her shrill voice. Her disapproval of the outdoor wedding had been public and harsh. "It is just like that Campbell family to fly in the face of tradition and decency," she had berated her husband.

She had taken every opportunity to heap criticism on Fanny and her family. She was particularly horrified and vocal about the Training Day when Fanny had raced. "Look at that child astride, racing like a boy. It is disgraceful," she complained. And now she was to ruin the wedding.

"You there, back in the trees." The crowd turned. "Seth Barker, I see you." Her voice became even more piercing. "You and your brother come out at once." In a small stand of pine, two men were clearly visible. They turned as if to run.

"Hold it right there, fellows." Constable Farnsworth strode toward the trees, rifle held loosely in the crook of his arm. "Seth, you and your brother Rob, drop those sacks."

"It wasn't my idea; I was just looking to have a little fun." Rob's head ducked up and down as he grinned.

"Oh, shut up!" Seth snarled. He shoved Rob, who would have fallen, except that Constable Farnsworth had him by the collar.

"We weren't gonna do nothing," Rob whined. "It was just a joke."

"Shut it." Seth raised his arm to whack Rob but thought better of it when the barrel of the constable's rifle found its way to his chest.

"I'm thinking it would be a good idea for you both to sit right there on the ground and put your hands on your head. Now!" he snapped. They both sat with a thud.

Fanny took two steps toward the trees in a fury, but Will caught her hand. "Let Mr. Farnsworth do his job, darling. The sooner they are gone, the sooner we are married. Besides, if you tear his head off, you might get that very beautiful dress dirty." Fanny looked at her soon-to-be husband.

"You know," she said, "this is one time when you are absolutely right."

"Thank you for noticing," said Will.

"No need to get melon-headed about it," said Fanny. "I said this one time."

Will touched his head to Fanny's temple, where a stray curl escaped her cap. "I will settle for that gladly." He squeezed her hand gently, and she let a tiny sigh escape.

Farnsworth kicked the burlap sack at his feet. "What have we here?"

"Uh, I don't think you want to do that," said Rob.

"Did you find out what they up to, Constable?"

"I'm about to, Mrs. Wilcox. Open the sack, Rob."

"Uh-uh, no, sir. I don't think you want me to do that." Rob looked at his brother Seth for support.

"I said open the sack. Do it now." Rob loosened the rope and let the neck of the sack fall open. Instantly, a nose-searing stench spread throughout the crowd. Those closest stepped back.

"What is that?" Will asked as he choked. "It's disgusting."

"Well," said Fanny, "that is pig manure. It has a much riper smell than cow or horse, and if you close it up in a sack, it gets even stronger."

"I did not need to know that." Will said, his nose wrinkling as he tried not to breathe in the heavy stench. "What were they going to do with it?"

"I imagine they were going to fling it at us during the wedding. Was that it, you disgusting little rodents? Did you think to shower us with dung?" she shouted. "Shall I come down there and make you eat it instead?"

"Fanny," Aunt Maude's shocked whisper cut through the silence. "We are ladies."

"Darling," Will grabbed Fanny's arm and hung on. "Do you mind if we get married first? Then you can give them what-for, and I will help you." Fanny glared. Sara looked beseechingly at Nate. He was down the hill in two strides.

"Constable Farnsworth, do you need a hand with those fellows?"

"Nope, I'll just march them down to the stockade to wait for the magistrate. Pick up those sacks, you drunken miscreants."

"But they stink," said Seth.

"Yes, and I might just leave them in the stockade with you for a day or two. Evidence, you know." He prodded them with his rifle butt, and they stumbled forward. "You folks commence with the marrying. I'll be back in time for the feast!"

"Thank heavens, they've gone," chirped Aunt Biddy. "They were quite rude."

"Will, you can let go of me now. I promise I won't hurt them."

"Good girl, I was starting to lose my hold."

Fanny laughed. "That will never happen. You are stuck with me, sir. But there is something I must do this minute. I'll be right back."

"I'll be right here," said Will. "Right here," he said at her retreating back, "looking for my wife-to-be. Where is my wife?" he shouted to the sky.

Joshua tugged at Will's coat.

"Don't worry, Will. She's just over there." Will picked up Joshua and gave him a hug.

"Thank you, Joshua. You are always a big help."

Fanny wended her way through the crowd, the hem of her dress flung over her arm, advancing on Mrs. Wilcox. The crowd held their breath. Fanny threw her arms around the startled woman and lifted her off her feet in a huge hug. "Mrs. Wilcox, you saved my wedding!"

"Alright, child, alright, put me down. People are staring."

"I don't care. Mrs. Wilcox, you are my hero." Fanny set her on her feet.

"Well," Mrs. Wilcox said, straightening her cloak, "a wedding is a sacred thing, even if it isn't in a house of worship."

"You are a peach, Mrs. Wilcox, and I won't forget it. You can count on that." Fanny kissed her cheek and ran back up the hill, leaving the pastor's wife pink-cheeked and flustered, but pleased just the same.

"Can we begin, please?" queried Pastor Wilcox. Fanny nodded, smoothing the folds of her skirt. "We are gathered here to witness the union of Frances Louise Campbell and William Marsden Lowell. They have posted their banns and are now ready to proceed in accordance with the law. Does anyone here know any reason this marriage should not be sanctified?" He looked around. Fanny held her breath. No one spoke.

"Well, thank goodness for that," said Aunt Biddy, breaking the silence.

"Hush, sister," hissed Aunt Maude.

"Who gives this woman?" intoned the pastor.

"I, Nathanial Hawkins, freeman, give the hand of Fanny Campbell in the name of her father, Gerald Campbell."

Joshua stuck out his chest. "That's my Daddy," he announced to the crowd.

Fanny and Will faced each other. Pastor Wilcox pronounced the vows with great pomp and ceremony. Fanny and Will said their "I Do's" with husky voices and shining eyes. Then the pastor asked for the rings.

"We have them. Come on, Dolly." Joshua stepped up to the pastor with Dolly at his side, wagging her tail. "Give him the rings, girl." Dolly dropped a small box daintily at the pastor's feet.

"Well, I never," said Mrs. Wilcox.

"Hush," said Aunt Biddy loudly.

Will scooped up the slightly damp box. "Good girl, Dolly." He held out the rings to Pastor Wilcox, who took them hesitantly, and then held them up. The sun glinted off their finish.

"These rings are a symbol of your union with each other and with God. May the circle never be broken." Fanny and Will slipped the rings on each other's fingers and stood with their hands entwined. The rings had belonged to Fanny's parents. Will and Fanny decided that this was a way to honor them and give even more meaning to the ceremony.

"Now, by the power given to me by God and his Royal Highness, King George, I pronounce you husband and wife.

What God has joined together, let no man put asunder. You may kiss your bride." Fanny and Will stood looking into each other's eyes. "Son, it's time to kiss your bride." Still, they didn't move. Joshua once again tugged at Will's coat.

"If you don't kiss her, I don't think we can eat, Will." The breeze picked up just then, lifting Fanny's veil and making a canopy over the couple's head. Will leaned in and put his lips close to Fanny's ear.

"I love you, Fanny Campbell," and then he kissed her for a good long time. Then he shouted, "Let's eat. The bride is starving!"

The tables were covered with enough food for an army, but by the end of the party, there were only scraps. Aunt Biddy's cake was a huge success. Donald Almy ate four pieces and swept her up for a dance when the music started, leaving Aunt Biddy pink-cheeked and breathless. Kevin O'Herlihy played the hand organ and sang in a fine tenor voice. Aunt Maude stood to the side and sang along. Will's crew were going back to Mrs. Da Silva's boarding house for the night, but for now, they were dancing and clapping with everyone else. Mrs. Da Silva had been thrilled to be invited to the wedding. She brought trays and trays of Portuguese pastries called *Pasteis de Nata*. They had been invented by monks in Lisbon in the 1600s, and she was very proud that she had the recipe. The tiny, sweet egg pastries were gone in an instant, and Mrs. Da Silva thought that she might have a new business. Everyone pitched in to clean up the field, but Sara and

Nate insisted that Fanny and Will go home. The gifts were all loaded into the wagon and off they went, back up the hill.

Later that evening, Fanny and Will sprawled on the porch bench, exhausted by the events of the day. The sky was a dark navy blue with no clouds, so the stars were out in all their glory.

"It was a great party, wasn't it?" Fanny whispered, not wanting to disturb the silence.

"It certainly was. I particularly liked the moment I spun you into a dance, and you almost fainted."

"I did not! I just had no idea you could dance."

"There are a lot of things you still don't know about me."

"Oh really? What, for instance?"

"For instance, I can name every star and constellation in the north sky."

"Well, that means nothing. I can do the same!"

"Then let's go! Ursa Minor."

"Oh, too easy. Orion." As they yelled out the names, they pointed, jumping around, and pushing each other out of the way.

"Pleiades."

"Oh, come on, the sisters? How obvious." Will sneered. "I name Capella."

"Not even the brightest. Vega."

As if it were planned, they grabbed each other's hands, and shouted together, "Polaris," and fell back onto the bench breathless and laughing. The bench creaked under the sudden weight.

"Oh, no! It would be awful if we broke this bench. Daddy built it for Mamma before I was born. They called it the snuggling bench."

"Well then, we had best to get to snuggling." Will tangled his hands in Fanny's hair and leaned in for a long kiss. Then he pulled back and said, "Perhaps we should continue this inside?"

"What a novel idea, sir." They both stood up, and at that moment, Fanny threw her arms round his neck and leapt into his arms. Will stopped himself from tumbling over the porch rail and barely kept his footing.

"My lady, what is this?" he gasped.

"This, Mr. Lowell, is where, in keeping with ancient tradition, you carry your wife into the house."

"And so I shall, Mrs. Lowell." Will kicked at the door but it remained shut. "Tarnation, this door is as ancient as your tradition." Will kicked at the door again.

"Put me down, you silly man."

"I will not. This is a tradition, and I will complete my task." Will held Fanny on his hip and fumbled at the handle.

"Don't you dare drop me!" Fanny tried to sound threatening, but she was laughing too hard.

"I shall not, my lady, I promise."

"How very gallant, sir."

Will finally wrestled the door open and swept Fanny back into both arms. She curled against his chest and sighed as they crossed the threshold into their new life.

SIXTEEN

THE GOODBYE

A SMALL BEAM of light came through the tiny window in the sleeping loft. Dolly whined at the bottom of the ladder. There was no movement from the pile of quilts on the pallet. Dolly placed her paws on the first rung. "Woof," first gently, then with more insistence. Getting no response, Dolly stretched her neck up and gave a window-shaking howl. Will popped up from the pile of quilts like a chipmunk.

"Wha', wha', what?" he spluttered. "Dolly, go back to bed." He laid back, eliciting another mournful howl. The quilts started to shake, then Fanny peeked out, laughing.

"Dolly, stop it. It's too early."

Will squinted at the window. "Actually, my darling wife, Dolly is right. The sun is well up. I'd best get to the ship."

"So soon?"

Will smiled down at Fanny. "What are you thinking, Mrs. Lowell?"

"Well, Mr. Lowell, I think we should pull the covers over our heads and pretend we are not here, so you don't have to go." She wrapped her arms around his neck and pulled him close to her face. "Must you go, Will? Really?"

"His Majesty's Navy likes her officers to be present at the sailing of their ship, you know. I don't think they will change that rule only because I am newly married."

"I could ask them," said Fanny. "I could tell them your helpless little wife will be lost without you, and you must stay home." Fanny gave her most sincere helpless look, causing Will to fall back laughing so hard, he hit his head on the window frame with a crack. "Well, now you can't go, you are wounded."

"Mrs. Lowell, I must, but have I yet mentioned today how much I love you?"

"No, sir, you have not." Fanny's face suddenly changed, and she became thoughtful. "I hate that you are going, Will, I do, but I am so proud of you. William Lowell, I will say to everyone, is the youngest officer sailing on the *Queen's Courage*, and he is mine."

"So happy to be all yours, but yours to share with King George for the time being. Here I go." Will slid down the ladder, narrowly missing Dolly's head. Will ruffled her fur and rubbed her ears. "Sorry, girl. Come down here, wife. I am in need of a hearty meal, and, as we all know, I am a terrible cook." Fanny hung her head over the edge of the loft.

"Oh, sir, do wait so I may dress to please you." She grabbed the edge of the platform and somersaulted out of the loft. "Well," she said, smoothing the sides of her nightgown, "I guess this will have to do." Will grabbed her waist, twirled her off the floor, swept an empty copper pot to the ground, and set her on the table.

"Wife, you scare me when you do things like that, but you certainly are beautiful."

"And you, my dear husband, are crazy." They kissed a long, slow kiss. "Now, take me off the table, if you would. I have breakfast to prepare, and you get to fetch wood and water."

"What, I don't get to lay about with my boots on the table? I thought that's why men got married." Fanny picked up the butter paddle from next to the table and cocked an eyebrow. "I'm going directly," said Will. "Come on, Dolly," he said as he headed out the door. "Our Fanny is quite strict this morning, isn't she?" As the door closed, Fanny lobbed the butter paddle against it with a thud.

"Next time it will be your head, William Lowell." She turned to the stove, smiling.

The night before, after the party, Sara laid out makings for biscuits and eggs. "There is a bit of bacon in the icehouse, and I saved the last of the chokeberry jam," she said as she bustled around the kitchen. "We will stay with Biddy and Maude until Will sails."

Fanny's shoulders dropped. "Oh, Sara, I was fine without him, and now I can't stand the thought of being without him for one second, let alone six whole months. What am I going to do?" She began to cry. "What is the matter with me, Sara? I don't cry. I never cry."

Sara put down the tin pitcher and gathered her into her arms. "Of course, you do. You must! Crying washes the soul, so you go ahead and cry away. You love him, you will miss him, and you will carry on. Cry away, dear child." Fanny smiled at the memory and cried again as she rolled and cut the biscuits, deftly sliding them into the cast iron skillet. The front door opened.

"You couldn't have chopped much wood that fast," she said without turning. She dabbed her eyes with a dish cloth. "What happened? Did you miss me?"

"Fanny," said Will quietly, "it's time."

"Oh, no." She took in a gulp of air. "They said afternoon, not morning."

"I know, love, but a boy was sent from the harbor. The captain wants to beat a storm that is brewing east, so we sail on the next tide."

Fanny pushed her tangled red hair off her forehead and took a deep breath. "Alright, darling, but you owe me a full wood pile when you get back."

"I promise." Will pressed his lips against her temple. "I will dream of you every night." Fanny laid her head in the crook of his neck.

"And I you." They held each other tightly for a long moment. A timid knock at the door pulled them apart.

"Sir, the captain said I should wait for you." A small tow-headed boy stuck his head around the door.

"Come in, son," said Will. "You can sit at the table while I get ready."

"Would you like some biscuits?" Fanny asked as she laid the skillet onto the coals. "It won't take a moment. By the time Lieutenant Lowell has buttoned all his buttons, they will be ready. What is your name?" Fanny asked.

"Colin, ma'am." The boy's face turned red from the attention.

"And how old are you, Colin?"

"Ten, ma'am."

"Well, Colin, my name is Fanny. I have a brother just about your age. His name is Joshua. I hope you get to meet him someday. Now, Colin, can you do me a special favor?"

"I'll try, ma'am."

"I want you to watch out for my husband while you are at sea together. Alright?"

"Aye aye, ma'am." Colin squared his shoulders and looked Fanny in the eye. "I shall."

Will stepped out of the alcove, brass buttons shining, boots gleaming black, gold braid laid across his chest.

"Oh, my," said Fanny. "You are a handsome one."

"Do you think so? Son, would you look away? I would like to kiss this woman."

"Yes, sir." Colin tucked his head under his arm and peeked out. Fanny took Will's face in both her hands and kissed him hard.

"Madam, what will my wife think?" Colin stifled a laugh behind his hand.

"She will think you are a lucky man," said Fanny. "Now, the two of you sit, and we will have a proper breakfast. Your captain and King George will just have to wait."

"Aye aye!" Will and Colin called out together. They sat around the table, laughing as they passed the biscuits.

Later that morning, Will stood on the open deck of the *Queen's Courage*. A flurry of activity took place around him as the ship glided out of the bay. Men pulled ropes, lifted sheets, and stowed and secured barrels of supplies. He supervised with practiced efficiency, but his attention was out to sea, fixed on a small sloop tracking the passage of the *Queen's Courage*.

"Sir, small craft off starboard bow." A seaman saluted sharply.

"Yes, I see it," said Will with a small smile. The boat cut in front of the *Queen's Courage* and came about at a sharp angle. Long hair whipped against the sail, dark red on white. A big black dog stood proudly at the bow

"Did you see that? What a bloody fine sailor," shouted another seaman.

"Indeed, I did," replied Will, "and watch your language, sir, that bloody fine sailor is my wife." This elicited a cheer from the crew as Fanny expertly maneuvered her craft up next to the huge ship.

"Don't get lost at sea, you big oaf!" she shouted.

"Don't swamp that little tub and drown while I'm gone!" Will yelled back.

"I love you!" they shouted in unison. Fanny heeled her boat around and headed inland as the crew lined the gunwales, watching Fanny in awe. Will tore his eyes from the speck as it arrived almost to the beach.

"Back to work, lads, we have a ship to sail."

Fanny beached her boat in record time and raced up the hill, Dolly nipping at her feet. A breeze had come up strong and the bay was covered with tiny white wavelets. The *Queen's Courage* had all sails stretched to the fullest and rode majestically on the wind. *What a ship. Gosh, she looks beautiful*, Fanny thought. *And strong. Will is safe on her.* She stood tall, straining to see until the ship was nothing but a shadow on the horizon. As it faded from view, she sat on the grass.

"Nothing left to see, girl." She buried her face in the deep fur on Dolly's chest, hiding her tears, even from herself. When she lifted her head, Dolly placed her shovel-sized paw gently on her arm. "I know, girl," said Fanny. "It's awful, but he'll be back before you know it." She leaned against Dolly's broad back, tears salty on her cheeks.

"Fanny?" Joshua appeared over the lip of the hill. "Mamma says come on down when you get cold, and we will all have dinner."

"Thank you, Josh." Fanny put her gaze back out to sea.

"Fanny, are you alright? Your eyes are all wet."

"I'm fine, Josh." Joshua crouched at her feet, looking skeptical. "I am. I am sad, but I'm fine too. I'll be right down."

"Fanny, what if Will gets lost?"

"Well then, I will go find him, won't I!"

SEVENTEEN

A DIFFERENT CHRISTMAS

FANNY STOOD UNDER the chestnut tree as had become her morning ritual. Today the sea and the sky were both so gray it was impossible to see the horizon. She wrapped her woolen shawl more tightly and repeated her vow. *Will, my darling, wherever you are, I am with you. We are never apart.* She took one last look at the gray sea. A slight wind whipped it up into whitecaps for a moment. She could almost hear his voice, promising to come home, not to die. "I hear you, darling," she whispered and turned to trudge up the hill.

At the cabin door, Fanny stomped the snow from her fur-lined boots and shut the door with a backwards kick. "I think I hate winter." She dropped the pine branches she had picked up in a heap and pulled a chair close to the fire. Sara scooped a ball of dough from an earthen bowl. She slammed it on the table, sprinkled it with a handful of flour and with a large rolling pin began to flatten it out.

"I'm sure you do," she said, "but if there was no winter, then there would be no Christmas. No cookies, no hot cider, no presents. Then what?"

"Alright, I will put up with winter just this once so we don't disappoint Joshua. I made him a great present and it would be a shame not to give it to him."

"We are all in your debt," said Sara dryly. Fanny laughed and snatched a piece of dough from the table.

"I love your spice cookies, almost as much as Will does. I don't suppose we could send them off on a mail ship to find him. No, that wouldn't work. They would be sawdust by the time he got them." Fanny's face dropped. Will had been gone almost two years now, and it had become harder to stay cheerful. "I'm worried, Sara, I haven't gotten a letter since spring and . . ."

"You know how unreliable mail at sea is," said Sara. "He's probably sleeping on a sunny beach dreaming of winter and you. Don't fret, dear. And I promise I will bake dozens of spice cookies his first day back." Fanny shrugged off her heavy, wool coat.

"Good, and make Will some too." They both laughed.

"Where shall we put these pine boughs? I want to finish decorating so Nate and Joshua will be surprised when they come home tomorrow. Do you think they liked spending the night with Aunt Biddy and Aunt Maude?"

"Of course they did. Biddy fussed over them and Maude gave them cakes. I just hope they managed to get all our supplies. I don't want to have to go back into town when the snow comes." Sara surveyed the room. "Let's pile some on the mantle and drape it with the new red cloth," she said. "We can hang those tin stars off it too, and the rest can go around the door." Fanny laid the branches end to end. Sara pulled a length of rich red cloth from the cupboard. "With luck, we can find some more of those chokeberries this spring. This is the best red we've made yet."

"I know," said Fanny. "I gave Aunt Biddy a little piece for her table and now she said she wants enough to make a cloak." Sara turned back to the table and picked up a carved cookie cutter.

"Look, Nate made a new one shaped like a bear. Isn't it cunning? He got the eyes and the snout just right."

Fanny clapped her hands. "That is my favorite."

"What about the tree and the turkey and the star and the gnome. They were all your favorites too." She laid the bear-shaped cookies in rows on a tin tray.

"I have an idea," said Fanny. "What if Nate makes dozens of these? I can help carve if he shows me. Then we can take them to the first Training Day Fair in March and sell them along with our cloth."

"It's a good idea," said Sara, "but let's get these baked first." Fanny opened the oven set into the stones on the side of the hearth. Sara slid the tray inside. "When the smell gets strong and sweet then it is time to take them out. Let's cut some more."

Fanny picked up the tree shape. "This one is for you, my darling Will."

At that moment, Dolly stood up from her spot near the fire. She faced the door and curled her lip. A low rumble came from deep in her throat. Fanny stepped away from the table and picked up the long rifle resting in the corner. With a practiced hand, she poured the powder and loaded the ball. She rammed it in with the long rod and shouldered the gun. Sara went to the door and listened intently. "I can't hear anything," she said.

"It has to be a stranger or Dolly wouldn't be at alert," whispered Fanny. "There were smugglers run off the bay last week. They could have come back." There was suddenly a light scratching sound at the door. The women froze. "Who is there?" Fanny made her voice deep as a man. There was another scratch. "Who is it? Answer or take the consequences." A scratch, followed by a thud. Fanny aimed at the door. "Open it," she whispered. Sara flung open the door and stepped to one side. A small bundle tumbled into the room.

"It's a boy." said Sara. She pulled him across the threshold with one hand and slammed the door shut. Fanny came around the table, rifle still at the ready.

"Do we know him? Is he from town?"

"I don't think so, but he's in a bad way. Help me get him to the fire. He's near frozen, poor thing."

Fanny laid the rifle in the corner and picked up the boy. "He weighs scarce more than a bag of flour," she said. Sara laid some blankets on the hearth. Fanny gently placed him on the blankets and covered him with a large beaver skin.

"What do you suppose he was doing out in this weather?" she said.

"And not dressed for it, either," said Sara. "Look at his shoes."

Fanny looked down and caught her breath. "Oh, my God, Sara, he's off Will's ship. I recognize him. He's here about Will." Fanny sat down hard and began to rock. "Oh, God, oh, God."

Sara took her by the shoulders and gave her a small shake. "Alright, Fanny, alright. If he is from Will, he will tell us. First, we must get him warm."

"Of course," said Fanny. "I wasn't thinking. I'll heat some soup."

"Good girl. I'll fill a skin with hot water. We can put it under the fur and he will warm up twice as fast." When the soup was hot, Fanny dribbled it slowly into the boy's mouth.

"Not too fast," Sara said as she tucked the skin around the boy's chest.

"He is so thin," said Fanny. "It looks like he hasn't eaten properly in a long time. Will he be alright, Sara?"

"I think so," Sara replied. "The young have an amazing ability to bounce back. Look at you. You were more than half dead from the pox when you were about his age, and look at you now. Being cold and hungry won't kill this boy,

I promise. Listen to his heart." Fanny did as she was told and laid her head on the boy's chest. "Do you hear that?" Sara asked.

"I do," said Fanny. "Strong and steady." She lifted her head and the boy's eyes fluttered open. "Hello, there," said Fanny. "Glad you came back to us. Are you Colin?"

The boy swallowed.

"Is it you, Mistress Fanny?" he whispered.

Fanny couldn't speak for a moment. "Yes," she finally said, "it is."

"Oh, good," said the boy and closed his eyes again.

"Ah," said Sara, "that is no longer a swoon. He is just sleeping now. He'll be fine."

"He is from Will, Sara."

"Yes, he is, child. Let's get dinner on, and when he wakes, he will tell us all about it." The dinner was cooked, eaten, cleared away, and still the boy slept on. Fanny paced beside the fire.

"What do we do, Sara?"

"We wait. You will want to sleep here on the hearth, in case he wakes in the night. I will bring down your blankets."

"Thank you, Sara. I will stay here, though I don't think I shall sleep at all."

The next morning, Sara arose to find Fanny asleep leaning against the fireplace holding the boy's hand in her lap. Dolly was stretched out against his back, her paw curled over him. Sara stoked the fire and looked out the window. Everything was sparkling white. The storm had passed and left a soft blanket of snow. She turned from the window and heard footsteps on the porch. Dolly didn't move. It was Nate and Joshua back from town. Sara opened the door with her finger to her lips. "Hush," she said, "we have company. Come sit at the table and have some breakfast and I'll tell you what we know so far."

As they sat, Dolly stretched her back legs and stood up. She licked the boy's face. He laughed and pushed her away. "So, you're awake," said Fanny from her place on the hearth. "Would you like some breakfast?"

"Yes, ma'am, very much. I haven't had anything but some hardtack for the last few days." He stood, swayed, and would have fallen if not for Nate's quick arm.

"Slowly, son," he said, easing him into a chair. "You'll get your strength back in time, don't you worry."

"Thank you, sir," said the boy.

"What is your name?" asked Joshua. "Are you going to stay? Where do you live?"

"Hold on, son, let the boy eat. Then we can talk."

"Sorry, Daddy." Joshua settled in his chair. Sara put a wooden plate down in front of Colin and piled it with potatoes, mashed squash, and eggs.

"When you feel a bit stronger, I'll give you some mutton," she said.

"Thank you, ma'am," the boy mumbled, his mouth full.

"Have a biscuit," said Joshua. He laid one on the boy's plate. "I like them best with jam," he said as he spooned out a heap. The boy's eyes lit up. He picked up the biscuit with both hands and put half of it in his mouth.

"Slow down there, son," said Nate. "You don't want to eat so fast your stomach can't keep up." Fanny watched the boy eat. She had a million questions, but kept her mouth shut. His blonde hair was ragged, but clean. There were shadows under his eyes, but as he ate and laughed with Joshua, they began to sparkle. He was twelve or thirteen, Fanny guessed. She was anxious to hear his story, but she waited until he pushed his plate away with a sigh.

"I never thought to eat real food again," he said.

"Shall we talk now?" asked Fanny.

"Yes, ma'am. I am Colin Richard Wilkens, cabin boy of Her Majesty's vessel, *Queen's Courage*.

Fanny breathed in slowly. "You were here before, weren't you?" she asked gently.

"Yes, ma'am, two years ago." He pulled himself to his feet and stood straight. "I have been charged by my superior officer to bring you a message." Colin struggled to stay standing.

"Sit down, boy," said Fanny.

"It's official business, ma'am."

"Just this once. No one will mind," Fanny replied.

"Thank you, ma'am. The boy sank into the chair and took a deep breath. "Mistress Fanny Campbell, I have been charged by your husband, William Lowell, to bring you the following message."

"Where is he? Colin, is he alright? What has happened?" The words tumbled out of Fanny's mouth before she could stop them.

"Fanny." Sara laid a hand on her arm. "Let the boy talk."

"I'm so sorry, Colin," said Fanny. "You tell us your own way."

"Yes, ma'am. Well, here it is, just the way it happened. We were off the coast of Cuba about to head for home. There was a mist on the ocean. The Spanish warship came out of it so fast we had no time to turn and fire. She laid all her guns on us broadside and the commander went down. His face was covered with blood and no one knew what to do. There was smoke everywhere, and some of the rigging was on fire. Suddenly, your husband appeared with his saber drawn.

"'Come on, lads, we'll take them hand to hand as they board. Colin, up the rigging now. We need your eyes aloft.'

"'Aye aye, Captain, sir,' I said, because for sure now he was the captain. I went up the main to the crow's nest and watched the battle. The Spanish ship got her hooks in us.

"'Colin, tell me when they are about to swing.' All the crew were at the ready. 'Now, sir,' I yelled. 'Now!' You should have seen it. Our crew outnumbered and attacking like we couldn't lose. Truth, ma'am, I was dead scared, but the captain was in the thick swinging away.

"'Come on, lads, show them your steel,' he shouted. Even when the Spanish had him pinned up against the mast, four blades at his throat, he laughed. 'Now that's English courage, lads. Good show, my friends.' And he marched onto that Spanish ship, his head all high like he had been invited. When they brought me down from the rigging, he said, 'That one is a stowaway. You can throw him back if you like. He's not one of ours.' At first, I was plenty mad, because I was not a stowaway, but he winked at me, and I figured out he had some plan. They took us all to a big castle on that island, Cuba. I never saw so many Spanish soldiers and guards. They put me in a cell by myself and didn't chain me up, so I figured the captain's plan was working. Then they took us all to this big room with a man sitting behind a tall desk. The captain told them they had no right to keep us prisoner or bring us to trial, but they all just spoke Spanish and never looked at us.

"We were all jammed into this prisoner's box, and they were looking at us and pointing and talking when all of a sudden, the captain began to shout at me, 'You little weasel, this is your fault! We should have hung you when we had the chance.' The Spaniards now were watching and laughing. 'Don't give me that look, boy,' the captain said. 'You are nothing but a puling little snake. What! Do you want to hit me? Go on, now is your chance. I'm in chains, you aren't. Now you can pay me back for all those beatings, you cowardly piece of trash!'

"Now I tell you true, he had never hit me once, never even said a cross word. In fact, he had stopped the first mate from kicking me when I lost a line. The whole crew loved him. Then all of a sudden like, I got it! He was fooling them. He wanted me to jump him. That was part of the plan. So, I did. And when I was on his neck, he whispered, 'Go to Fanny.' I knew all about you. He always talked about you and sometimes shared your letters with us. And then he shouted some more awful names at me, called me a pustulant toad. I wasn't sure what that meant, but I knew it was bad, and then he butted me with his head. The Spaniards were all laughing now, and I think taking bets. 'Put your hand over my mouth,' he hissed at me, and when I did, would you believe, he spit this into my hand. Colin pulled a scrap of cloth from his pocket, unwrapped it carefully, and laid it on the table. This for you, ma'am."

Fanny picked up the gold ring. "This is Will's wedding ring," she said in wonder.

"Yes, ma'am. He hid it from them in his mouth the whole time." Fanny held the ring tightly. "So, after he spits the ring in my hand he whispers, 'Hold tight.' He winks, and then he bites me. It hurt fierce and I jumped back and yelled. I fell down in the box, and all the crew rolled me to the back. Then the judge said something in Spanish, and the guards took them all away. Nobody paid me any mind at all, so I snuck out the door with the crowd, ran down to the harbor, and hid out.

"A Portuguese ship came into the harbor bound for the Americas, so I talked my way onto it, again as a cabin boy! It took me to Boston and then I walked here. It took a long time. I hope the captain is alright. He saved my life, ma'am.

He bit me hard so it would look real. I'm glad for the scar. I don't want to ever forget what I owe him." He held out his arm. Fanny ran her finger over the faint bite mark.

"I'm sorry he had to hurt you," she said.

"Not to worry, ma'am. But I almost forgot the most important part. When they were dragging him away, he said, 'Tell Fanny I will keep my promise.' Do you know what he meant, ma'am?"

"Oh, yes, Colin, I know." Fanny let her tears run free. "Thank you, Colin. When Will comes home I will tell him how amazing, brave, and faithful you are." Fanny hugged Colin hard. When she released him, she asked, "Do you have a family?"

"No, I am an orphan."

"No longer," said Fanny. "You are family to us and we to you. You shall stay with us as long as you like or forever, if you wish."

"For true, ma'am?"

"Of course," Joshua piped up. "Fanny never lies. Everyone knows that." The tension that had been in the room left as they all laughed.

"How would you like a brother, Joshua?" Fanny asked.

"I would very much. Come on, Colin," Joshua pulled at his sleeve. "I'll show you the toy boat my father carved. Maybe he will make you one too." The boys ran into the corner as though they had been playing together for years.

"Are you alright, Fanny?" Sara asked.

"I will be," said Fanny. "You know what he promised? He promised not to die."

"So, what will you do, Fanny?" Nate took her hand. Fanny stood and looked out the window at the chestnut tree on the hill for a moment. She turned around smiling.

"Why, I'll go get him, of course!"

EIGHTEEN

THE PLAN

FANNY WOKE WITH a start. She heard murmuring in the cabin below, but it was not yet light. She climbed down when she saw Sara and Nate at the table. It was covered with cloth, leather, and papers.

"Have you been up all night?" she asked.

"We could never allow you to start this venture unprepared," said Nate. The night before, Fanny told them she had decided to dress as a man, get on a ship going south, and find Will. It wasn't much of a plan, but it was the best she had.

"Look what we made for you." He handed her a folded piece of parchment. She looked inside and saw an official-looking form identifying her as Frank Campbell, able-bodied seaman, and an accompanying letter from Captain Thomas Charles from the British warship *Orion's Belt* with a commendation for bravery. Fanny was dumbstruck.

"How did you do all this?" she asked in a soft voice.

"Your dad and I had lots of practice when we went to rescue Sara. Your mother made so many great documents. Do you remember? She used pyrite and glue for the seals and imprinted it with a button from your father's uniform. I just did the same. This will certainly work for a sea captain. Now look at what Sara did! These are clothes of mine she altered to fit you, but that is not the best part. Show her, Sara!" Nate beamed proudly as Sara held up several pieces of clothing.

"This is your doublet. It goes over the shirt and is well padded. Here is a reworked leather belt to hold up your pants, and this is the best part: a leather singlet to go under your shirt to hide your breasts. You are slim, so it won't be too much of a problem."

"It is a good thing I am not ample like my mother. There is no way we could have disguised me as a man." Fanny laughed as she spoke.

"No, indeed. Now look at the trousers. I was thinking about having to relieve yourself, so the front button flap goes all the way around. You unbutton the four buttons, then tuck the flap in your belt at the back. You won't have privacy on a ship, so your shirt is extra long to cover the front so no one will see what you are missing."

Fanny held up the pants and looked at the work with awe. Then she took all the clothes behind the privacy curtain in the corner. She tried on the singlet first. It fit perfectly. She could see no evidence of her breasts. She put on the rest and came out fingering the seams.

"I look just like a boy," she said. "Sara, you are a genius. I would never have thought of any of this. Shall we cut my hair now?"

"I would wait." said Nate. "You want to go to the Admiralty as a woman first to check on the status of Will's ship. Then you become a man and search the harbor for a ship for yourself."

"Nate is right. Here, I will show you how to cut it when the time comes." Sara sat Fanny down and pulled all of her hair to the nape of her neck and wrapped it with a long leather tie. "Now, when you want to cut your hair, you go about a hand length from the tie and cut it straight across. Your hair is curly, so it will end up exactly the right length this way. Make sure you pull it back tight so it doesn't come loose from the tie. What's the matter, dear?" Fanny had turned her head away. Dolly dropped her big head on Fanny's lap.

"My precious family, I can't believe I have to leave you, but I promise that Will and I are going to come back together." She looked back at Sara and Nate with tears in her eyes. "Once again, you are saving me. You did it when my parents died, and you are doing it again." She crossed to the hearth where Joshua and Colin were still sleeping. She knelt down and touched their heads. "I won't wake them until it is time to go. Then we can have a happy goodbye. Shall I take Fiona?"

"Yes," said Nate. "I have a friend working in a livery stable in Boston. You will go there and tell him to hire a rider to bring her back. You can ask him for a place with a single room you can rent for the night. These coins should be sufficient to pay him. Also, Sara has sewn coins into the seams of your trousers and your doublet. We don't want you to be stranded without currency. When you return from the Admiralty, you must be very careful when you become a man. You mustn't let anyone see you leave the boarding house."

"Nate, you have thought of everything!"

"I have had much practice being on the run and hiding. You must very careful. If you are found out, there will be terrible consequences."

"Don't scare her, Nate! Fanny is a clever, brave girl. She will take all of your counsel and she will come back to us, whole and happy."

"That is one of the things I love most about my wife," Nate said to Fanny. "She can look for a positive outcome in the direst of circumstances."

"Indeed, I can and I am most always right," Sara said tartly. "Now, let's get Fanny's knapsack packed." She picked up a large canvas bag with leather straps and started to fill it. "Fanny, get those clothes off and dress for traveling."

Fanny did as she was told. She chose a skirt and a blouse with a vest, and her boots to be comfortable while riding. Sara also put in a soft bonnet and some flat shoes in her bag. At the end, she slipped in a volume that was one of Fanny's favorite books, *Don Quixote*. It was a gift from her parents on her tenth birthday. She had always been fascinated by the imaginary world he had immersed himself in and had read it over and over. Sara thought it might be a comfort to Fanny when she was on her own. Nate went out to saddle Fiona, and Fanny sat at the table, watching Sara store bits of dried beef, biscuits, and fruit in her sack.

"It will be a long time, Sara. Please stay safe until I am back."

"And look who is talking about staying safe. We will be fine. And we will keep you in our hearts as we are in yours, until you return. You will return, I have no doubt. On occasion, Nate claims I have second sight. This is one of those occasions. All will be well. I am going to wake the boys so we can wave you down the lane."

Dolly came over and once again put her head in Fanny's lap. She knew that something was happening. Fanny buried her face in Dolly's fur. "I will miss you, my beautiful beast. But your job is to stay here and protect our family while I am gone." Dolly looked deep into Fanny's eyes, as if she understood every word. Fanny was sure she did.

As she road down the lane, Fanny sat on Fiona with her back straight, wiping the tears from her eyes. She looked back to the porch and saw Nate, Sara, and the boys all waving madly. Dolly sat next to Joshua, who put his arm around her neck. *They will be fine*, Fanny thought. *They will keep each other safe, and this will be the picture in my mind.*

Fanny arrived in Boston and followed Nate's directions to the livery stable. His friend Henry took Fiona in and directed Fanny to a boarding house near the wharf. He told her it was a place that was clean and secure, where no one would notice her. Fanny found her room, washed off the travel dirt, and pinned up her hair. She put on her pretty jacket, bonnet, and shoes. *I look like a nice, respectable girl*, she thought.

At the offices of the Admiralty, she was kept waiting for several hours. When she was finally admitted to talk to the man responsible for tracking the ships, he acted as if she were a silly girl with no brains. He told her there was no way to track Will's ship, and she should go home and tend the fire. Fanny was furious.

"A wink is as good as a nod to a blind horse," she said.

"What exactly does that mean?" said the official behind the desk.

"It means you, sir, are a horse's ass and need to pay attention to what I say. I am going to find my husband, and when I do, you will apologize for your cavalier attitude." She flew out of the office and on to the street. She threw off her bonnet and stomped on it as if it were the official's face. Then she strode briskly along the Long Wharf in search of the right ship. It was quiet on the wharf at this moment, but Henry had told her about the rising tensions between the British and the colonialists. She knew she needed to find a ship fast. Near the end of the wharf, she spotted a four-masted barque. It was not pretty or well cared for, but it looked sturdy. She walked past it, turned around, and came back to view it from another angle. *Well,* she thought, *it won't sink!* She returned to her room and dressed in her man clothes. She used the cream Sara had made to roughen her skin. The last thing to do was cut her hair. She took her dirk out of her sock. She hacked through the thick red curls and was left with a tidy knob. She surveyed herself in the tiny mirror. *Sara,* she thought, *thank you for your help. I am now a man.* She packed her woman's clothes and her length of hair in bag and dropped them with a note and a coin at the doorway of Henry's friend. He was to return them to Henry to carry when he took Fiona home.

"Ahoy, the *Mary of Leeds*. Permission to board."

"What is your business?" A man with a scar that seemed to cover half his face looked over the bulwark.

"I am looking for a berth. I am an experienced, able-bodied seaman. I have references from my last captain."

"What happened to him?"

"He died." The man gave a snicker and waved Fanny on board.

"What is your name?"

"Frank Campbell, sir." Fanny thought that in this situation it would be prudent to be extremely polite. "I have letters."

He took them and knocked on the door of the aft cabin. A short man appeared.

"Sorry to disturb, sir, but I think we found a replacement for that imbecile we lost at sea. This is Frank Campbell, sir.

Seaman Campbell, this is Captain Browning." The captain walked around Fanny as though inspecting a side of beef.

"Climb up and release the main," he ordered.

Fanny made it to the mast in two leaps and clambered up the rigging. At the top, she released the ropes, rode one down, and let the main unfurl as she touched the deck. She stood in front of the captain and tried to look humble. The captain eyed her for a moment and then said, "He will do, get him sorted out."

The bosun, who introduced himself as Jonas, took Fanny below deck, showed her where to stow her bag, and said, "Don't leave anything you want to keep down here. It will be gone tomorrow."

That night, Fanny lay on her pallet with her bag under her head. In the dark she felt a hand reaching for it, twisted the wrist, and put her dirk at his throat.

"That is a dangerous thing to do if you want to stay alive," she whispered. "I will not cut your throat this time, but you might tell your shipmates that if they are looking to filch, I am the wrong person to try it with." In the dark she couldn't even see who the sailor was, but she knew that her message was received. She fell into a light sleep and started awake at first light. For a moment, she didn't know where she was. But then she recognized the foul smell and wished she were dreaming. *Wretched Mary of Leeds! I hate this ship already!*

NINETEEN

ABOARD THE MARY OF LEEDS

"SEAMAN CAMPBELL, WHAT do you see?"

Fanny looked down from the crow's nest to the deck below. "Empty sea ahead, sir."

"Good, carry on."

Silent Jonas, the bosun, only spoke to give orders. She wondered what he would do if he knew. She reset her grip on the frozen rope. The salt spray burned her cracked lips. She looked to the horizon and said her daily prayer: "God, keep my Will safe 'til I find him."

"Seaman Campbell!" The bosun was back at the bottom of the mast. "Come down at once. The captain wants a word with all the crew. Lenton will relieve you."

She made her way down the mast with easy swings on

the rigging. *Lenton was a boy*, she thought. *What could be so important that he would be trusted as lookout while we wait on the captain? Please, God, let it not be me.* She dropped to the deck in front of Indigo Sam, the first mate. The blue birthmark covering half his face had given him that name. He didn't seem to mind, but woe to the sailor stupid enough to stare. Sam had flogged one fellow to death and chalked it up to a weak constitution. No one did anything. The captain just read some words, and they threw his body overboard.

The crew stood on the heaving deck while the ship plowed through the breakers made by some faraway storm. The door to the captain's cabin opened. They all felt the rush of warm air and smelled some sort of meat cooking. The crew hadn't had meat for nearly two months. The smell made her stomach growl. Captain Browning pushed his bulk into the door frame, but no further. He was pasty-faced and round, with a nasty temper. The crew had often speculated as to how he got his commission in the first place. The most popular explanation was he married into it, but then who would marry such a pompous jackass?

"Cook brought to my attention that several kegs of grog are missing from the stores. Whoever stole them has taken grog from the mouths of his fellow crewmen. Step forward and admit your crime."

"He probably drank it himself." The voice in her ear made her start. Silent Jonas was looking straight ahead, but no one else was near her on that side. She took care not to smile.

The captain continued to sweep his eyes over the crew. *What an idiot*, she thought. *His eyes look like tiny, dried currants in a puffy milk pudding. Does he think we don't know? He has us on half rations and sells the rest in port.*

"We are starving while he eats what he likes. When we lose our next battle, it will be his fault." She hadn't meant to say the last bit aloud, but Silent Jonas turned his eyes toward her, and she knew she had. *Fiddlesticks*, she thought, *he'll report me, and I'm done.* Then he closed one eye. *Oh, my God*, thought Fanny. *Did he just wink?* At that moment, Lenton yelled from the crow's nest, "A black flag sir, a black ship with a black flag. Pirates!"

TWENTY

A LOSING BATTLE

"LENTON, KEEP CLOSE watch now; they are turning. Crew, prepare for a broadside!" Silent Jonas was silent no more, yelling orders while the crew stumbled in disarray, and Captain Browning ducked into his cabin, slamming the door.

"Coward!" Fanny shouted at his back. She hustled the gun crew below deck to prepare the cannons for firing. "Work faster. We will probably only have one chance to fire!" she yelled as she raced topside. She was just in time to see a cannon ball punch through the main sail and another one hit the aft deck.

"They are aiming high!" shouted Jonas. "They don't want to sink us. Prepare to be boarded!" The on-deck crew pulled out their swords and started to load the muskets. Although they were not well trained or loyal, they were at least willing to fight for their lives. Fanny could see the pirates in the rigging of their ship, changing the trim on the sails as their ship started a turn.

"How are they turning so fast?" Fanny shouted to Jonas.

"Good crew, great ship. Here they come!"

The sleek, black pirate ship was headed right at them and somehow, at the last minute, turned again and scraped against their hull. Grappling hooks came flying across, and now the ships were effectively bound together. Lenton gave a shout from the crow's nest, "They are swinging!" And pirates began to drop like giant albatrosses and swarmed the deck in an instant.

"Lenton, get your head down now!" The boy did as Fanny said and disappeared into the bottom of the crow's nest. Fanny engaged with her first pirate, exchanged blows, then caught him on the side of his head with the flat of her blade. He fell to the deck unconscious, and she turned toward the next one. She crossed blades with an angry looking Moor, who laughed menacingly, perhaps thinking Fanny's size was a hindrance for her. He soon found himself with her blade across his throat. Then she jumped in the air and kicked him in the head. He hit the deck like a sack of bird seed. She wasn't trying not to kill anyone; She just didn't see the necessity if she didn't have to. She scooped up the fallen blade and now had a blade in each hand. Fanny felt movement to her right, spun, and put her left foot behind her. She fended off an overhead strike from a massive Black pirate. He didn't get through her block, but his power was so great she would have fallen except for a slight pressure at her back. With a quick glance over her shoulder, she was astonished to see Silent Jonas. They stayed back-to-back and moved in a circle, protecting each other as though they had done it for years. The fighting was intense; they were surrounded by thrusts, overhead strikes, wide arm slashes. They were on their feet, but they were the only ones still fighting, and they were both flagging under the onslaught of multiple blades.

"Enough!" A voice rang out. In an instant, the circle of pirates fell back. Fanny and Jonas kept their weapons high. A figure, tall with broad shoulders, came into view. There were bigger men on deck, but his presence filled the space completely. He had a long, black braid down his back and thick sideburns but no beard. And a strong square chin. He wore the same clothes as the rest of the crew—canvas breeches, leather vest, cotton shirt, and a worn, long blue jacket that Fanny thought could be Royal Navy. He had in his belt two pistols and across his chest there was strung a powder horn and a bag of musket balls. But while most of the rest of the men had short sabers and cutlasses, he carried a long sword with an ornate pommel. Fanny had seen this sword at work during the battle. This man was no common sailor, that she was sure of.

"That was some excellent swordplay, young man. Where did you learn it?"

"My father," Fanny panted, trying to regain her breath.

"And who, pray tell, is your father?" The British accent was rich and highborn.

He is clearly an aristocrat, Fanny thought. *What is he doing on a pirate ship?*

"Why do you care? You are going to kill us anyway!" Fanny wiped the sweat from her eyes with her sleeve.

"Don't be so sure, young man. We on the *Bloody Rose* have our own way of doing things."

Fanny squared her shoulders defiantly. "Fine then! My father was the finest and youngest armorer in all of Scotland."

"Aha, then not much love for the English, I take it. From where do you hail?"

"Massachusetts." Fanny thought it better no one knew where she was really from.

"Ah, the rebels! I've half a mind to join them if they ever decide to throw off the yoke of King George." He turned his attention back to the crew from the *Mary of Leeds*, who stood huddled against the rail. Fanny followed his gaze. The brief battle had left them bloodied and exhausted. The pirates guarding them looked fierce, with multiple swords and pistols bristling from their sashes and belts. The massive pirate who had almost killed her looked particularly dangerous. He wore a leather vest with multiple pockets down the front full of daggers. His muscular black arms were bare and covered with scars, and there were scars around both of his wrists, broad bands like bracelets. He did not threaten or glare like the other pirates. He stood, legs apart, hand on his saber, still, like an ebony statue. Fanny did not relish the idea of crossing swords with him again.

"Can we just get on with it?" she said crossly. "Whatever you are going to do, let's just get it over with."

"Impatient, aren't we!" Why did Fanny have the feeling this man was laughing at her?. He turned his back and addressed his crew. "What do you think, men? Shall we throw them overboard, put them adrift?" The men laughed and shouted suggestions.

"String them up! Keel haul them! Run them through and feed them to the sharks!" *Was that how they amused themselves before killing us?* Fanny wondered.

"All excellent suggestions, very creative," said the pirate captain. "I will take them all under advisement, but first, some protocol!" He turned again and with the full force of his deep brown eyes, he scanned the *Mary of Leeds* crew.

"Allow me to introduce myself. I am Captain John Thorne of the majestic pirate ship, the *Bloody Rose*. This is my gallant crew. We are fiercely loyal, but only to each other." Fanny looked around again at the pirates who had gathered the rest of her crew against the bulwarks at sword point.

"Gallant seems an odd word, sir," Fanny replied scornfully.

"Perhaps, but you don't know them yet," Thorne said with a smile. "Gentlemen, those of you with a sword at your throat, pay attention. It is a tradition on some pirate ships to kill the crew of the captured vessel and throw them overboard.

We follow an alternate tradition. We vote. If the vote goes your way, you will have a decision to make. You can join our crew and sail with us as we hunt vessels like yours. You will be subject to all of our rules and regulations. You will become one of us, with equal rights to vote and share in the plunder and also the consequences of wrongdoing, same as any man on our ship. Or we can put you in your longboats with provisions and send you adrift off toward land. The choice is yours. Think well before you decide. Who will speak for the prisoners?"

"They fought hard, but not well," said a bearded pirate in a green bandana. This brought a raucous burst of laughter.

"Their captain must be an ass," said the one with the eye patch.

"So true, Moor!" said Thorne. "Let us find out for sure. Where is your captain? Show yourself!" Silent Jonas pointed with his sword to a carved doorway. Two pirates flung open the door, dragged Captain Browning out, and threw him unceremoniously on the deck. The elegant pirate began to laugh, as did his crew.

"So, you were hiding, like a little baby, while your crew fought valiantly for their lives. That is reason enough right there to allow them to join us."

"My men will never join with you." Browning's face was red and his voice high and shaky with fear.

"Shut your yob before I dispatch you this instant!" Thorne was not joking now; Fanny heard the steel in his voice. "Who speaks against this crew?"

"We took them fast. They never got their ship turned away."

"True, but that doesn't mean they are all bad sailors. It just means we are better. Anything else?"

"They can't fight . . . and their captain is an ass."

"Once again, the best reason to take them on. Let's vote. Do they get the choice?" The pirates all gave a resounding "Aye!" Fanny thought again that is might all be for sport or for show. Thorne fixed a baleful glare on Browning. "I am going to give them a generous choice. In case you did not hear, you have been captured by the *Bloody Rose*. I am her captain, John Thorne. This offer is for all your men, but not for you, captain. I will not have a coward on my ship. We hunt and capture mostly English ships. Yours, being American, was a slight accident. Men, you are welcome to join our crew. To do so, you must sign a contract and agree to abide by our rules. You will also share in the booty, the division of which is set forth in the contract. Or you can go in one of your longboats with your captain. We will provide you with water and provisions, and you can make your way to land, which, by the way, is in that direction." He pointed west. Everyone looked, but there was no land in sight. "What say you?"

Lenton popped his head up from the crow's nest where he had been hiding this whole time. "Sir, do you beat your crew?"

"Of course not. That would be ridiculous."

"Don't you dare, boy!" Captain Browning sputtered, his face redder still and practically apoplectic. Lenton swung easily down the rigging and landed on the deck in front of John Thorne.

"I would like very much to join you, sir." The pirates cheered lustily. "May I have a sword?"

"You shall have a sword, I promise you, but first we have other matters to attend to. Who else?"

Fanny stepped forward. "I, for one, see no need to hold false loyalty. This captain starved us while he gorged, beat the weakest among us for sport, and, worst of all, let us down in battle. You, sir, are not a captain. You are an incompetent fool." Turning to Thorne, she said, "I would like to join as well." Fanny dropped her blade to her side and stepped forward. The Black giant who almost killed her glanced at his captain. Fanny thought he may have nodded.

Indigo Sam flashed her a look of pure hatred as Browning began a tirade. "Traitor! You will hang for this." Captain Browning's rage kept mounting. He was so furious, he forgot to be fearful for a moment. The rest of his crew shrank before his intense glare. Silent Jonas ignored him, stepped in beside Fanny, and sheathed his sword.

"Anyone else?" No one moved. They were all too afraid. "Fine, let's get the rest of these cretins into a boat and resume our hunt." The longboat was lowered, a few kegs of water and a canvas bag of hard tack were handed down. "You are not so far from the Carolina shore. We will not waste sails on you, but oars work quite well. You can probably make landfall before your food runs out, if you put your backs into it."

Indigo Sam shouted back, "You will pay for this! Curse you and the cowards you sail with!"

Captain Browning pulled on his jacket. "Sit down, shut up, and row!"

"Row yourself, you fat cow. You ain't captain here!"

The pirate crew gave a cheer and began to place bets.

"I put a wager on the ugly one. In a day, he will dump the fat one overboard." Bill took a coin from his pocket and waved it about.

"I would take that wager," said Jim, "but how would we know?"

"He would float by before the sharks ate him." The pirates laughed again, but with a glance from the quartermaster, got back to the business of stripping the ship of everything of value.

"A word, sir!" The giant Black pirate came to Thorne's side.

"Of course, Q, and please remember, we are not at battle. You do not have to call me 'sir.'"

"This ship is in terrible shape. We should finish stripping her and then scuttle her."

"Done! Sink the scow! Let's get everything useful onto the *Rose*. It's time to be underway. The three of you, come with me."

"I'd like to retrieve my sack, if I may." Fanny took a polite tone just in case this pirate captain changed his mind.

"Be quick about it, then." Fanny ducked into the hiding place she had discovered at the bow of the ship, grabbed her sack, and planted herself in front of the captain in a flash.

"Hmmm," said the captain. "Follow me." He led them across a plank and onto the pirate ship.

TWENTY-ONE

THE *BLOODY ROSE*

FANNY WAS AMAZED at how clean and well-ordered everything was. The brass sparkled, and the wood was polished. This was not what she had expected. She looked up and saw the black flag and recognized it instantly from Will's story.

"You are called the *Bloody Rose*?" she queried.

"Yes, we are. You have heard of us? I like to imagine we are famous." The flag snapped in the breeze, a red rose against black silk with a single drop of blood falling from its petal.

"Infamous, maybe," Fanny said under her breath to Jonas. The captain laughed again. Fanny would come to find that he laughed often.

"I heard that. I will happily settle for infamous." Thorne led them into what was clearly his cabin. There was a large window aft, and shelves and shelves of books. *A pirate who reads?* Fanny was having to reassess her preconceived idea of pirates. Thorne went behind a large desk littered with charts. He pushed them to one side and leaned forward. "Do any of you read?" Lenton and Jonas shook their heads.

"I read quite well," said Fanny.

"Good. What is your name?"

"Frank Campbell."

"Well, Frank Campbell, read this contract to your mates. Anything you don't understand, ask me. Then you will sign, and we will all have dinner." The three looked at each other. Dinner? They turned back to the captain. "Cook always makes a feast after a capture. This one wasn't very rich, but we will celebrate anyway." Fanny remembered Will's story about the long tables on deck, with white linen clothes and silverware. "Meet me on deck as soon as it is signed."

"Well, lads, it looks like we may have fallen into the cream." Silent Jonas grunted, which Fanny thought might have been his way of agreeing, but she wasn't sure. "Alright, here are the terms:

"Number 1: During battle the captain's word is law. Disobey on pain of death.

"Number 2: No stealing. No touching of other's belongings. It is possible to be marooned or perhaps lose a hand if this rule is broken.

"Number 3: Even division of spoils. Exception made in the case of injury."

"What injuries?" asked Lenton. There was a little quaver in his voice.

"Let's see, loss of a hand, fingers, a foot, a limb, an eye, both eyes. Compensation is for different losses."

"Go on, keep reading," said Jonas. "I have no intention of losing anything."

"I agree; no need to dwell on the unlikely." Fanny continued reading.

"Number 4: The crew votes on everything that does not pertain to battle. Where to go, when to go, when to rest, who stays, who goes, and what ships are attacked.

"Number 5: The crew votes a captain in. If he does not perform well in battle, he can be voted out."

"Is there more?" Lenton was clearly impatient. He grabbed the quill. "I can't write, but I want to sign."

"I read all the important things. I can read the rest if you like."

"No, that's enough. Let's sign." Jonas was just as impatient as Lenton. Fanny showed them both where to make their X and then wrote their names underneath.

"That's my name," crowed Lenton. Jonas rolled his eyes but gave a tiny grin.

"It certainly is," said Fanny, "and I will teach you to write it as soon as we have time." Fanny signed *Frank Campbell* with a flourish and blotted the ink on the contract. "Now, I think we should go eat!"

On deck, the tables were set exactly as Will had described. She had been half certain he was making up a story, but here they were. At the head of the table, Captain Thorne stood up. "Any injuries?"

"Bill cut his thumb on our own hook." Liam, the pirate speaking, made weeping sounds. Bill was not amused.

"It wouldn't have happened if you had set the hook properly, you clumsy land rat!" Everyone laughed. This was clearly good-natured teasing among a tightly knit group. Fanny wondered just how they were going to fit in.

"This fight was almost too easy," said Bill. The others murmured in agreement. "There were no fighters, save these two."

"Very true. Let's welcome them to our little family." The captain raised his glass. All the pirates did the same and cheered, "Huzzah! Huzzah!"

"Cook Gio, tell us what we are about to eat!" The captain urged the man to his left to stand up. He was a tall, thin man with black hair and a scar across his eyebrow that gave him a rakish air.

"We have a good store of food from our last visit to Genova," said Gio.

"They like us fine there because they hate the English, and so do we," said Thorne. "Gio is Italian and likes to go home every now and then to see his family, but the great thing is that he brings amazing food on board. Our stores are packed with dried beans, smoked meats, candies, dried fruits, and flour. Oh, and lots and lots of garlic. Gio swears that it keeps us healthy, and he seems to be right." The captain was positively beaming at his cook. "Go on, Gio, tell us the rest."

"I caught lots of squids, so I made a sauce for them with the black ink and dried tomatoes. As you can see, it is on top of the pasta. I also baked focaccia and a panatone, with raisins and dried candied fruits."

"What are those things that he baked?" Fanny asked Bill, who was on her right.

"Focaccia is a kind of Italian flat bread he makes with lots of garlic, olive oil, and salt. Gio says it's really ancient; I say it's really good. And the other thing is a sweet sort of bread with all kinds of dried fruit inside. Wait 'til you taste it! I don't know how he does it."

They fell to eating with gusto. Fanny was in a bit of a daze. The food was wonderful and abundant. The grog was strong, and the atmosphere was extremely convivial. *How could this possibly be a pirate ship?* Fanny wondered. Bill got up for another drink. Fanny studied the captain as he joked with his men. Q sat down beside her.

"Don't let his highborn speech fool you. He is the best fighter of us all. He is a man among men, fair and kind as well."

"Has he no faults at all?"

"Oh, yes, he has a sneaky sense of humor and pretends to cheat at chess. But the one thing he has no patience with is lying. He always wants the truth."

"I will remember that," said Fanny. *I am the biggest liar of all*, she thought to herself. "May I ask you a question?"

"You can ask, and I can decide not to answer, if I so choose. Go ahead."

"Why are you called Q?"

Q laughed, a deep rumbling from his chest. "I am called Q because my full name is impossible for you white people to pronounce." He said his real name, which sounded to Fanny like 10 or 15 consonants strung together with clicks and whistles.

"You are right. I can't say it. I am happy to call you Q!"

"Good! Follow me. I will show you the important places. Where you eat, where you sleep, and where you piss." He led the way to the bow of the ship. "You probably recognize the head."

"I do," said Fanny, "but it was not so elegant on the *Mary of Leeds*."

On either side of the bowsprit were smooth, polished wooden boards with holes in the center. There were also buckets and sponges. "You are expected to change the water after you use it. The captain is very keen on hygiene. He is a doctor, you know. He has us cleaning the decks and emptying the bilge whenever we have free time. He says it keeps us healthy, and he is right. No one on this ship ever gets sick."

"That's why this ship doesn't smell of sewage like the *Mary of Leeds* did. And that crew were sick all the time. I think I wasn't sick because I spent all my time aloft."

Unexpected and quite pleasant, this ship! she thought to herself.

Below deck, he showed her to a hammock at the end of a long row. "This is where you will sleep. And this is your chest."

"Why do I have a chest?" That was something Fanny had never heard of aboard her other ship.

"The captain believes every man should have some place for personal items. We all have one."

"But what if someone steals out of your chest?"

"You have read the articles. On this ship, if you steal from your shipmates, you are marooned. No mercy. It is actually more merciful than on some ships, where they cut off your hand for stealing."

"I will not steal, I promise you, as I prefer to stay on board, and as it is I have one thing to put in my chest." She took out her copy of Don Quixote and placed it gently in the chest. Q cocked his head. "My father gave it to me," she said softly. She put out her hand to Q. He looked into her eyes. She thought he was going to say something else, but he didn't. He just shook her hand, and they returned to the deck.

Fanny stood alone at the rail. Behind her, the music played raucously, and the men began to dance and pound buckets and mop handles on the floor in tempo. *Ah, Will, darling*, she thought. *I am a pirate. If I will reach you sooner or later, I do not know, but I am on my way, I promise. Only now I am a pirate. I wonder what you will think of that.*

She was startled from her revery by the twins, Fallou and Sallou, who peeked out from behind the main mast. Fanny had seen them at dinner. They were very young and very tall, with skin the hue of strong coffee. Their identical deep brown eyes shown with curiosity.

"Good evening, gentlemen," Fanny said with a little bow.

"Hallo, sir. Thank you, sir." they said in unison, mimicking her bow.

"That is the extent of their English so far. Men, up deck!" Q strode forward and motioned with his hand, and they disappeared.

"They were very excited about new crew members. They came to us with no skills, but you should see them in the rigging now. They can swing and drop a sail with the best!" Q spoke with admiration and pride, a combination that Fanny found most appealing. *This is a man I want to know better*, she thought to herself.

"Have a rest," said Q. "Tomorrow we will sort out your duties."

"Thank you, sir. I am sore and tired from the events of the day. But I have one more question: Why is the ship painted black?"

"The captain thinks it is better to strike terror into the hearts of the pursued at the beginning. That way we may not have to kill them. The captain prefers not to kill."

Q gave a grin, Fanny returned it, and he left her.

She was bemused by the thought of a pirate who didn't like to kill. What was this strange ship she had landed on? On the berth deck, she took her out her copy of *Don Quixote*. She stroked the cover, then placed it carefully back in her chest. As she was drifting off to sleep in her hammock, amid the snores and snorts of the rest of the crew, it occurred to her that she did not know where they were headed. She hoped it was south toward Cuba. Her last thought was of Will's face smiling down at her from the chestnut tree.

TWENTY-TWO

THE LONG JOURNEY TO SMUGGLER'S COVE

THE *BLOODY ROSE* had been at sea for many days. The men were kept busy with chores, but in truth they were bored. Fanny now knew most of them by name and some of their stories. Fallou and Sallou had been captured in Senagambia and rescued off the slave ship with Q, along with several other men from the Ivory Coast. The Moor refused to tell anyone his name or his history, which included his missing eye and the angry red scar from his forehead to his collarbone. Wilbur and Ben were young English boys who Thorne felt sorry for. Wilbur was built like a bull and Ben was tall and thin. They had been press ganged onto a Naval ship in London, escaped in Genova and were sleeping rough in the bowels of Genova's dark alleyways. Fanny had not yet heard the whole story, just bits and pieces, but they, like the rest of the crew, were loyal to a fault. The bosun, Jim, had also been on Thorne's English crew and was an expert and honest sailor. Bill was jocular and a very fine musician. He was Irish, and a deep historical hatred of the English made him become a pirate. Attacking their ships filled him with fierce joy. Right now, he was agitated and bored. He stomped around the deck in his bare feet, swearing under his breath. The Moor climbed down from the rigging where he had been lounging.

"Bill, yer shakin' the deck with all yer clamor. Bring your bottom to anchor, ya gromit." The insult was all Bill needed to smash his head straight into the Moor's midsection. He was a much smaller man, but clearly didn't care. He pummeled away until the Moor caught him by the neck and began to squeeze. The crew on deck had gathered round and begun placing bets. The odds were on the Moor for his size, but Bill got a few wagers for his angry determination. Fanny thought it was strange to see them fight, because most days they were good friends. As she was wondering if she should intervene, there was a shout from the helm.

"Belay that this instant!" The captain's voice rang out cold and firm. The combatants wrestled for another second and then obeyed.

"It is quite a shame that boredom can make good men act a fool." He stalked down to the deck and stood between them. "What shall be done about this?" Bill hung his head.

"Captain, it was me, my fault. Moor is my mate. I was out of me skull for that second."

"Ah, shut it. I have regret for being a jackass. But I woulda won if we had kept going." Moor ducked a wild punch from Bill and laughed. "I'm joshing you, fool!"

"I am thinking a coin from each of you into our common fund will settle this. What say you, men?"

"Aye, captain," Bill and Moor shouted together. The crew dispersed, and all was calm again.

Captain Thorne leaned against the rail. He had an intuition that there would be slave ships to empty along this coast, and he was looking forward to it. He couldn't take the captives back to their homes, but he could free them before they were sold and send them north with a bit of coin and food. He scanned the horizon in frustration.

Where are the iniquitous rogues? I know they are out there, he thought to himself.

The fact was that they had not seen a ship for days and days as they sailed south.

During this long drought from battle, Fanny kept herself busy acquiring new skills. Jonas taught her how to carve cunning little animals. In turn, she taught Jonas and Lenton their letters, as promised. She also took Lenton aloft and taught him how to walk the crossbeams, swing and catch in the rigging, and how to release the sail with a drop. Her knot tying became legendary for its speed, rivaled only by Abreu, the Cuban. They had contests and although he beat her soundly in the beginning, now they were about even. The crew loved to wager, and these contests gave them a chance. Other crew participated, but they were left behind early as Fanny's and Abreu's hands flew. And although she had no musical skill at all, she sang along with gusto when Bill played his hand organ. At one point, a sleek black cat appeared on deck and rubbed against Q's leg.

"Hello, Shadow, you beautiful beast."

"I thought cats were bad luck on ships," said Fanny.

"Nay, just women!" Bill chimed in and the rest of the men laughed. "Gio told us that if we didn't let his little kitty on board, we would have rats and all manner of vermin. Turns out he was right. This is the first ship I was ever on without rats. She is our little assassin." He stroked her ears gently.

"All the men are quite fond of her," said Q. "She doesn't come up on deck unless the seas are calm. Doesn't like to get wet, I think. She picks which hammock she wants to sleep in and woe to the man who rolls over on her. Her claws are right lethal. Gio says her name is Ombra, but since we don't speak Italian, we are allowed to call her Shadow."

"Hello, Shadow," said Fanny and reached out to touch her shiny fur.

"Captain, a sail!" came the shout from the nest, and Shadow disappeared down the hatch.

"Where away?" Thorne grabbed his spy glass.

"South," came the answer. Thorned spotted it in an instant.

"Spanish, high in the water, not much cargo." Q gave his assessment.

"I agree, but let's take her anyway, for practice! Men, prepare to attack." The activity on the ship became almost frenetic. The crew were aching to engage.

The Spanish ship surrendered after the first broadside. The men swung aboard and were disappointed not to be met with any resistance. The Spanish sailors surrendered without raising a single sword. Q asked one of them why as they loaded them on to their long boats. He said they had heard of the evil black ship and knew they were doomed. Thorne laughed when Q told him.

"You see, our reputation precedes us. If ships are terrified at just the sight of us, our job is much easier. Make sure we take all the cannons before we burn her. We will take them to one of our favorite spots. Smugglers Cove!" The men cheered heartily, and Fanny was confused.

"What is a smugglers cove?" she asked Q.

"I will let it be a surprise. It is on a small island off the Carolinas. Looks like just a deserted little spit in the ocean, so small it doesn't even have a name, but it is quite the haven for the likes of us. It isn't many days' sail from here. You will like it!" Fanny fumed at the lack of details, but knew it was Q's sense of fun, so she let it go.

They arrived at the island and into a hidden inlet in record time. They anchored next to a rocky cliff and went to the base of the cliff with their long boats. Guards came out of a cave mouth with their muskets raised, but when they saw Thorne, they waved them in. They climbed a set of steps carved into the rock. Next to the steps hung an elaborate set of pulleys and ropes. The other men had been there before, but Fanny, Lenton, and Jonas were in awe. The long passageway, lit with torches, led through many curves, with guards stationed in hidden spots along the way. They reached a huge cavern with what looked like an entire village spread out along the massive floor. Torches were everywhere, but some sunlight filtered in through natural tubes in the ceiling.

"I wonder how that happened," Fanny said, pointing to the ceiling.

"I know," said Jonas. "I explored caves for fun when I was a boy. When stalactites become very old, sometimes they drop. You can see that if one hit you, you would be dead." He pointed to the needle-sharp rock formations hanging from the ceiling, like deadly missiles. Lenton looked askance at the ceiling and moved to the other side of the path.

"Don't worry, boy, you will have time to jump if one comes at you." Jonas gave Lenton a push, laughing, and then tripped over his own feet and fell on his face, to which Fanny said, "You see what happens when you are a fool? The gods turn right around and smack you down." The conversation ended when they came across the first stand. It had knives of all kinds and shapes. The Moor picked up a double set of curved hand blades.

"These will be very useful. How much?" And then began the time-honored tradition of bartering. Lenton stayed behind to watch, but Fanny and Joshua kept walking. There were tables with every kind of arms you could think of. Crossbows, spears, short swords, long swords, muskets, and blunderbusses. They wandered for an hour or so, amazed by other stands with an abundance of molasses, cotton, coffee, tea, sugar, spices, and rum.

"Where does all this come from?" she wondered aloud.

Thorne had come up behind and answered, "It is all plunder from various ships. Anything the British put a tariff on, colonists steal and smuggle. Our cannons will fetch a nice bit of gold for us. I think the colonists are collecting them for when they go to war."

"Do you think that is soon?" Fanny asked.

"Certainly in the next year or two. Everyone I have talked to here says most of the colonies are disgusted with the behavior of the crown. When they have finally had enough of the way they are being treated, they will revolt, no doubt. Which means, for us, more British ships to attack!" Thorne looked almost gleeful at the prospect. Fanny thought about Nate, Sara, and the rest of her family and began to worry. She hoped the coming war waited until she rescued Will.

Thorne interrupted her revery, "Now, over there, by the fire, is a spot where you could get a bit to eat, but I would say Gio's food is much better, so I would wait if I were you. We will return to the ship as soon as I have finished our business. Q, have the men haul in the cannons."

"I will help," said Fanny, rolling up her sleeves.

"Not this time," said Thorne. "The cannon crew are the largest, heaviest men on the ship, and although you are certainly the most capable, you are not heavy enough for this work."

That was fine with Fanny. She was fascinated by the cave and all its contraptions and set out to explore. There were rope ladders to higher levels and more stone steps carved into some of the walls. There were smaller caves and passages everywhere, some open and some with man-made barriers. She figured those for storage spaces and wondered how they were assigned. In fact, she wondered, who was in charge of all this? She climbed a rope ladder to the highest level. There was a shelf there and also a natural window in the wall looking right out to the sea. She realized that the whole top of the hill that sat in the center of the island was hollow. What a find this place was for people involved in illegal activities. A young man climbed up the ladder and joined her.

"This is my lookout. Are you new?"

"Yes," said Fanny. "My captain comes here for business, but this is my first time."

"Oh, well, I don't mind you being here, but I need to be at the window."

"Sorry," said Fanny and moved to the side. "Could you tell me how this place functions? Who is in charge?"

"There is a smugglers' council that is elected, and then they appoint a leader. We all vote on everything."

"It is the same on our ship. I never knew much of the importance of democracy until I went to sea. Now I think I would fight for it."

"You may have to, sooner than you think. My family is from Boston, and things are getting really difficult. Did you hear about the attack on the *Dartmouth* and the *Beaver*? The Sons of Liberty emptied all the tea from both ships into Boston Harbor. As a result, the British are taxing more and more and forcing us into resistance. That is why I became a smuggler. Our family's business could no longer pay the taxes and survive."

"My family is on a farm in Rhode Island. I hope they are alright." She and the boy stood quiet in thought for a moment, then he turned back to the window.

"Rhode Island has some fearless patriots. Were you there for the burning of the *Gaspee*?"

"I've been gone for a while, so no."

"It was a revenue ship that was chasing one of our smugglers in Narragansett Bay. It stupidly ran aground. Boatloads of citizens rowed out, fought down the crew, put them out in a long boat, and set fire to the ship. Such a strike against the British. It was a great moment of civil disobedience. I would have liked to have seen that!"

"Are we at war now?" Fanny asked the question with trepidation.

"Not yet, but it does feel like it's coming." Fanny felt a small shiver down her back. *I have to find Will and get home somehow*, she thought.

"I'll leave you to your post, Good luck to you and your family."

"Thank you, same to you." He turned back from the window. "Listen, I am doing a smuggling run to Providence in a few months. Would you like me to get word to your family that you are well?"

"That would be a kindness. Ours is the Campbell farm in Lymington. I am Frank Campbell."

"I can't make a guarantee, but I will try."

"What is your name?"

"We usually don't share names here, but since you have told me yours—I am William Dawes the third. My father is a patriot and one of the Sons of Liberty."

"Thank you, William. I hope our paths cross again."

Smugglers and pirates, honorable men and patriots? Maybe not all of them, but certainly enough for me to rethink my opinions, Fanny mused as she climbed down to the cavern floor.

She was just in time to hear Q shout, "Back to the *Rose*! We have concluded our business, and the captain wants to get back to sea!" In an aside to Fanny, he said, "The captain says this isn't a smart place to stay with a full bag of gold. After all, we are all criminals." He winked at Fanny and they began the treacherous descent to the beach.

TWENTY-THREE

THORNE & Q

THORNE CONTINUED TO be a pleasant enigma, but one day, when she and Q were on watch together, she asked Q how a clearly cultured and highborn man like Thorne became a pirate. On this particular day, Q decided to be forthcoming.

"It is a long, sad story with a happy ending for all of us," said Q. He sat back against the bulwark and as his hands continued to tie knots, he related the complicated tale.

"Thorne was a captain in the Royal Navy, but his first training had been as a doctor. On a voyage along the coast of northern Africa, his ship was hailed by an East India ship. Their captain had been wounded, and their doctor had died and had not yet been replaced. Captain Thorne went on board with four marines and treated their captain's wound. It seems he had fallen, and somehow put a hook through his hand. Thorne suspected he was probably drunk at the time, as he seemed to be now. The wound was festering. Thorne treated him while pondering man's stupidity. As he left the captain's cabin, his nose was assailed by an awful stench from below deck. Immediately suspicious, he quietly sent for a full complement of marines, all the while maintaining a pleasant demeanor and chatting with the quartermaster. As soon as his men boarded, he scattered them across the deck with their guns and demanded the hatch be opened. The quartermaster protested, but Thorne's dagger at his throat convinced him to comply. The smell immediately grew much worse. Under the filth, he could also smell death. He ducked into the hatch and when his eyes adjusted to the dim light, he was horrified to see rows of African men chained together, some dead, others half dead, and all those alive looking at him with despairing eyes.

"'Unshackle those men this minute,' Thorne demanded. The quartermaster made a move toward Thorne but was discouraged by Thorne's blade, once again at his throat, and the guns from the marines trained his way. He got out his keys and climbed into the hold followed by two marines. The men from the hold emerged slowly and painfully, blinking in the sunlight. They were scarecrow thin, mostly naked, and all African. Thorne was angrier with every second passing.

"'Get these men on board our ship and give them water, some soup, and something to wear.' I was the last to come up the ladder because I had stayed behind to help the others. When he saw me, Thorne said, 'I don't know if you understand English, but you are free now.' They approached the last long boat when an East India sailor stepped forward. He had broad cheekbones and copper skin.

"'I would like, if permitted, to come with you. My name is Abreu.' His voice had a light accent Thorne didn't recognize.

"Thorne was about to refuse when I told the captain that Abreu had helped us. 'He brought us water and snuck us bits of food. It would be a mercy to bring him on your ship. The rest of the crew hate him because he is from Cuba, and they think he should be a slave.' Thorne was thunderstruck to be spoken to in perfect Oxfordian English by a naked black man on a slave ship.

"'I will trust your assessment,' he said. 'To the ship.'

"That night, after the freed men were sorted out with blankets and places to sleep, I went looking for the captain. 'Why did you do this?' I asked him. 'It is likely there will be trouble for you.'

"'I find slavery to be a moral offense, and the men that ply it are no more than beasts. No other reason. May I ask, what is your name?'

"You may call me Q. That is what my friends in London settled on.'

"'Well, Q, would you care to share why your English is so perfect and how you ended up on that terrible ship?'

"'First, you tell me where we are going!' I wasn't yet sure if I completely trusted the captain.

"'I will take you all home, once we figure out where that is.'

"'I was snatched right off the street in London, bashed on the head, and thrown in the hold. My father was the chief in our village. He sent me to London to learn English and go to school. He thought it would help with the trade in our community. He might have been right; we will never know. The East India snakes had already filled the ship's hold in Africa. They had made a supply stop in London and were about to leave for the colonies to sell their captives. It was my bad luck to be in the wrong place at the wrong time. Two of the boys who died in the hold were from my village. They told me the slavers wiped out our village and killed all who resisted, including my father. No use taking me home. Nothing there now. Others will appreciate going home.'"

Q continued the story, "With my help, Thorne ascertained that most of the men would be happy to go to the Ivory Coast, so that is where he headed. Twin boys from Senegambia, Sallou and Fallou, also had nothing to go back to, so Thorne agreed to keep them on the ship. The marines took up collections to have the men disembark on the Ivory Coast with some clothes and a bit of coin. That done, Thorne headed his ship north.

"'Where shall we be going now?' I asked.

"'Genova, Italy, for supplies and then on to England. I will probably have some explaining to do for my actions.'

"I looked at him askance. 'No doubt, sir!'

"Captain Thorne told me he always loved sailing into the harbor in Genova. It was beautiful, very large, and full of Genovese ships, with their unusual blue sails. He docked his ship at Molo Nuovo in front of Capo di Faro, around a curve in the harbor where the beautiful ancient lighthouse sat atop a pile of granite.

"In Genova, Thorne sent his quartermaster, Seth, and Jim, the bosun, to find provisions. He, too, disembarked and began to stroll along the harbor looking to see if he recognized any other ships. Before long, he encountered an officer with whom he had graduated. He hailed him happily. He had been at sea a long time, and it was nice to see a familiar face from home. William was very English with blond hair and pink cheeks. 'William, it's me, John. How are you?'

"'John, this is a surprise.' William stuttered for a moment, and then he continued, 'I am very glad to see you, but what are you doing here? It isn't safe.'

"'What are you talking about?' asked Thorne.

"'You don't know! I am afraid I have some very bad news.' He looked sadly at Thorne. 'I don't know how to say this.'

"Out with it, man, waiting is more painful than not knowing.'

"'You have been accused by the East India Company of attacking their ship and stealing their cargo. You have been found guilty of piracy by the Crown. There is a price on your head, and your estates have been confiscated.'

"'What? No, absolutely not. That cannot be. I have a spotless record.'

"'They have witnesses who say you attacked unprovoked and injured their captain. John, I know it isn't true, but sentence has already been passed. If anyone spots you, they will turn you in.'

"'Villains! Are you here on a ship? Can you take my crew back to London?'

"'Of course I can, but what will that do?'

"'Save them from a charge of piracy. I will tell them to say I forced them and then booted them from their ship in Genova.'

"'That is good for them, but what about you? Can you hide somewhere? Maybe this will pass.'

"'William, my old friend, you know it will not pass. I will take care of myself. Now, to protect you, wait until you see me leaving the harbor, then raise the alarm. The Italians won't care. They won't do anything. They only tolerate us for the duty we pay them on their flag.'

"'What are you talking about?'

"'See that beautiful flag flying over the lighthouse?'

"'The one with the red cross. Yes. Why are the Italians flying our flag?'

"'Because it is theirs. It is the flag of Genova. We bought the right to fly it so that they don't attack our ships. They protect us for a price. So, don't worry about me, William. I will leave the harbor unscathed, and I will land on my feet.'"

TWENTY-FOUR

THE ESCAPE

Q STOPPED TALKING and looked down at his hands. The knot-tying had ceased.

"Thorne saved my life, gave me purpose, then the adventure really began. Let's get a drink for the rest of the story." He yelled down the hatch, "Gio, any chance of two coffees?"

"How much will you pay me?" Gio yelled back.

"A handshake, and I will let you live."

"Sounds fair. On its way."

Fanny shook her head in amazement. "I have never been with such a passel of fools. Do you ever not joke?"

"This is a hard life, Frank. You know that. This is our way of making it bearable, making it fun. Captain Thorne encourages all this silliness, except when it comes to business. Shall I continue the story?"

"Yes, please," said Fanny, settling back against the bulwark. "I cannot wait to hear what happens next."

Q resumed the story, "'Q,' the captain said to me as he leapt back onto the ship. 'I need your excellent brain. We have some immediate planning to do.'

"The captain told me of the treachery of the East India Company and asked if I had any thoughts.

"'Well, sir, there is no legal path out of it once you are convicted, so since they think you are a pirate, why not be a pirate? I would like nothing better than to hunt down an East India ship and sink it, wouldn't you?'

"With a ferocious grin, the captain replied, 'Nothing better, Q, nothing better. First, I will need a new crew. I have a few contacts here in Genova. Let's see where we can find some disreputable men.'

"We headed into the center of Genova, full of dark alleyways and passages. We went into the lowest taverns we could find. Then, along the dock, in a loud, smelly, wooden house called The Sailors Rest, we found a bar full of men in various stages of inebriation. Thorne stood up on the bar and shouted, 'Anyone who has a yen for piracy, talk to me here at this table while we drink some excellent Italian wine.' He gathered a few Irishmen, some Italians, and someone called the Moor. The Moor had a scar and was missing an eye.

"'Why should I listen to you?' said the Moor. 'An Englishman took my eye.'

"'Then it is a good thing that I am not English.'

"'You sound English.'

"'Am I English, Q?'

"'Certainly not, sir. You are a man of the seas.'

"'I like that. Good! It is settled. I am not English.'

"'How would you like to make your fortune attacking English and Dutch ships?'

"'That would suit me fine.'

"'Why do they call you the Moor?'

"'Because people are too stupid to know that Tunisians like me are not Moors.' He put his finger next to his nose and thought for a second. 'I have another friend who has no love for the English. You should meet him.' He took a step toward the bar and shouted over the din. 'Hey, Liam, this fellow has a good proposition.' A tall man with black hair and the rolling gait of a sailor strolled over.

"'Liam O'Shea of County Cork, at your service.' He seemed a nice enough fellow, but he was quite drunk, and Thorne wasn't sure where this was going to go.

"'Are you a sailor?' he asked bluntly.

"'I am a bonny fine sailor, but what for would I want to sail with you?'

"'To sink English ships, you daft bugger!' I clapped him on the shoulder, and he was so drunk I nearly knocked him down.

"He fell to one knee and said, 'In that case, I am your man. Drunk or sober, I am the best sailor in this port!'

"'I doubt that,' said I. 'My people were sailors before your precious Ireland was even a country.'

"We would have kept arguing, but Thorne didn't have time, so he stepped in and said, 'Continue this debate another time. We have some more berths to fill, and we need to catch the tide.'

"At another tavern, he broke up a fight between a few woe begotten English boys and a Scotsman and offered them all a berth. He took them all back to the first tavern near the ship and told them to wait and try not to get completely drunk. He would be back by day's end. His Genovese contact headed him toward one last rude tavern to find a cook named Giobatta. This cook was highly recommended, but the contact said he had a tendency to be volatile, and he certainly was. They found him with a barstool in one hand and a club in the other. He was attacking a large group of drunks at the bar over a perceived insult. We dragged him out by his arms, shouting and kicking. When we reached a stone quay, I flung him into the water. He emerged sputtering and swearing in both English and Italian.

"'*Porca miseria*, you English! I kill you for this!'

"'Wait a minute!' I said. 'Clearly, I am not English.'

"'Well, you sound English, and the other *cretino* is definitely one!'

"The captain laughed and replied, 'I used to be, and if you come out of the water, I have a proposition for you.'

When the man had climbed back onto the quay, the captain began to talk, 'I am told you are an exceptional cook. Your name is Giobatta, but your friends call you Gio. Until a few months ago, you and your mother cooked together for the dockworkers. Then she died, and you haven't cooked since. I am very sorry about your mother. I know what that is like. I have a hole in my heart that will never go away, and my mother died years ago.' Gio shook his head and made as if to go. 'Now listen, this is a good offer.' Thorne used his command voice and, oddly enough, Gio stopped. 'I want you to cook on our ship. We are pirates, and you would have a great chance to hunt the Dutch, Spanish, and, of course, the English.'

"Gio looked confused. 'You hunt your own ships?'

"'They are no longer mine. I am no longer English. I am a man of the seas, of the world, as is my friend Q. What say you?'

"Gio stared at the floor for a long minute and then glared at Thorne and took a deep breath. 'Can I cook whatever I want?'

"'As long as the men will eat it, yes.'

"'They will eat it. I make a guarantee! My mother is gone. I have nothing here. Why not? It can't be any worse than this.'

"Gio stayed with the other men while the captain and I returned to the ship. He loved the crew of the *Cornwall Rose*, and it made him sad to leave them behind. He walked slowly up the gangplank in deep thought. His bosun welcomed him heartily.

"'Nice to see you, sir. The men have been cleaning the decks, coiling the lines, and repairing the sails as you asked, and the stores are filled."

"'Thank you, Jim. Please call the men, all of them, at once.' The men gathered, curious as to what this was about. Maybe a bonus, some of them hoped.

"'Men, I need you to gather all your belongings. You are to leave the ship and go across the harbor to HMS *Accension*. It is tied up right under the lighthouse. The commander is William Taylor-Shaw. You will present yourselves to him and say that I have mutinied and thrown you all off the ship.'

"'Sir, you did no such thing,' said Jim, 'That is ridiculous. What is this all about?'

"'I have been accused and convicted of piracy for releasing the captives on the *East India Man*. If you stay, you will be accused as well. Most of you gentlemen have families. Please do as I ask at once. No discussion, please. There is no time to waste. Now go!'

"'Sir,' asked Georgie, the cabin boy, 'what will you do?'

"'Well, Georgie, I am going to take to the high seas and that is all I can tell you. Off with you now!' The men did as he asked and left the ship, some of them with their heads down, some of them looking back over their shoulder. They each gave Thorne a thank you and a fare thee well as they left. Jim was the last on deck.

"'Sir, I have no family and nothing I care about more than you and this ship. If it would be alright, I would like to stay.'

"'Jim, you understand that it means you become a criminal. There is no turning back.'

"'Sounds good to me, sir.' They watched as the last of the men disappeared around the bend of the harbor, and I boarded the ship.

"'Ah, that was hard,' said Thorne. 'That crew and I have traveled well together. Q, can any of our new crew actually sail?' I thought for a moment.

"'Well, the Irish fellows and the Italians are all seasoned sailors, also the Moor. Plus, we have Sallou and Fallou, who don't know sailing but are wicked smart, and Abreu the Cuban, who is a fine sailor, all on board already. Don't know about the Scotsman or the English boys. That Wilbur seems to be a strong one.' Wilbur was not as tall as Q, but he had a massive chest and forearms that seemed to be made of iron. In contrast, his face and demeanor were that of a boy. He kept his head down and did not speak.

"'I suppose we will find out when we try to sail out of the harbor. Jim, you stay as bosun; Q, you are quartermaster. We will sort out the rest later. Let's collect the men and leave as soon as they are all on board.'

"The new crew explored the boat and prepared to sail. Thorne could see that some of them knew what they were doing.

"'We can't leave yet,' said Gio. 'I need to check the stores.' He slid easily into the hatch and came back almost immediately. 'There is nothing there to cook with or eat.'

"'Yes, there is!' Jim said indignantly, 'I just stocked it myself.'
"'Is there any olive oil?'
"'No.'
"'Then how do you cook? No Parmigiano, no basil, no pasta, no nothing. Captain, I need to do a very fast gathering of food. It will only take an hour. You and you come with me.'

"He pointed to me and the Moor, who were clearly the biggest men and could carry the most.

"'Fine,' said Thorne, throwing him a bag of coins. 'An hour, and don't be late.' Gio returned in less than an hour with several wheelbarrows piled high.

"'Every time I thought he was through, he bought something else. You should have never given him so much money. I did not sign on to be a donkey,' the Moor grumbled as he started handing things onto the ship. Giant wheels of cheese, several huge barrels of olive oil, barrels of olives, barrels of vinegar, barrels of wine, fresh and pickled vegetables.

"'What is all this?' asked Thorne.

"'Don't worry; you will be happy when you eat!'

"I arrived with four huge sacks on my shoulders and threw them down on the deck.

"'That is the last. And it is?'

"'*Ceci* flour, farina, and dried pasta. Now we just need somewhere for it to stay dry.'

"'The aft hold is the driest spot,' I said. 'Let's put them in some empty barrels for protection.'

"Gio gave me a wide smile. 'You know you will have good food, don't you?' he said. Just then a small sound came from the pocket of his jacket. A sleek, tiny black head with huge golden eyes peeked out.

'Is that a cat?' asked Liam. 'No cats on a ship! Bad luck.'

'She is the best ratter in Genova. She will keep this ship clean. No cat, no cook!' Gio started back down to the shore. Thorne stepped in front of him.

'Gentlemen, no arguments, the cat stays. I do not believe in good or bad luck. Nor do I believe in King George or God. I believe we make our own luck. We need to leave before someone on board the *Ascension* decides to arrest me for the price on my head.'

'You have a price on your head? So do I. I am now inclined to trust you.' The Moor gave Thorne a particularly sardonic grin, which he returned.

'So, that's all it takes? We are settled with the cat?'

'For now, yes!' The rest of the men nodded reluctantly.

"Jim had assigned the men positions, the anchor was up, and we were ready to sail.

'Men! Avast ye! Sails away! Hoist the mizzen and sheet it hard to the right,' Thorne shouted his commands, and the crew responded, slowly, but accurately. The mainsail dropped, and the ship inched away from the quay. As she picked up speed out of the harbor, we all saw a complement of marines running down the quay. Captain Thorne's friend William had given him just enough time to get away.

As we watched Genova disappear, the captain said, 'My ship needs a new name. She was called the *Cornwall Rose*, but I am now a pirate. From here on, she will be known as the *Bloody Rose*!'"

TWENTY-FIVE

THE STORM

THE DAY HAD a strange feel to it. The wind was changeable, and the sky had a strange yellow cast to it. The men were keeping busy doing chores. Jonas pretended he was sharpening his dagger, but, in reality, he was carving a small whale for Lenton. He had taken quite a liking to the plucky boy and almost felt like a father to him. *Don't get soft, Jonas*, he said to himself. *It's just a whale.*

"Sir, there is a dark band of clouds just over there," Lenton pointed as he shouted to Captain Thorne from the crow's nest. Thorne checked the horizon through his glass.

"Lenton, descend immediately. Men, prepare for foul weather; a hurricane will hit us shortly." Thorne began shouting directions to the crew, "Reef the main sail! Break out the storm jib!" They worked with practiced efficiency. There was no sense of panic, just order and speed. Lenton swung down on the ropes from the crow's nest just the way Fanny had taught him.

"Did you see that?" he asked Jonas with a grin.

"Shut up, boy, trouble on the way!" Lenton's face dropped but brightened again when Jonas added, "Not bad for a first drop."

"Jonas, Bill, Lenton, get below, start covering the gunports and securing the cannons. Take Wilbur with you. Don't leave anything to break loose," Jim shouted orders as he began coiling ropes.

On deck, men were stationing themselves at various points to release and secure the sails on command. They also attached safety lines to the rails and around their waists. They had seen men washed overboard before and no one was taking a chance to be another. Fanny made a harness to secure herself halfway up the mast. Her job was to give advance warning of the wind or waves. She made it tight enough to hold her firm but loose enough to get out of if they started to sink or the mast broke.

"We will head for Cumberland Island," said Thorne. "We probably won't make it, but we might get a bit of shelter if we can round the point." Cumberland Island was a barrier island off the coast of Georgia. It had changed hands many times but was currently unclaimed and unoccupied. "All hands ready?"

"Aye aye, sir," the men shouted as the winds picked up.

"Here she comes!" shouted Fanny. "This is a bad one!" The wind slammed into the ship like an invisible avalanche, unstoppable and brutal. Q and Thorne wrestled with the helm together while the men downed the sails and tried to lash them to the masts. They couldn't hear themselves above the howl of the wind, so Fanny used hand signals to indicate a huge wave rolling toward them. Q and Thorne tried to turn the ship into the wind, but there was no time. A thundering waterfall washed over them. The ship was in danger of foundering, but, by some miracle, the wave swept over the deck, and with a shudder, the *Bloody Rose* righted herself. It was as though she was fighting back, refusing to be vanquished. Below, Lenton was thrown across the deck. Wilbur caught him with a massive forearm just before his head would have bashed into a cannon. Bill and Jonas wedged Lenton between them, hard up against the hull. Wilbur pressed his back against a cannon, and they all waited for another hit.

"Yer not scared, are ya, boy? This is nothing, just a little shake up. I seen lots worse. One time a ship we was on turned complete on her head and half the crew drowned." Bill was trying to reassure Lenton in his own gruff way.

"Shut up, Bill. Ya ain't helping!" Lenton's face had turned a ghostly white.

"The wind has stopped. Why has the wind stopped? Is it over?" Lenton tried, unsuccessfully, to keep his voice from shaking.

"Not likely," said Jonas. "It's most likely the eye."

"Yep, the eye," Bill repeated. "It's that strange place in the center of a storm where everything feels calm-like. Sometimes it's big, sometimes it's small. But don't let it fool you. The storm is right there on the edge, waiting to pounce like a tiger." Lenton shuddered, and Jonas gave Bill a punch on his shoulder. "What was that for?" said Bill. "I was just explaining things so the kid wouldn't be so scared."

"What do we do now?" Lenton looked from one face to the other, on the verge of panic.

"We wait. We just hold on and wait. This is a strong ship, and we have the best captain and crew on the high seas. Captain Thorne will not let a storm take his ship." Lenton looked a bit mollified and took in a deep breath.

"Shall I sing us a song?" Jonas and Bill exchanged glances. Had fear made the boy lose his mind? "I am going to sing us a song. That is what my mother would do during thunderstorms, and this is a heck of a big thunderstorm." Lenton began to sing in a sweet tenor voice, "Sing a song of six pence, a bag full of rye." After a moment, Wilbur joined in with a low rumble. "Four and twenty naughty boys baked in a pie."

"Wait a minute, mates, you have outgrown those children's rhymes. Let's have a good, old-fashioned sea tune." Bill began to sing raucously, "What do you do with a drunken sailor early in the mornin? Ho, ho, and up she rises, ho, ho, and up she rises, ho, ho, and up she rises early in the morning.

Sing, you worthless scoundrels!" The four of them sang the chorus again and again, getting louder and louder.

Above deck, there was a flurry of activity, but the men heard the song from the hold and pretty soon everyone was singing as they worked. The whole ship reverberated with song, "Ho, ho, and up she rises!"

"Raise the mizzen, we may catch that light wind before the vile storm returns!" shouted Thorne. "We are almost around the point. There is a small passage to the west if we can get that far."

"Sir, I see it. Is it wide enough?" Fanny had climbed even higher up the mast.

"Just barely, but if we don't try, the next gust could blow us to bits." The ship inched slowly toward the narrow passage that could lead them to safety. Q tweaked the mizzen sail to use every breath of the almost nonexistent wind. Thorne stayed at the helm, he and Q a perfect duo of sailing expertise. They inched into the passage just as the wind began to roar once again.

"Hold the sail!" Thorne shouted. Q hauled at the rope, and the Moor took it up behind him. Q gave him his ferocious grin, and together they manhandled the sail up the mizzen mast. The sides scraped as the ship careened forward, but not the bottom. This was a blessing because if they ran aground in the passage, the ship would most definitely shatter. The *Bloody Rose* made it through the narrow neck and popped into a small bay like a cork from a bottle. The men all cheered wildly. No one could believe they made it to safety. Thorne opened the hatch. "Come out, you four. Did I hear singing down there?"

"Yessir, you did. The little gromit here was trying to keep our spirits up and did a right good job, I say!" Jonas almost knocked Lenton over, clapping him on the back.

"Good then! It's time for a very small celebration. Hear that I said 'very small.' We are not out of the soup yet! We will drop anchor, batten down the hatches, and wait for the rest of this monster to pass." Thorne authorized a measure of grog for all and sent most of the crew below to rest, but kept watch on deck with Q, Fanny, and a few other men in case the weather deteriorated again. The rain was heavy, and the wind howled all night, but the *Bloody Rose* floated serenely in the shelter of the bay.

In the morning, when the skies were clear, Thorne asked Jim to have the crew check for damage and repair all sails, rails, and the hull. He then strode toward his cabin indicating to Fanny and Q to follow.

"Let's check the gunpowder." *Gunpowder?* Fanny wondered why they were going into the captain's cabin.

In the captain's cabin, usually well-ordered and pristine, everything was turned over and in shambles.

"Blast! Our chess game is gone!" Thorne set the small table upright, and Q began to restore the chess board.

"It's just as well," he said with a grin. "You were beating me again, and it was starting to hurt."

"No more than you beat me. Frank, do you play? We are getting to know each other's moves too well. We need new blood." Frank took a king from the board.

"I play a little, sir. Shall we have a go?" Q uprighted some kegs, and the three of them sat around the small inlaid table. Fanny looked at the kegs. "Rum, sir?"

"Gunpowder. The rum is in the hold." He pulled back a curtain and revealed a wall of kegs, still intact. This is the only place it will stay dry and, as you know, wet gunpowder is as useless as a glass cannonball."

"Of course, this is the first place that will blow up in a fire."

"Astute observation, Q. Would you like to change cabins?"

"No, thank you, sir. I prefer to be as far away as possible from your wall of death. Just be very circumspect about your lanterns!" Fanny enjoyed listening to the banter between these two men. They interacted as equals. It reminded her of Nate and her father, and she suddenly felt a deep wave of homesickness.

"Frank. Frank?" She was jarred from her contemplation by the captain's voice.

"Sorry, sir. I was daydreaming for a moment. What did you say?"

"I asked what color do you choose?"

Fanny picked up the white king. "When I played with my father, I always chose white. He said it was because I was afraid of my dark side. He should see me now." Fanny gave a wry smile and made her first move, pushing a pawn forward.

"Aha," said Thorne, "setting up a defense I see."

"How can you tell from one move?"

Q leaned forward and whispered, "He is a mind reader. That is his secret. Don't tell him I told you. That is why he is impossible to beat."

Thorne snorted derisively. "That would be one reason. Another one is that I cheat." They all laughed at that. A few moves later, Fanny viewed the board with dismay. She had walked right into a trap and could see no way out.

"Tarnation and corruption! My father taught me better than that."

"You can still wriggle out with one very clever move." Thorne watched as Fanny stood up and surveyed the board.

"I keep hoping if I look at it from another angle, I will find the move you are tormenting me with." Fanny clenched her jaw in frustration. Just then, there was a knock on the door, and without waiting Gio came in with a tray.

"Have some *farinata*. I made it before the storm hit." They all took a piece of what looked like this flat golden bread. Q dropped a whole piece in his mouth and smiled. Fanny nibbled around the edge before doing the same.

"This is delicious. What is it?"

"Just chickpea flour, salt, and water. It has a great history. My father told us that a Genovese ship carrying bags of chickpea flour was hit by a storm, and everything in the hold was soaked. Those of us from Genova are known to be very frugal, and not wanting the flour to go to waste, when the sun came out, the captain had the crew spread the flour and salt water on the deck in a thin layer. It cooked in the bright, hot sun, and now we have *farinata*." Gio finished his story with a bow and sauntered out the door. "I will be back with more after I feed the crew," he said over his shoulder.

"Gio was quite a find, wasn't he?" Fanny said with her mouth full.

"You have no idea. He was just a boy, well, a young man. His mother ran a small food stand that the sailors loved to eat at when they came to Genova. He helped her with the cooking, but then she got sick. She would sit in her chair and direct him in making the various Genovese dishes she was famous for. She wouldn't let him take her home, and she refused to lie in bed, saying that was for people who were really sick, and she was just having a bad spell. She died in that chair, and Gio was drowning in grief and refused to cook. He also took out his frustration in bar fights. That's where I found him, in the middle of a huge brawl, swinging a stool in one hand and a club in the other. Q and I got him out of there just in time. He had been recommended, and we didn't want to lose a good cook."

"That part is true, but he also felt sorry for the boy. He never wants anyone to know about his soft side." Q poked Thorne in the arm.

"That is not true. I am a black-hearted scoundrel through and through."

"Yes, sir, of course you are. What was I thinking?" Q's sarcasm was heavy, and Fanny laughed out loud.

"Are you still thinking? Make your move!" Thorne was hoping to divert attention from all the fun Q was having at his expense.

Fanny finally moved, and Thorne laughed and snatched up her king.

"Checkmate!" he crowed like a little boy.

"He does this to me all the time. It's wretched annoying for sure," said Q, shaking his head.

"I'll get you next time. Now I know your tricks."

"You might. You only lost by one move. You are a good strategist, I can tell."

"Thank you, sir. My father would have been pleased to hear that. I was just getting better when he and my mother were taken by the fever. I haven't played since." As they talked, they came out of the cabin into the hot sunshine.

"What now, Captain? Do we go ashore?" Lenton had gotten over his fright and was almost dancing with anticipation.

"We finish the repairs and then we go hunting for game! Lads, you will love this place. It is one of the wild secrets of the Georgia coast. Welcome to Cumberland Island!"

TWENTY-SIX

CUMBERLAND ISLAND

CUMBERLAND ISLAND LAY stretched out before them. It was about a mile across and eighteen miles long. This particular bay had a wide, pristine beach of white, white sand bordered by a dense, green forest of palmettos and tall, spindly live oaks. A shorebird plunged into the water off their bow and came up with a wriggling fish. Gio stood at the rail, grinning.

"Lots of fish. Good! What else can we find?"

"This island is home to deer, wild hogs, and turkeys, for a start. What do you think, Gio? Can we make a feast?"

"More than a feast, sir. We will have a *baccanale*!"

"Gio, what is a bacca-nail?" asked Fanny.

"It is as I said, more than a feast." He disappeared down

the aft hatch and came back up with his crossbow. "Sir, may I take a hunting party?"

"Certainly. I will join you. Lower the boats!"

Thorne left a small crew on the ship to finish repairs and stand watch. The rest beached the long boats, and, armed with muskets and sabers, headed into the interior. "The *Bloody Rose* landed here once before to take on fresh water, but we didn't stay too long. There was still a British fort at the other end. We didn't know if it had guns or was even manned, but we had a load of booty from a Spanish ship we had just taken and didn't want to chance it. Several years ago, the British finally abandoned it. I'm sure they will take it back at some point, but for now, we probably have it to ourselves."

"Sir, are those horses?" shouted Lenton.

"Yes, indeed. Aren't they beauties?" Three small, sturdy horses were grazing on some marsh grass at the far end of the bay. They had shiny coats and long manes.

"How did they get here?" asked Fanny. "I know they didn't swim."

Thorne scratched his beard and smiled. "They probably could have—they are amazing animals—but common knowledge is that the Spanish left them here several centuries ago and somehow they thrived." The horses looked up at the sound of their voices but didn't seem to be afraid.

"Can we pet them?" Lenton asked innocently.

"Don't be fooled, son, these are feral horses. They could easily stomp you to death with their hooves." With that, Thorne turned away and led the hunting party off the beach, into the dark, mysterious woods. Fanny looked at the horses and thought of her beloved Fiona. She hoped beyond hope all was well for her entire family. Sara, Nate, Joshua, and Dolly were never far from her thoughts. She was almost happy for the moment, however, to be pushing her way through the tangled ferns and low-hanging branches. The foliage was different from that at home in Lymington, but Fanny could still imagine Will at her side, traipsing through the sun-dappled forest. Thorne held up his hand, and the group instantly halted. Ahead was a majestic three-pronged stag. He had not yet heard them when Thorne took aim with his long gun, and the deer fell.

"Nice shot, sir," said Gio. His crossbow had raised in front of him, but now it hung at his side.

"I know, Gio, you could have taken him, but you know the rule: Whoever sees them first!"

"Yeah, well, I will get the next one."

"If you can. If you can!" Fanny loved listening to this well-rehearsed exchange. *This is another game they all play*, she thought. *I like these men.* When they came out on the other side of the island, they were faced with towering dunes and vast salt marshes. They stood at the top of the highest one and looked out to sea.

"How far is Cuba, sir?" Fanny asked wistfully.

"Not too far. A straight shot down the coast of Florida. It could take anywhere from five days to three weeks, depending on wind and weather. Why do you ask?"

"Just curiosity sir. I always wanted to visit Cuba."

"Well, maybe we will. There are usually some very rich ships sailing out of Cuba. We shall see." Fanny was secretly delighted with that answer. *Will*, she thought, *I am on my way.*

The party made their way back through the woods, picking up their catches on the way. Gio had bagged a wild hog with his crossbow, and the men strapped that and the deer onto poles for easy carrying back to the beach. At one point, Gio bent down, inspected the ground, and crowed.

"Mushrooms. Lots of mushrooms. Look. These with the feathery edges are delicious. See if you can find more. We can pickle them in vinegar, and they will last a very long time."

"How about these?" Jonas held up a large mushroom cap with white spots."

"That one will kill you in an instant."

Jonas dropped it and wiped his hand on some leaves. "Crikey, there are more things here that can kill you than on the streets of London," he grumbled.

"Quiet," Fanny hissed. She raised her rifle to her shoulder, took sight, and fired. A large wild turkey fell from a tall pine in front of them. She ran over and held it up by its feet. "More for our backnail!"

Gio laughed. "You almost pronounced it correctly. Say *bak-uh-nuh-le*. You have to feel the Italian music when you say it."

"*Baccanale*," said Fanny, pronouncing the word slowly and carefully.

"Perfect, you are almost Italian. This meat will fill our stores for months to come. Tonight, we will eat it fresh, and then I will prepare it for the future. I will smoke some and cure some with salt and some with vinegar." Gio was in his element, directing the men to build several large fires as he butchered the stag. Fanny joined him and went to work on the hog. She had done this many times on the farm and expertly carved out the hocks and the belly. She laid the hooves aside for soup and buried the head in the hot embers the way Sara had taught her. She remembered Sara saying that this would make the cheeks crispy and delicious, and the rest could be used in a stew. Sara believed nothing should be wasted, and Fanny carried that lesson with her.

Thorne and the other men went back to the ship to bring everything they needed for this feast. They came back with planks for the tables, the cutlery and plates, rounds of cheese, jars of olives, a sack of galettes, and a cask full of grog.

The crew gathered round the table, sitting on stumps and makeshift benches. Thorne proposed a toast.

"This is to celebrate surviving a storm that by all rights should have killed us, but it did not. And why is that? It is because we are the *Bloody Rose*, and we make our luck!" The men lifted their tankards and cheered.

"To the *Bloody Rose*!" they all shouted and fell to eating the steaming slabs of meat with gusto. When the meal was over, they hauled the detritus back to the boats, including extra portions of meat and grog for the watch crew left on board. Gio stayed on the beach to tend the fires for the smoking of the turkey and the hog. Fanny opted to stay with him. She had come across a stream deep in the woods on the hunt and she took this opportunity, which she seldom had, to be alone and to wash in fresh water. She didn't mind the dark at all as she picked her way through the fallen branches and over grassy hillocks. In fact, she reveled in it. All the better to hide if someone came after her. But no one did. The stream was where she had remembered, and she sat down on the bank, took off her shoes and dangled her feet in the water. She took off her clothes and laid them in the water, held down by stones. Then she slipped naked into the stream. *I have never been this dirty in my whole life*, she thought. *Will this wash off or am I to be permanently stained brown?* She picked up handfuls of sand from the stream bed and scrubbed and scrubbed. She scraped at her scalp and rubbed every part of her body until it felt raw. Then she laid back and let the water drift over her. It felt delicious on her skin, her hair, over her breasts, between her legs, and down to her toes. She looked up at the tiny lights dancing in the treetops above her. *Fireflies*, she thought. *Will and I loved the fireflies in the chestnut tree.* She thought about their wedding night and how gently Will had touched her, like the touch of the water. And then how eventually they both exploded with light like comets across the sky. She gave a small shuddering sob and sat up. She shook her head to dispel the vision of Will. *I can't think about that now. I have to stay strong, stay Frank.* She picked up her doublet from the stream and scrubbed that as well as the rest of her clothes. *This will probably be the last chance for a while, so I had better do it well.* She hung her clothes on a tree branch for a bit but realized that the sun was just coming up. She put on her trousers, singlet, and shoes. She draped her shirt, doublet and socks over her arm and went back to the beach. Gio's fires were nicely banked, full of hot embers. Fanny hung her clothes on sticks she placed around the fire. She stoked it and sat down beside Gio, who was snoring gently. He woke with a start, but Fanny said, "Go back to sleep, Gio, you work harder than any of us. I will watch the fires." Gio eyed the fires, smiled at Fanny, and drifted back to sleep. A bit later, Thorne arrived alone in a small dinghy. He beached it and threw himself in the sand beside Fanny.

"You smell better than the rest of us. What did you do?"

"What do you think? I had a wash. You should try it. It is very refreshing after all that salt water. There is a stream right through there." She indicated the path she had taken. He laid down his cutlass, his blunderbuss, and his jacket beside her.

"These will be safe here with you. I will take my dagger, just in case." He disappeared into the woods and came back later, just as Gio woke up.

"Sir, you are all wet."

"Yes, I am and much the better for it. Now, what shall we eat this morning?" Gio had already thought this through during his long night by the fire. He dug out the hog in the pit and shredded the meat onto a long plank of wood. Fanny scraped the head out of the embers and did the same.

"I'm sorry, sir, the turkeys smoking will need a few more hours, but then we are ready to go."

"Good," said Thorne. "Let's get the crew fed, top up the water kegs, and get ready to sail. I have been on land long enough." Fanny hailed the ship, and the men came to the beach in the long boats.

"Who is on watch, Q?" Thorne asked.

"The Moor on deck and the twins and Lenton up the mast. They love it up there."

"Excellent. Frank, show the men the stream to fill the water kegs and have a wash, then we will eat." The men moved with alacrity. They ate their fill, helped Gio pack up the meat, loaded the boats, and were off.

Back on the ship, the crew went to their posts. It was a gloriously sunny day, with an azure sky and puffy white clouds. The bosun shouted orders, the anchors were hauled up, the sails were unfurled, and the majestic *Bloody Rose* was underway once more, her sails full and her flag snapping in the breeze.

TWENTY-SEVEN

GHOST SHIP

THE *BLOODY ROSE* slipped easily out of the inlet, through the passage, and into the open sea. They were headed south under full sail when Lenton, atop the mast, spotted a ship dead in the water.

"Sir!" he shouted. "One ship, mast down, no sign of life." Thorne looked through his glass at the tattered ship.

"The boy is right. It appears to be abandoned. The name is *Dromeda*. Looks English. Q, take us broadside and let's have a look." Q expertly maneuvered the big ship next to the smaller one. The men rigged lines and planks and went aboard. It was eerie on the deserted top deck.

"What could have happened?" Fanny wondered aloud. "I suppose they could have been hit by a rogue wave like the one that tried to topple us. If they weren't prepared, everyone could have been washed overboard." Bill came up from below deck, a sour look on his face.

"There's two fellows down there smashed to bits. Looks like they got rolled over by a loose cannon. It's a real mess."

"Tarnation," said Thorne. "Alright, do we tow her, sail her, or sink her? Q, what say you?"

"There is one good sail. With a bit of luck, we could take her back into the inlet and see what there is to salvage."

"That's it, then. Frank, you and Jonas sail her. Do you need more men?"

"Just Bill to help with the sheet. That will be enough," Fanny replied. They rigged the sail, Fanny took the helm, and they followed slowly in the wake of the *Bloody Rose* back into the bay. The sun glinted off the water and Fanny felt, for a moment, quite content. Just as they were about to drop anchor, a disheveled figure rose from a pile of fallen sails and lunged at Fanny, stabbing her with a short sword. He would have done it again if Jonas had not cut off his head with one swipe of his cutlass. Fanny felt a searing pain in her side, fell backwards, hitting her head, then lay still. Jonas hailed Thorne in a panic.

"Sir, sir, Frank is injured, badly! This piece of vermin Englishman stabbed him, he hit his head, and now I can't tell if he's even breathing." At his first shout, Thorne and Q had readied the dinghy. Thorne rowed, and Q manned the tiller. At the *Dromeda*, Jonas and Bill gently handed her down and climbed into the boat. They laid Fanny at the bottom, Jonas holding his shirt against the wound in her side. She was bleeding profusely and was still unconscious.

"The head wound doesn't look too bad, but we need to stitch up this side wound right away. Let's get him onboard and take him to my cabin." The crew gently passed Fanny hand to hand onto the ship. They carried her into Thorne's cabin and laid her on the chart table, where Thorne had stitched many a wound before. He poured rum over his hands and began to thread a sail needle with hemp. "Everyone out. Back to work. I promise I will let you know as soon as I assess his condition." The crew backed out of the cabin, whispering with heads lowered. They all liked Frank and did not want to see something happen to him. "Q, take off his shirt and turn him on his side for a better angle. Put a pillow at his back." It was quiet as they worked but then Q coughed.

"Sir, I think you should see this," he said softly. He had removed Fanny' leather singlet and there were her breasts. Both men looked down, astonished. "Did you have any idea?" Thorne shook his head.

"No, did you?"

"Of course not. How would I know?"

"You are completely right. But we had better sew up this wound before he dies . . . she dies . . . he dies." Thorne splashed more rum into the wound and began sewing with neat precise stitches. "Q, we will tell no one. He is a brilliant seaman, a master swordsman, and a gallant man.

He must have a reason. I do not care that he is a woman. Do you?"

"No, sir, I do not, but some of the men might."

"We will not tell them. It is our secret. We have never seen these breasts. They are very nice breasts, but we have never seen them."

"What breasts would that be, sir?"

"Exactly! Lace up his singlet, and we will wait for him to wake up." Thorne went out on deck to reassure the assembled men.

"Sir," said Jonas. "How is he? Will he be alright?"

"He is still unconscious. I tended the wounds, and I believe he will awake in due time and be in fine fettle. No need to worry, he will be back among us in no time."

"Ah, thank you, sir. We were all sore worried. Bill there was almost in tears."

"Was not, you daft bugger. That was you cryin', ya big baby!" Bill took a wild swing at Jonas's head. "Will I have to pound you?"

"Enough," said Thorne. "We can't afford any more injuries, so get back to your work. Let's get that ghost ship stripped and get underway."

Back in the cabin, Fanny opened her eyes slowly.

"Back among the living, I see. How do you feel?" asked Q.

"Like I have been kicked in the head by a mule. What happened?"

"The only survivor on the ghost ship decided to try and lay you out. You were busy piloting and didn't see him."

"Where is he now?"

"Jonas sliced off his head and threw him into the sea. He was very angry that you had been hurt." Fanny fingered the laces on her singlet. They were tied straight down instead of crossed, the way she did it, to keep them tight. *Oh no, what do I do now?*

"Q?" she cocked an eyebrow in question. Q gazed at her, his eyes filled with sympathy.

"Frank, some secrets are not meant to be told."

She put her hand on his arm and breathed a sigh of relief. "Thank you, my friend. And the captain?"

"He did the sewing. It will be a very impressive, but tidy scar." Fanny laughed and then winced.

"Here, drink this. It is a bit of laudanum for the pain, and it will help you sleep. It works a bit better than rum." Fanny smiled wanly and did as she was told. As her head fell back against the pillow, she thought, *What great luck that I would fall in among such righteous men.*

She woke up, still in Thorne's bed, to dazzling sunlight streaming through the vast window at the stern and Shadow, the black cat, curled against her back. Thorne sat at his desk writing. The quill made light scratching noises that Fanny found very pleasant. She rested a moment longer, then sat up and groaned. It felt as if a hammer had hit the back of her head. Shadow sat up and licked her hand.

"Aha, awake at last." He looked at Shadow. "She stayed in the bed with you the whole time. She likes either you or the smell of blood. Hard to say. You have been quite a lazy slugabed these last few days."

"Have I now? It might have been that powerful draught you kept forcing on me."

"Well, that was only because you let yourself be slashed like a beginner."

"I would have been fine if you hadn't blocked my view!"

"Blocked your view? I wasn't even there."

"I know, sir, I just thought it would be fun for something to be your fault for once. You are annoyingly perfect. Like my stitches. Thank you, by the way." They grinned at each other. Fanny swung her legs out of the bed.

"Your trousers and socks are on the chair. Put them on and we will chat." Fanny gathered her clothes. *Chat?* Her mind froze. *Will he throw me off? Will he tell the crew?* Fanny's mind raced as she dressed. When she had slipped on her shoes, she turned to face him.

"Sit down, seaman. I have some questions," he said sternly. Fanny took a seat on the other side of the large carved desk. "The most reasonable place to start is why. What made you dress up as a man and sign onto that scow, *Mary of Leeds*? That was asking for almost certain death."

"Long story, sir. The shorter version is that my husband, Will, was captured by the Spanish and has been imprisoned in Cuba for over two years now. My only thought was to rescue him, and I could see no other way. I was not going to leave him there. The British government abandoned him and his men."

"They do that, don't they," said Thorne bitterly. "And what was the plan?"

"No plan, sir. I am going to get to Cuba and figure it out there. If this ship isn't going south, I will have to find another one."

"You are determined."

"I love him, sir. He is my other half. The only man who saw me as I am and didn't run away in fear."

"I understand that. You are a formidable man and an even more imposing woman. I think I would like your Will very much."

"Q, I need you," Thorne bellowed. Q stuck his head in instantly. Thorne gave him a look that Q read and replied to the unspoken reprimand.

"I was at the door awaiting your call. I was not listening," Q spoke with quiet sarcasm that made Thorne and Fanny laugh.

"Good man. What say we sail for Cuba? Rich pickings in that corridor."

"I like the idea, sir. Let's put it to the men for a vote. Frank, you need to come out for the vote. Can you make it?" Fanny leapt up from the chair and twirled around, landing in a fighting stance.

"What do you think?" Q just shook his head and went out the door to call the men for the vote.

Thorne stood by the helm and waited for quiet.

"Men, as you can see, Frank is in fine fettle, but right now I need a vote. There are rich Spanish ships to be had toward Cuba. I propose we head in that direction. We can do this vote with just a show of hands. Is Cuba a place we can agree on?" All the hands shot up. A promise of rich pickings was music to the pirates' ears. Abreu's eyes began to tear as he thought of his home. He brushed them away and stood stoically with his hand raised.

"Then it's done," said Thorne. "We refit, clean up, and head south!" As the men went about their business, chatting happily about the new plan, Fanny took Thorne aside.

"You are a good and kind man. You want people to think you have a black heart, but I know better. Thank you."

"Nonsense!" Thorne brushed off her words, but as she walked away, he smiled to himself. "Q, take the helm! To Cuba!"

TWENTY-EIGHT

A HERO LOST

"SAIL, HO!" LENTON'S shout from the crow's-nest made everyone look up from their work. "It is an East India ship."

"Are you sure, boy?" Q asked with a ferocious growl as he grabbed the spy glass from its stand.

"Yes, sir. It's their flag."

Q steadied his gaze on the name of the ship. "*East India Man*, there they are!" Q spat the name out of his mouth like something foul. "The idiots give all their ships that same stupid name."

Thorne was standing at his shoulder. "I think we should attack. They are lazy and arrogant and won't be expecting us," Thorne said with a dangerous grin.

"Sir, I hate them as much as you do. It was their lie that turned you to piracy, and their evil that stole my family.

However, I do not think it would be prudent to attack at this time."

"Q," said Thorne, "remind us all why you speak the King's English better than the king himself." Thorne never tired of the story of Q's beginnings, plus he loved putting him on the spot.

"Sir, if I may say so, don't be ridiculous. This is not the time or the place. I will give you one sentence. Oxford would not have me; they would take any prince from any country as long as his skin was white, so I read and studied on my own, and here I am today!"

"Q, I am proud to call you friend."

"As am I, sir, but about this ship," he said, indicating the horizon. "Not to be discouraging, but I would like to point out that they have over a hundred men and at least forty cannons."

"And we have forty men who are vastly superior in skill and heart, plus a ship that can outmaneuver them in an instant. Shall we put it to the men?"

"Oh, blast," said Q, and sighed in resignation. "Let's put it to the men." He gave a great shout. "All hands on deck!"

The men appeared from all over the ship. Below deck, up the masts, and from behind the sails, where they were repairing the shrouds. They gathered in a clump, all eyes on the captain, bright with anticipation.

"How go the repairs? he asked the bosun.

"Done, sir," replied Jim. "We was just making sure she is pretty."

"Good job, men. Over there on the horizon is an East India ship. We are outgunned and outmanned. Who would like to go hunting?" The crew cheered lustily, raising their fists in the air and rattling their sabers. They had become restive and were looking forward to another skirmish.

Thorne looked at his ship, then looked at the crew with pride and shouted, "What say you, men? Shall we crush these weasels?"

The crew cheered again, ready for a fight. Thorne turned to Q with a crooked grin. "You see?"

"You are almost always right, sir. I find it most annoying." Q shook his head and laughed. Thorne was in his element, directing the movements of the crew.

"Frank, take the gunners below and prepare the cannons. Lenton, back to the mast. Gentlemen, sails away! Let's get this beauty moving!" The brisk wind carried them straight and swift toward their target. The sea was flat and sparkling blue, with a few puffy clouds in the bright sky. "A fine day for a fight, aye, men?" Thorne shouted.

"Aye aye, sir!" came the resounding response. Q expertly maneuvered the *Bloody Rose* into their favorite position to begin battle. They were next to the lumbering *East India* almost before their crew could reach battle stations.

"Gunners, away," Thorne commanded. "Give them a broadside they won't forget!" The object was not to sink the ship but to disable it and discourage the crew from fighting back, so, as usual, the aim was high. The cannons boomed, and giant splintered holes appeared where there used to be gun ports. The *East India* crew was in complete disarray. Several pirates dropped onto the deck and secured the ships together with thick hemp ropes. Then planks were placed, and the rest of the pirates boarded with ferocious yells. Some sailors had regrouped and tried to fight back, but they were cut down almost at once. Thorne was, as usual, in his glory, a cutlass in one hand and a saber in the other. Q was at his back slashing with his preferred daggers, Fanny next to him, wielding her favorite sword.

A sailor came at Thorne with his own dagger extended, but over Thorne's shoulder, Q downed him with deadly accuracy, a dagger to his throat. Thorne dispatched the two on either side, but as the last one fell, he rolled under Thorne's feet. Thorne tripped and fell forward onto the pirate Q had just killed, but he righted himself instantly. The fighting died down and the remainder of the *East India* crew surrendered. Thorne looked around triumphantly, but then swayed and almost fell. Q and Fanny were instantly at his side.

"Sir," said Fanny quietly, "there is a dagger in your chest."

Thorne looked down at the hilt protruding from his doublet and gave a slight smile

"So there is. I hadn't noticed. Get me back to the ship and we shall deal with it. Men, haul and list the booty, we will divvy later. Put that crew off in boats. I will have no *East India* scum on my ship. Then send this ship to the bottom of the sea." He sauntered slowly across the planks, onto the *Bloody Rose*, and into his cabin. Q helped him sit.

"What shall we do, sir?" There was a small hint of panic in Q's voice.

"Well, here is the problem. I believe this dagger, that I fell on like a fledgling, has gone directly into my heart. If we take it out, I will die. If it moves one tiny bit, I will die. For the moment, what say we leave it where it is? In fact, there is no doubt I am going to die shortly. But there are a few things I would like to say first. Q, you have been my right hand from the beginning. Shall I put you forward to a vote as captain?"

"Most of the men like and respect me, sir, but all of them would follow Frank into battle without hesitation. I would say Frank. But I refuse this discussion. You will not die." Thorne stifled a laugh and gave a slight cough.

"The fact is, my old friend, I am already dead, my head just won't believe it."

"And neither do I," said Fanny. "There must be something we can do!" Fanny was also feeling the flutters of panic. Thorne was the *Bloody Rose*. How would the ship continue without him?

"Here is what we shall do. Gather the men, I shall talk to them, and we will decide together what to do next." Q went out the door and Fanny tried to help as Thorne struggled to his feet. He brushed her off, the blood draining from his face, but he walked forward with purpose. Fanny stopped at the door and turned to Thorne, tears in her eyes.

"Sir, I would be proud to lead the ship for you if that is what you and the men want, but what of our secret?"

"That is yours to keep for as long as you wish. Now, stop that. Pirates don't cry . . . ever!" He winked and walked through the door.

"Men, listen carefully, I have some things to say that are of vast importance to your future." The crew eyed the dagger in Thorne's chest with dismay, but they listened. "You have been the finest group of sailors I have ever had the honor to command."

Lenton could contain himself no longer. He ran up to Thorne and would have hugged him if Q hadn't grabbed his arm first. "Sir, are you going to die? You can't die!"

"Yes, I can, and I will, very shortly, so pay attention now." He draped an arm around the boy's shoulders and continued to talk. "You will vote for a captain when I am gone. I have a suggestion for you. Frank Campbell as captain, and Q as his second in command. As always, the choice is your democratic decision to make. Make a smart choice, sail well, and watch over my ship, you bunch of scurvy blackguards! Now, give me a huzzah!" The crew cheered weakly, most of them looking at their feet. "What a bunch of puling sissies! I deserve a real one. Show me what kind of pirates we truly are!"

The men raised their weapons into the air and shook the air with a prolonged cheer. "Now, that is what I like to hear. I will see you all in heaven, if there is such a thing, because, no doubt, that is where all righteous pirates end up." He laughed and a tiny spray of blood escaped his lips. "Inside please, now!" He motioned to Fanny and Q, who practically carried him inside and back to his chair. "The blasted dagger moved when I was shouting. That's what I get for being a clown." His voice started to lose strength, and he gestured them closer. "Q, my dear brother, I have treasured our time together. I will miss you. Frank, you are the son, or daughter if you prefer, that I never had. Thank you for that. You both make me proud." He spoke softly with a faint smile. "Bury me at sea with good words and take good care of my ship! If you happen to sink her, I will come back from hell, or wherever I land, and haunt you to the end of your days." He coughed again and was quiet. Fanny and Q each held a hand and watched as the light slowly left Thorne's eyes. They held a long look between them.

"I know we should tell the men, but I would like to stay here with him a bit longer," said Q.

"As would I," said Fanny. The sun slowly set, filling the room with a golden light from the aft windows. Fanny and Q sat with their heads bowed, tears from their eyes dropping on the dagger that had killed their captain and altered their lives forever.

TWENTY-NINE

THE VOTE

THE NEXT MORNING, the sky was cloudless and impossibly blue. The sea was as flat and shiny as a mirror. The crew gathered silently on deck. No one felt inclined to chatter. Bill and Jonas stood close to Lenton, whose eyes were red and swollen.

"Remember, boy, pirates don't cry," Bill whispered, and Jonas gave Lenton's arm a pat. Lenton nodded and squared his shoulders. "Good fellow!"

Jonas, heretofore known as Silent Jonas, had been chosen by the crew to speak for them. It seems Bill had discovered that Jonas had been a traveling actor before he was press-ganged onto a merchant ship. One night when they were a bit drunk, he began to orate Hamlet's last speech. Bill was delighted and amazed. Jonas wouldn't do it again sober, but Bill spread the word, and when the crew asked him to speak, he couldn't say no. He stood silent on the deck for a moment. The breeze ruffled his hair and dried his tears, for which he was grateful. It wouldn't do to be seen crying at this moment, or any moment, for that matter. He listened to the call of a sea bird and the ropes singing against the mast. Finally, he spoke.

"This quote from Shakespeare I think is fitting, 'Cowards die many times before their deaths; the valiant never taste death but once.' To our valiant captain! The best sailor, the best fighter, the best doctor, and a particularly righteous man. He never let us down, and he died a good death. He wasn't a religious man, but I suggest we all bow our heads for a moment and send his spirit on with your own version of a prayer. Mine is this: Sir, I will be proud to stand with you at the gates of heaven or hell, whichever you prefer. May your sword stay sharp, and the wind always be at your back."

After a long moment of silence, Q asked if anyone else cared to speak.

"I'll speak," said Fanny. She stood on the foc's'le and surveyed the crew. "Thorne took me in as a prisoner and made me a mate to you all. He treated me with respect and kindness. But he treated everyone the same. He was an honorable and forthright man. He was fearless and very funny. He was our captain, and we were lucky to have him. He was the pirate among pirates."

The men cheered and slowly lowered Thorne's canvas-wrapped body over the side. The canvas was a new, white sail, lovingly stitched around his body by a group of solemn sailors. As his body hit the water and the attached anchor carried it to the dark blue depths, all stood silent at the rails. Then Gio broke the silence, "*Basta*! Enough! A drink to our captain. That is what he would have wanted." Bill and Lenton passed out cups, and Gio knocked a hole in a barrel of rum and began pouring. Once all the cups were filled, Q raised his and shouted, "To the captain!" The crew raised theirs and responded, "To the captain," and they all knocked back their shots together.

Q jumped handily onto the quarterdeck.

"Men, we have an important item to attend to before we all get stinking drunk. The matter at hand is the vote for captain, so everyone have a good think about it. As you heard, Captain Thorne suggested Frank Campbell, so let us begin with that vote." The men murmured to each other and glanced at Fanny leaning against the rail. Bill brought out a wooden box and two bags of small smooth stones, black and white. He placed them behind the wheel at the helm of the ship. The men filed up one by one and dropped a stone in the box. Fanny pushed off the rail and joined the line. When it came time, she picked a white stone, dropped it in the box and thought to herself, *Whichever way this goes will be fine. If not me then Q, and we shall continue toward Cuba. That is all that matters.* Gio and Jonas were at the end of the line.

"I think this is how they vote for the pope," Gio whispered to Jonas.

"I thought they burned white smoke," said Jonas.

"No, no. I think that is how they announce the winner, *ridicolo*. The voting comes before, I'm sure."

"Some Catholic you are, not even sure of how they vote for the pope!"

Gio smiled and shook his head. "I'm not even sure I'm Catholic!" With that, he punched Jonas in the arm, and they began to fake punch each other.

"Hey, you rascals, go and vote, we are waiting on you!" Q hurried them along to the helm. Gio dropped his stone immediately, but Jonas made a show of pondering the two bags.

"Vote, you bloody bugger!" came a shout from the crowd. Others joined in chanting, "Vote! Vote! Vote!"

"Ah, come on, ya lubbers, I was joshing. This is easy!" He dropped the last stone in the box and jumped down. "Give us the answer, Q!"

Q retrieved the box and shook it before he emptied it onto the deck with a flourish. Everyone gathered round and stared for a moment, then Lenton yelled. "Hooray for Captain Campbell!" The rest of the crew took up the cheer. Every one of the rocks was white. It was a unanimous choice.

Fanny leapt halfway up the mast and raised her sword and shouted, "To Captain Thorne, the *Bloody Rose*, and on to Cuba!" The ship's decks shook with the resounding cheer of the crew. "To Captain Thorne, the *Bloody Rose*, and on to Cuba!"

THIRTY

THE JAIL IN CUBA

WILL JERKED AWAKE, the smell of Fanny's hair in his nose, the taste of her lips on his mouth. For an instant, he was happy. As he rolled over, the heavy chains snapped him back to reality. He felt the filthy straw under him and smelled its rancid odor. In the early morning light, the damp wall behind him glistened and moved like a living thing. He struggled to his feet and shuffled forward.

The chain fastening him to the wall just barely let him reach the barred window. He could see the mast of a ship and the edge of the harbor. He touched the bars, then tried to shake them. They were corroded and flaking, but firmly in place. He gave a ghost of a laugh. What did he think, that they would magically loosen during the night, thus allowing his escape? He didn't think he would even fit through the window, although at the rate he was losing weight, that might not be a problem for long. As was a ritual every day, he scratched a line on the wall next to the window with the shackle on his wrist. There were now too many to count, but doing it seemed important somehow. He wasn't sure why. He was in a hot, damp hole in Cuba. He was not likely to leave. No one knew where he was, unless by some miracle Colin really managed to escape. He kept that as his small glimmer of hope and continued with his daily routine. He shuffled back to his pile of straw, shook it out and made a pile against the wall. He ignored the lice that were his constant companion. Now the bed was made and on to morning exercise. He wondered if Fanny knew where he was. Not likely. Colin was probably dead in a ditch somewhere. Mustn't ponder such things. That way lies madness for sure. He picked up the heavy chain at his feet and began to lift it, up down, up down. The rhythm numbed his brain. Faster now, up down, up down, up down. He hadn't seen a soul in months, just a bowl of slop shoved through the slot at the bottom of the door on some odd days. He wanted to try to stay strong, just in case. One day, when someone walked in, he would wrap his chain around their neck, lock them in his cell, and find his way off this accursed island. Back to Fanny, back to her flashing eyes, sharp tongue and joy for living, back to her sweet lips and wonderful strong body, back to her fierce, unending love.

For a moment he stopped lifting the chain and brushed at a tear in the corner of his eye. No, no despair, not today, not any day while there was breath in this body. He began lifting again, this time with Fanny's face fixed firmly in his mind.

THIRTY-ONE

BECALMED

THE WEATHER WAS beautiful, a light breeze filling the sails, the sea a shimmering clear aqua. Lenton was hanging over the side with Fallou and Sallou, looking for sharks or manta rays. The three of them had become fast friends. Lenton was helping them with their English, and the twins were showing him some Senegambian fighting styles when they weren't racing up and down the riggings. Fanny was at the helm, and Q and a few others were dragging a net behind the boat for fresh fish. Gio had informed everyone that they needed fresh fish at least twice a week to remain in peak fighting form. The crew weren't sure they believed him, but he was right about Shadow, the cat, and the impact she had on the rat population, plus they liked his cooking, so they fished.

Abreu approached Fanny at the helm.

"Sir, do you know how far we are from Cuba?" Abreu was anxious to get home and spent much of his free time scanning the horizon.

"I don't know exactly," Fanny replied. "We are past the tip of Florida and if the wind stays fresh, it couldn't take more than a week." Abreu gave a faint smile and went back to scanning the horizon. Fanny knew he couldn't wait to see his family. She felt the same way about finding Will. It felt like it was taking forever to sail south.

Just then, the wind lessened. Fanny tweaked the helm to find more breeze, but the sails began to luff and then lay flat. Q came forward, shaking his head.

"I felt it in the air," he said. "I am afraid we are becalmed."

"I disagree. I'm sure the wind will pick up again soon."

"Sir, you know better than that. You just don't want it to be true. Shall we have a wager?" Like the rest of the crew, Q liked to bet on anything and everything: How long it would take Shadow to catch the rat she was after, how long Bill would snore before he woke himself up with a start, or who would break into song first. They were silly wagers, but they kept the spirits of the men light, so Fanny went along with them every time.

"Yes, let's wager. Whoever loses has to scrape the hull for an hour."

Q cocked his eyebrow. "You hate scraping."

"So do you, so you had better not lose!" They shook on it, and both stood watching the sails. When it became clear that the wind had deserted them, Fanny called the crew to the foredeck.

"Men, it is possible, I say *possible*, that we are becalmed. As you know, this can last an hour or weeks. Let us hope for the hour. However, if Q is right and I am wrong, we are going to have a plan of action. First of all, we will take this opportunity to clean and repair whatever needs looking after. Q and Jonas will assess and assign jobs. I will likely be scraping marine growth off the hull, if Q has his way. Next, we will begin doing sword drills. You are all good fighters, but we can all improve and share new techniques. My father drilled my mother and myself almost every day."

"Your mother?" Wilbur was astonished. He came from a very traditional English background where a woman would never even hold a sword.

"Oh, yes," said Fanny. "My mother could probably beat any one of you in a fair fight. She was fierce as well as beautiful. So, drills, every day. I will organize them. Also, you will all learn your letters. Being a pirate is no excuse for being uneducated. Bill, can you go below deck with a few men and pull some slate out of the ballast? We can use it to write on. Captain Thorne left me a good store of chalk. I'm not sure why he had it, but we can use it to write on the slate."

"I never wanted to go to school, and I certainly don't want to now." The Moor grumbled under his breath.

"Really? Is it fine with you that you can be cheated and robbed by clever men if you can't read or do sums?" Fanny's tone got just a bit sharp. "I want you men to be able to handle your own fortunes, if you ever return to land. Of course, with no wind, we may never see land again." Most of the crew laughed at that, but Lenton and the twins looked worried.

"Sir, is that likely?"

"No, Lenton it is not. We may get stuck for a bit, but the wind always finds us again, don't you worry." Bill followed up Fanny's pronouncement with a punch to Lenton's shoulder.

"The thing to remember, son, is that Captain Campbell is just like Captain Thorne. Neither would ever lie!" Fanny ducked her head at that and thought, *If only they knew, they might just throw me overboard.*

"Gio, let's speak." Fanny called out. "I am sure it won't come to that, but how is our water supply? Should we begin to ration a bit?"

"We have plenty of fresh water right now, but it wouldn't hurt to be cautious. I will pour less and mix it with rum at meals. Also I will use less for cooking."

"Good, let's just hope the wind comes up tonight."

The next morning, the sun was hot and bright, but there was no wind. Q looked at Fanny and shrugged.

"It feels to me like it could be several days, maybe a week," he said. "I really didn't want to win that bet, sir."

"Don't worry, there really shouldn't be much to scrape. I want to make sure the *Bloody Rose* is as fast as she can be, so any marine growth that will slow us down needs to be cut away. Who wants to dive with me?" Fanny shouted.

Fallou and Allou were the first to step forward. Not to be outdone by a couple of boys, the Moor stepped to the rail as well, and Bill, always wanting to best the Moor, joined them all.

"Hey, Moor, I didn't know you could even swim."

"What idiot lives on a boat and doesn't learn to swim?" The Moor gave Bill a glare. Some of the men exchanged furtive glances. Regardless of the Moor's opinion, it was quite common for men on ships never to have learned to swim.

"Let's get some lines under and around the boat for us to use as a guide. said Fanny. "Q, please take care of that. Jonas, get us the sharpest heavy, short blades. When all that is done, we will dive."

"This is crazy," said Lenton. "They could all drown."

"That's why we have the lines, so we don't." Bill reassured Lenton with a smile.

When all was prepared, the group stepped up to the rail and prepared to jump. They had all removed their shoes and anything heavy. Fanny was in her singlet and trousers. Just before they began, Q stepped forward.

"It wouldn't be right to let you do this without the real expert along." He said with a grin.

"We shall see about that," Fanny retorted. "Whoever brings up the biggest cluster wins!" She dove over the side, entering the water without a splash. Everyone else jumped feet first, and the race was on. The men on deck couldn't see what was happening underwater, but every time someone's head emerged, there was a great cheer. Fanny came up first with a great hunk, followed by the Moor and Q. Bill came up empty-handed, sputtering and coughing. The last to resurface were Fallou and Sallou, who seemed to be having a wonderful time; they threw up some clusters of marine detritus and went right back down. Fanny followed them and, after about an hour, they were all exhausted and climbed the ropes back to the deck with difficulty.

"The hull looks pretty clean," said Fanny. "I think that is enough for now."

The Moor threw himself on the deck. "Good, now I think I would rather learn to read." Fanny laughed along with the crew. "That is nice to hear. Tomorrow, first class and first sword drills, but tonight, Gio, please feed us very well."

"Don't I always? But tonight I will try even harder, in honor of the lack of wind."

The second day of no wind dawned. The gray, airless sky felt heavy and dry. Fanny had the crew on deck at first light. They lined up in two rows facing each other, following her instructions.

"Men on the port side attack, starboard side defend, using only the strikes I call. First strike, thrust, pass back, now lunge, pivot, overhead strike, slope, and stand down. Sloppy, but not bad for the first attempt. You are all good fighters, there is no doubt, but don't think for a second you cannot improve. We could become the finest fighting unit on the seas with just a little more work. Trade sides, and let's do it again." By the time Fanny called for a break, they were all panting and sweating like racehorses at the finish line. "Gio, put out a very light lunch. We will eat, then we will resume." The men groaned in unison but picked themselves up off the deck and put up the planked tables to eat. It was a tradition that Captain Thorne had initiated, and Fanny meant to continue it along with all his other traditions, like singing after dinner. It kept the men in a routine, but more than that, they were good ideas, and every time she implemented one of them, she felt John Thorne at her side. She missed him fiercely, as did the rest of the crew, and these rituals honored his memory.

Gio laid out pickled vegetables, smoked turkey, and galettes, which were rock hard biscuits that lasted forever. Gio preferred to make focaccia or farinata, but right now it was important to preserve their stores, just in case.

"Gio, these are dry as a bone. How are we supposed to eat them without breaking our teeth?" The Moor growled as he gnawed at the galette.

"Don't bite, nibble, yah daft bugger." Liam held up his half-eaten galette. "It tastes pretty good with the olive oil."

"Thank you, Liam," said Gio. "At least one of you has a taste for finer things."

"Finer things, my granny, this is peasant food. It's good, but it ain't finer things." Jonas shook his galette in the air and a rain of crumbs landed on Gio's head.

"Who are you calling a peasant, you *pezzo di rumenta*!" Gio jumped up ready to fight, but Jonas slipped under the table, out the other side, and shot straight up the rigging.

"Catch me if you can, ya wanker!"

Fanny sat at the table and watched the antics. Bets were laid on who would go down first. Her crew took great delight in winding each other up, but it was all in fun. They were a diverse lot, but they functioned spectacularly as a unit when it was time. She was proud to be their captain. She wondered again what they would think if they knew she was a woman.

"Enough!" she shouted. "All I need is for one of you to get injured acting the fool. One half hour of rest and then back to drills." The half hour went far too fast, and the men grumbled as they straggled into two uneven lines.

"We are going to do something different this time. Two volunteers, please." Sallou and Fallou jumped forward, practically vibrating with excitement. They had been practicing their swordplay with each other for some time and were looking forward to displaying their skills.

"I will go first, but you will all take a turn in the middle. Gentlemen, I want you to attack me from both sides and see if you can disarm me. Please do not cut me if you can avoid it." They squared off and attacked. Fanny, with a blade in each hand, kept them at bay, but she was amazed to see them jumping and spinning as they thrust. It took all her concentration to keep track of where they were. Finally, she flipped Sallou's blade out of his hand with one sword and put the other to his brother's neck. The crew cheered, as much for the twins as for Fanny. "That was amazing," she said. "I want to know where you learned that style of fighting."

"Sir, we made it up. At home, all the men would dance with spears and pretend to fight. Then, when there was a real fight, we were ready." Sallou punctuated his pronouncement with another spin.

"We had never done it with swords before, but it seemed like it might work." Fallou, the quieter of the twins, gave a shy smile.

"Well, it did! Good job, gentlemen. Who is next?" The Moor stepped up and shook his sword.

"Don't kill me, ya little twerps." The twins leapt into position and off they went. It was a glorious afternoon. The crew traded off who would defend and what pair would attack. There was betting as usual and lots of heckling from the sides. The favorite moment for all was when Bill and Jonas, two of the smallest men, decided to take on Q, who was, without a doubt, the largest man of the whole crew. They nipped lightly around him and got in a few blows, but Q kept smacking them with the flat of his blades, first on the head, then the legs.

"You are like little rat terriers. You never know when to quit. Stand down before you get hurt." Q had had enough, but not Jonas and Liam. They continued to flail away as their arms got heavier and heavier.

"Never! This is a fight to the finish!" Liam barely got his sentence out, his breath coming in short gasps.

"Nah, I'm done." Jonas dropped his sword to his side and Q gave a final smack to his backside. Then he drove Liam backward with a flurry of strikes. Liam windmilled his arms, trying not to fall, but ended up on his back with both of Q's blades crossed at his neck.

"Enough?" Q put his face close to Liam's and smiled.

"Enough!"

"Good, I didn't want to have to kill you." Coins changed hands as the wagers were paid off.

"Who was stupid enough to bet against Q?" Fanny asked.

The Moor raised up his hand.

"I was just hoping he would trip and fall."

"Too bad for you," Q retorted. "If you had ever paid attention, you would know I never fall."

"Ah, well, there is always a first time. I will just have to wait."

"A long wait for you, but perhaps I will trip and fall on your grave." With that, Q launched one of his daggers into the mast behind the Moors head. The Moor did not flinch.

"Your aim is getting better," he said and strolled away.

It was now the third day of no wind. Fanny wrote a letter to Sara and Nate before she came out of her cabin. She had no idea how to send the letter, but it made her feel better to write it. She emerged to an amazing sight. The men were gathered quietly in two groups. One was around Q and the other around Bill. They were all scratching away on the slate slabs from the ballast. Bill was teaching letters, and Q numbers.

"Bill, is this an *L*?" Wilbur asked.

"No, eejit. It's an *I*. The *I* comes before the *L*. Pay attention."

"I am, but it's hard sometimes to tell the difference. Like a *D* can look like a *P* if you ain't careful." Wilbur's already ruddy cheeks were flaming red from embarrassment. He wished he had not spoken at all. He was very shy and hated attention. He was not the best sailor. He couldn't climb the masts or drop the sails, but he was strong like an ox, could move cargo around like it was nothing, and although he couldn't raise the anchor chain by himself, it was a lot easier to reel in if he were pulling. Bill tried to rescue him by bringing attention back to the lesson.

"Right, and then you would write *die* when you were askin for *pie* and that might get you in a barrel of trouble." Bill wrote out both words. "Does everyone see the difference? Lenton began to laugh.

"What is so funny, gromit?"

"I was just thinking that if you sent a mean letter that said, 'I hope you die,' but you spelled it wrong, you would say 'I hope you pie!'" He kept laughing and rolled over on his side, trying to catch his breath.

Fanny overheard the last exchange and started to laugh. That made all the men in Bill's group laugh as well. Q looked over and yelled, "What is so bloody funny?" This made them laugh all the harder. That kind of laughter being quite contagious, soon the whole ship was ringing with hilarity, but no one could remember why.

The fourth day was the same as the ones before. The sea stretched out around the ship, gray and unmoving. Not even a small wavelet disturbed the surface. It was getting harder to keep in good spirits, but Fanny maintained order with lessons in cartography and celestial navigation. Q and the Moor gave lessons in knife throwing, and Abreu challenged all comers to knot tying. When asked why he was so adept, he said that it was a tradition in his tribe to make fishing nets, hammocks, and baskets, all with intricate workings of knots. Soon everyone was copying his technique, and new hammocks appeared on the berth deck.

On the fifth day, Lenton called to Fanny with great excitement.

"Sir, sir, come look what Wilbur did!" At the back of the ship, Wilbur had fashioned a platform from which the men could fish. At this particular time, Shadow, who had grown into a robust and muscular cat, was perched on the end of the platform staring into the water. Then, without blinking, her claw swooped down, snatched a fish by its tail and tossed it back onto the deck. Fanny shook her head in amazement, but not at the cat.

"Wilbur, I need you now!" she called out in her command voice. Wilbur appeared, hanging his head. He was sure he was in trouble. "How did you do this?" she asked.

"I found some broken anchor links, some iron bolts, a few planks, and I just made it. I'm sorry."

"Sorry? This is brilliant. You made it out of nothing. Do you think you can repair some of the cannon straps on the gun deck?"

"Yes, sir, I think so."

"Good fellow." Fanny clapped him on the back, making his cheeks flame once more at the unexpected praise.

Later, Gio decided it was time for a treat and broke out some cured ham, parmesan cheese, mushrooms, and olives in oil. He declared that this was the best prosciutto that he had ever made, and it was sure to lift their spirits. As they ate, Q lifted his head and sniffed the air.

"Storm is coming," he declared, "about three or four hours away."

"How does he do that?" Lenton wondered aloud. "There are no clouds, no sounds, no wind. It's like magic. Is it magic, Q?"

"No, lad, it's just knowing the air, the smell, and the feel of the atmospheric pressure. You just have to pay attention. I will teach you, but right now we have to prepare for departure."

"Let's make ready the sails!" shouted Fanny. "We want to catch the first wind and be off." Almost without warning, the wind freshened, the sails puffed out full, and they were underway once more.

THIRTY-TWO

ON TO CUBA

THE *BLOODY ROSE* raced across the waves like a sleek black arrow. The fresh breeze billowed the sails to their fullest. Fanny spun the wheel ever so slightly and then back to coax a bit more speed.

Q clapped her on the shoulder and asked, "Where did you learn that trick? I shall be using it in the future." Fanny looked around to make sure no one was in earshot.

"Will showed me. We were comparing sailing styles, and I was moving my boat as fast as I could. I was making fun of his giant boat and said that it could not possibly go as fast as my little sloop. He said, 'Let's make a bet. If I can get your little tub going faster with exactly the same wind, you owe me a pie!'

"I agreed and he took over, threw my boat into a slamming turn, tweaked the tiller a few times, and got her going faster than I ever had."

"What did you do?"

"I had no choice, I had to make him a pie." She laughed at the memory and then turned her head as her eyes began to fill.

"Q, we have to start making a plan, but first I have to convince the men that this is an important mission. I hate lying to them, but I am afraid there is no way to tell them the truth just yet."

Q was quiet for a moment, his eyes automatically scanning the horizon for sails. Fanny glanced at him and was about to speak when he raised his hand. "I have a thought. What if Will was your brother? We tell them the truth about everything except his identity."

"How do I explain why I have never mentioned him?"

"You were angry because he chose to sail for the British. But when the British abandoned him in a Cuban prison, you had to set aside your feelings and save him."

"That is a good story! Did you just think of that now?" Fanny looked at Q in amazement. She thought she knew him but there were clearly hidden depths behind those dark eyes.

"Oh yes. I was an excellent liar when I was young. I called it storytelling, but my father said I was just a liar, and when he would catch me in one, he would find a very creative punishment. Once, I had to clean out and rebuild the pig enclosure by myself. No one was allowed to help. Another time, he dressed me up in my sister's wraps and jewelry and had me sit outside our hut all day."

"Oh, my, were you upset?"

"Not a bit. I got to nap while everyone else worked. I even got a marriage proposal from a fellow passing through from a neighboring village. He told my father he needed a big strong wife to help work his farm."

"Q, is that all true, or are you lying again?"

"The honest truth. My father was a man with a real sense of purpose and great humor. We always laughed about it in the end."

"Alright. We will tell the crew the true story with one small lie. Will you gather them now?"

Q nodded and whistled loudly up the mast and down the hatch. The crew straggled on to the foredeck. It had not been a battle whistle, so they took their time, joking and laughing as they formed a group.

"Men, we have some decisions to make. I will explain the situation, and then we will take a vote." Fanny laid out the facts and ended by saying, "I must rescue my brother. This is not your fight, but I would be beholden to you if you would join me." She paused, pursed her lips and continued, "I will also give my shares of the next two ships we take to be divided equally among you all." With the mention of the shares, everyone looked much more cheerful. The men turned their backs and talked quietly among themselves for a minute, and then Jonas stepped forward.

"Captain, you have never steered us wrong. We are behind you to the end, so if this is what you need to do, we are with you. What say you, men?"

The entire crew raised their fists into the air and shouted, "Aye!"

Fanny let out the breath she had been holding. She called to the Cuban sailor Captain Thorne had rescued.

"Abreu, I need you to tell me everything about Cuba, Havana, and the prison. Q, Jonas, join us in my cabin. We have plans to make."

In the cabin, Fanny laid out a map of Cuba. Captain Thorne had been a collector of maps, and this proved to be a boon. "We need to get to the prison so we can blow it up," said Fanny.

"Isn't that a bit extreme?" asked Q with a twinkle in his eye.

"We won't blow up the whole thing, just the back wall as a distraction. Lenton and I will reconnoiter a day or two before so that we know exactly where the prisoners are. When the wall blows up, we will go right out the front door, onto our wagon, and away we go."

"Wait a minute, what wagon and away to where?" asked Jonas.

"You and Abreu will be in charge of procuring a wagon. I will explain the rest as we go. Abreu, show us a route."

Abreu stood over the map and began to trace.

"This is a small harbor on the opposite side of the island. There is no beach, only marsh and jungle, so no ships ever go there. However, it is deep enough for us to anchor. Straight up this rise is my village. It is well hidden, and no one bothers us. The Spanish think we are all dead or enslaved. The path through the jungle is difficult, but we can make it in two days. There is also a secret path from the end of the road that cuts to our village. We can rest there with my people. They can take the mule and the wagon to the road, with the captain. The rest of us can continue to the back wall of the prison. That wall is the barracks for the guards. The prisoners are kept in the other wing of the building. They stupidly built their barracks right up against the jungle, so no one will notice anything until it is too late."

"This is outstanding, Abreu. We will be in good hands with you. Q, would you ask the Moor to join us? He has some deep knowledge of explosives."

The Moor was delighted that he would finally be able to blow things up. He practically leapt into the room and began his explanation.

"I learned this technique from a Chinese sailor. It involves glass balls filled with gunpowder, lime, and sulphur. You can throw a passel of them against a wall and then launch a single torch. They will then all catch fire, explode, and emit a sulphurous fog."

"Is that dangerous to breathe?" asked Jonas timidly.

"Nah," said the Moor. "It just smells like pig dung."

"That will be perfect," said Fanny. "After the wall blows up, you will gather the prisoners, disappear back into the jungle, and regroup at Abreu's village. We will take the wagon out of town and cut through to the jungle at the lower end of the island to join you. This should work." They all looked at each other over the chart table. They knew it would take a miracle!

"Now, Abreu, you need to teach me the important Spanish phrases I will need. I will say I am Italian, which will explain my bad accent. We have some days at sea. Let's get started."

Two days later, Lenton yelled from aloft, "Sail, ho!"

Fanny grabbed the glass. What she saw amazed her. A Spanish galleon riding so low in the water it moved like a snail. It reminded her of the attack Captain Thorne had made and what a rich haul they had gained. At her command, Jonas whistled the battle sound, and the men rapidly gathered.

"We have a chance for a very rich strike," said Fanny.

"Once again, we are outgunned and outmanned, but we are faster and sneakier. What say you? Shall we attack?"

"Aye!" Their shout shook the sails. Fanny grinned and called to the Moor.

"Do we have enough of your little sulphur bombs to throw a few at this Spanish ship?" The Moor bared his teeth in his version of a smile, "We just need to be close enough."

Bill stepped forward. "I have an idea. We could use leather slings, so we can land them from a bit further away. We light them with a little wick and, with any luck, they explode on impact."

"Good idea," said Fanny. "See to it; take whoever you need to help you. We need those slings in an hour."

Lenton and Jonas helped Bill along with five others. They cut squares of leather, made pouches with two long cords attached, and brought twelve slingshots on deck.

"This is just how David killed Goliath. We used to make these as kids and pelt each other with rocks," Bill said gleefully. "Let's kill us a Spanish treasure ship."

The *Bloody Rose* maneuvered swiftly into position and unleashed a barrage of cannon balls into the upper deck before the Spanish crew knew what had happened. The galleon tried to make a sluggish turn, but the pirate ship sped around to the other side. Q's adroit sailing put them right next to the *Santa Teresa de Avila*, as her name proclaimed on the bow. The pirates lined up on the rail in twos, and as one lit the fuse, the other flung it to the far deck. They landed with a satisfying loud boom, blowing holes in the deck and emitting a creeping yellow fog. The Spanish crew, in panic, started to cough and choke and threw themselves off the rail into the deep water below. Fanny's crew covered their noses and mouths with wet kerchiefs. They swung onto the other ship on ropes and laid on planks to run across. Their sabers at the ready, they charged the Spanish crew as the frightened sailors descended into chaos. Between the fog and the expert swordsmanship, the Spaniards were disarmed and lined up at the rail in no time.

"Thanks to the Moor, we have triumphed against insurmountable odds. This is a huge achievement. Thank you, men!

Now, let's search this ship." Clearly, this was a ship headed back to Spain. They found gold, jewels, fine cloth, and spices.

The canvas bags of spices thrilled Gio. "You have no idea what I can do with all of this."

Fanny couldn't let him or any of the others bask in their bounty. "Move faster, men. If she was part of a fleet, we are in trouble. Abreu, question them and see what you can find out. One more thing, let's take some of these cannons. Captain Thorne found them very valuable at the smugglers' market."

Moments later, Abreu ran across the deck. "Captain, I have some information. They were blown off course in a hurricane two days ago. They aren't even sure where they are. The captain is quite agitated. He thinks we will slaughter them all."

"Bring him here, Abreu. You translate." The Spanish captain had on a blue velvet waistcoat closed with gold brocade frogs, tight silk pants, and shoes with large brass buckles. Fanny wondered how he could fight in such a restrictive sort of dress. He was red-faced and angry. The yellow fog had blown off, but his eyes were still tearing.

"What do you intend to do?" he shouted. "Get on with it, *gillipollas.*"

Fanny didn't understand him exactly, but she got the gist. The captain then drew a dagger he had hidden in the pocket of his coat. He was quickly disarmed, but Fanny admired him for the attempt and made some fast decisions.

"I am Captain Frank Campbell, and here is what we intend: We will take as much of your cargo as we can carry. We will leave you alive with one mast and one sail. With a bit of luck, you might reach Florida, but you will never catch us."

She ordered her men to chop down the two smaller masts and left the main. The Spanish captain watched with a mixture of dismay and hatred. Then they collected all the shrouds but one. They ripped them with their knives, threw them overboard and stove in the longboats. When all the booty was stowed, the pirate crew returned to their ship and hoisted sail.

"Lets head north for a bit to throw them off, just in case they do reach Florida," Fanny said with a twinkle in her eye. "Then we will turn toward Cuba."

"Captain," said Q, "you are one sneaky fellow."

What was left of the Spanish crew stood forlornly at the rail of their crippled ship, wondering what to do next, as the *Bloody Rose* disappeared over the horizon.

THIRTY-THREE

THROUGH THE JUNGLE

THE *BLOODY ROSE* anchored in the inlet Abreu had guided them to, on the opposite side of the island from Havana. They left a watch crew on board and took two long boats to the shore. They hid them under piles of marsh grass and waded through the mud flats to the shore. Abreu assured them no one ever came here, as there was nowhere to land and nothing to see.

He led the crew, hacking through the dense growth of the jungle with a dangerous looking machete. The foliage was so thick that almost no sunlight could reach them. This fact alone made for a tense and uncomfortable trek.

"There is a spring toward the end of this part of the jungle. We can pause there for a short rest when we get there," he said. "But it is important that we keep moving."

Fanny followed Abreu at the front of the straggling line. She kept her sword in constant movement, clearing pieces of jungle. She wiped the sweat from her eyes and repeated to herself, *This plan will work. I know this will work*, as if saying it would magically make it so. She kept her fears to herself. *If he were dead, I would know. He is alive. I can feel him.* The other men followed behind, slashing with their sabers. The air was so thick it was hard to breathe. The dampness made their clothes heavy and, worst of all, the trees were filled with clouds of mosquitos. Bill practiced his most colorful Irish swears.

"A bad ending on ye, ye bloody rogues." He windmilled his arms around to no avail. They kept swarming and biting. "*Mallacht mo chait ort!* Ye sops!"

"What's that one, Bill? It sounds dirty," asked the Moor.

"It means a cat's curse on you, you bloody doddypoll. Why aren't they biting you, ye mangy lout?"

"I'm from the desert. Bugs don't like sand, and my veins are full of it." He was right. While the bugs bedeviled everyone else, he walked through the clouds of bugs as though he were in a bubble. Bill couldn't stand it. He picked up a glob of mud from the jungle floor and threw it at the Moor's back.

"Ya cretinous slime!" The Moor turned and hacked a hanging vine from a tree. "Now ya done it. If my gunpowder is wet, it is all on you. You are in for a thrashing for sure." He shifted the huge sack on his back and advanced on Bill, waving the vine like a whip, but was stopped by Fanny's voice.

"Quit it, you eejits!" she yelled. "We have a hard day's hike without the two of you making it worse." The two grown men hung their heads like schoolboys.

"Sorry, Captain," they said in unison. The party surged forward in silence, everybody needing all their air just to breathe.

"Captain, we are at the spring. We can stop for water and maybe get some relief from the bugs." Abreu shouted from further into the jungle. They all suddenly moved faster at the prospect of relief. They gathered at the spring, which was nothing more than a small mudhole fed by a little gurgle of water. Abreu showed them how to smear their arms and faces with the red mud, anywhere not covered by clothes.

"Can we drink this?" Fanny asked.

"Yes, it tastes of iron, but it is safe," Abreu replied. They all went to their knees and gulped handfuls of water.

"It will be easier from here. Ahead there is a tunnel through the trees." As the group lurched forward, they were amazed to see Abreu was right. Huge mangroves had grown towards each other on either side of a deep stream, making a leafy tunnel. "This is how we have stayed hidden and alive all these years. We have many secret trails. Both the Spanish and the British have tried very hard to find us and wipe us out, but we Taino are strong people. We refuse to die." He smiled as though it were a joke, but everyone knew he was serious. "We will reach my village before nightfall. You will have a chance to rest, and you will have real Taino food. Gio, you are going to like this food. Maybe you will find some new recipes." Abreu was trying to lighten the mood, and it worked. They began talking about real cooked food, clean, dry clothes, and meeting Abreu's family.

"I hope we don't scare them," said Jonas. "We are not a particularly savory lot."

"Speak for yourself, sir," said Lenton. "I am very savory, whatever that means."

"It means wholesome, ya gob, which you certainly are not." Bill couldn't help but chime in. He loved causing trouble almost more than attacking ships. "I know you got press-ganged because you were a thief."

"I was a thief because I was trying not to starve. I was right good too, until someone ratted me out, and the constable came looking for me." Bill started to laugh, but it strangled into a gulp. A very large spider dropped onto his knee. It was as big as an orange and had long hairy legs. Bill froze, as did everyone else. Abreu picked the spider off of Bill's knee and laughed.

"Look, she is just a little guaba, a tarantula. Nothing to be afraid of. She is actually beautiful. See the long, golden hairs on her legs and that design on her back? When she is pregnant, her belly turns red." Abreu turned the spider over and her red belly was clear to all. "Looks like we have a mother here."

"Get that thing away from me." Bill backed up so fast he fell over. The men didn't laugh, all eyes fixed on the huge spider in Abreu's hand.

"She can't hurt you." Abreu stroked her back and she waved her legs around. Smiling, he said, "Well, she can bite and it will hurt, but it won't kill you."

"Oh, well, thank the rats for that!" Bill spat out angrily. Abreu placed the tarantula on a branch to the side of the stream and she ambled away.

"Enough, let's move out," said Fanny.

"Come on, move out, you lazy slogs!" Q berated them, and slowly they waded through the stream in the tunnel of trees.

Time seemed to stand still in the jungle. Birds sang continuously, and every once in a while, they would see a flash of brightly colored feathers in the tree branches.

Fanny kept her mind on the task ahead, Will's face in front of her eyes at all times. *He promised not to die. I pray I am not too late.* She shook her head to dispel the thought that that might be possible. She looked up at the beautiful awning of green made by the mangroves. *I am coming, my love. I am almost there.*

A tiny multi-colored hummingbird flew past Lenton's face. He made to brush it away but stopped himself. "Look, look! It seems like a bee, but it isn't. It's a bird!" The hummingbird darted around Lenton's head, shimmering in the bit of sun that cut through the green canopy. He was entranced, a big smile breaking the red mud coating his face. "Look how beautiful." He was so excited that the other men couldn't bring themselves to tease him.

"Yeah, boy, that is a right amazing sight," said Jonas.

The rest of the crew murmured in agreement and Fanny smiled. *Look at my crew. In spite of themselves, they have become a family.*

THIRTY-FOUR

A SECRET VILLAGE

THE HIKE SEEMED to never end, but the air filtering through the mangroves felt cleaner and lighter. As the light faded, the birds' songs became small, occasional peeps. The group moved from jungle to a dense forest of tall pines. The trees reminded Fanny a bit of the pines at home in Lymington, except that the trunks rose up naked and then formed a canopy of feathery branches at the top. The young trees almost seemed like bushes, but the pine smell was the same.

"Abreu, can we stop? Something has hold of my leg and I need to free myself, but I can't see what it is." Q was eerily calm. Abreu came back to where he stood and saw that Q's right leg was wrapped in the thick coils of a boa.

"This is our largest snake. He can bite, but he isn't poisonous. He can't really hurt you."

"Tell that to my leg. It is slowly being crushed, I think." Abreu took hold of the tail of the boa. Hand over hand, he unwrapped the coils from Q's leg. When he got to the head, he grasped it a few inches behind its mouth and lifted it. The entire crew gasped. The snake was almost twenty feet long and as thick around as a hawser. Q still hadn't moved, other than to shake his leg to make sure it was free. He slowly turned round and looked at the snake.

"I really hate snakes," he said softly.

"So sorry. I think he was just curious." Abreu walked the boa a few yards into the forest and placed it at the foot of a tall pine. The snake hissed softly, twisted slowly up the tree trunk, and disappeared.

"Can we please put some distance between us and that legless abomination?" asked Q.

"Of course. We are almost there." As they continued forward, the trail through the forest widened into a well-worn path. Abreu stopped the party with a wave of his hand.

"Wait here. I will prepare the village for your arrival." He stepped out of the jungle and into a large open square, surrounded by round buildings. From where she stood hidden, Fanny could easily see the clean-lined, round buildings with thatched roofs and bamboo walls. There was one very large rectangular one with a porch and eight or ten smaller ones. Abreu stopped in the middle of the square and chanted softly. It sounded to Fanny like a song she might have heard before. There was an answering chant, a different song. Abreu stood still and suddenly a tall, beautiful woman with straight black hair to her hips came streaking across the square from the large house and threw herself into his arms. She was naked except for a small woven apron tied across her hips. She wore earrings and strands of gold and coral draped around her neck. He wrapped his arms around her, and they stood frozen like a statue until their shoulders shook as both wept. Then the village exploded with activity. People streamed out of every house. Abreu stroked the woman's hair and whispered in her ear as people gathered around laughing and crying.

"The woman is his wife," Fanny quietly told the crew. "He has been missing for four years."

"Sir, they are all naked," said Lenton, unable to take his eyes off the group around Abreu.

"It is their custom. Now stop staring; it is not polite." Fanny tried to sound annoyed, but she understood the shock of seeing so many naked bodies. Some of the men wore loin clothes, but not many. A few of the women had little aprons around their waists, but most wore nothing. Everyone wore beautiful jewelry, and some had tattoos. The only person Fanny had ever seen naked was Will and that was only for a moment in the dark. Bill smacked Lenton on the side of his head.

"That's right, boy. Don't stare; you might go blind."

"Bill, you shut your yob and be respectful." Q slapped the side of Bill's head in exactly the same manner. "We are guests here. Don't forget that."

"Thank you, Q," Fanny said loudly. "You saved me from pulling my blade." She winked at him. Bill didn't see the wink and became instantly quiet, staring straight ahead. The idea that Fanny might pull her sword on him actually scared him.

"Moor, Moor, so you think he meant that? Would he draw on me?" Bill whispered out of the side of his mouth.

"Why wouldn't he? You are a loudmouthed fool!" Moor started to laugh, and then he saw Bill's face, which made him laugh harder. Fanny shushed him just as the whole village turned to look at the edge of the jungle where they were hiding. Abreu walked closer, his wife at his side, and gestured.

"Come out, you are welcome." Fanny stepped out first and bowed to Abreu's wife.

"I know you can't understand me, but Abreu has told me so much about you and the rest of his family. We are privileged to be here." Abreu translated into his wife's ear, and she smiled. Then she gathered Fanny in for a long, strong hug. The rest of the men emerged slowly. They were in filthy clothes, their skin was covered with red mud, and they were heavily armed. The villagers didn't seem to notice. They smiled, nodded, and touched their hands to the men's faces.

"This is how we greet friends," said Abreu. "Because you brought me home, you are their friends forever. This is my wife, Anacaona, and her sisters, Luysa and Yahima." They were both as beautiful as their sister, with long shining hair and sparkling golden eyes, but Luysa was tiny while Yahima was as tall as Anacaona. "Please go now with them into our house. You can bathe and will be given fresh clothes." The sisters walked the crew to the porch of the large house. Inside was a huge open room with enough space for at least fifty people.

"Abreu and his wife are both *caciques*, chiefs. The tribes have been so decimated over the last century by disease, slavery, and war with the Spanish that they decided to join together. This is one of the last enclaves of Tainos in existence." Fanny told the men in a hushed voice.

"Sir, how do you know all this?" asked Bill timidly.

"Abreu told me everything about himself and his family while he was teaching me Spanish. They stay hidden, but they farm tobacco, flax, cotton, and maize, they weave beautiful cloth, and they are more skilled with dyeing and colors than anyone. One of the ways they make money is selling black cotton cloth to the priests for their cassocks. The tribe has a few contacts in Havana that deliver the goods. It is the highest quality, even better than the cloth from France. The priests don't care where it comes from, and they pay well in gold."

Just then, a group of women arrived with large baskets so tightly woven they held water right up to the brim. Each man had his own basket. At the women's direction, by hand signals, they stepped into the baskets and the women began to remove their clothes. All of the men stood like statues, their eyes as wide as saucers.

"Captain, sir, are we really going to do this?" Lenton was mortified at the idea of being naked, much less bathing.

"We are guests, we follow their customs. Now, all of you, behave decently, or you will answer to me. I am going out to find Abreu." Q craned his neck around and gave Fanny a desperate look as Luysa began to unbutton his shirt. She had to stand on her toes and giggled as she fell against his chest. Fanny took no notice. Out on the porch, she gave a heavy sigh and then a took deep breath. She had to figure out what to do about this communal bathing.

Just then, Anacaona mounted the porch. She took Fanny's hand and walked her around to a small, enclosed shed. There was a large basket of water already there. Anacaona looked into her eyes and put her hands on Fanny's chest. Then she put both of her hands over her mouth. She ended by putting her hand on Fanny's heart and Fanny's hand on her heart. Then she smiled and ducked out of the curtain that covered the door of the shed. *She knows.* Fanny thought to herself. *She knows, and she just promised not to tell. I am a very lucky woman to be sure.* Fanny felt secure enough to take off all of her clothes. She rinsed them out and scrubbed her body with the large natural sponge Anacaona had left in the basket. Then she relaced her vest, pulled on her pants, and went outside to dry by the huge bonfire that was now burning in the square. She wanted to go over the plan with the crew, but she saw that this was not the time. They were all seated on logs around the fire. They were dressed in light cotton pants and draped tunics.

Where did the clothes come from? she wondered. Abreu approached her with a pile of clothes.

"These we make to sell. Our cotton is better than anyone else's and our friends in Havana take them to market. Please, try them."

"Abreu, isn't the fire dangerous? Might it not give away your position?" Fanny asked.

"No, we are safe. First, we only let it flame high at night, when the smoke won't be seen. During the day, we keep it at smokeless embers. Second, the Spanish soldiers are too lazy to search through trackless jungle for a puff of smoke. Last, we have spies in Havana, so if they were to ever launch a search, we would know far in advance. Don't worry, they will never find us."

Fanny took the pile of clothing and went back to her private spot. She put on the trousers and marveled at their softness. The shirt, however, didn't cover her vest well and she didn't want to risk questions. Just then, Anacaona peeked her head in. She handed Fanny a second shirt that was thicker, with the front covered in embroidery. Fanny put it on over the first shirt. The problem was solved. Once again Anacaona had saved her. Fanny hugged her tightly, and they walked together to the fire. Food was being passed around in coconut shells as the whole tribe gathered to eat. There were puffs of dough stuffed with plantains and pork and wrapped in banana leaves, called *bacan*, sitting on large wooden trays. Gio sat next to Abreu and made him explain everything.

There were *teti*, small fried fish smothered in coconut milk and with pieces of sweet peppers and onions. Tiny shrimps swam in a spicy sauce on top of steamed corn and something that tasted like spinach. It was a feast for kings. Fanny decided that any plans could wait until morning. Everyone, including herself, was too full and too tired even to speak. It had been a very long day. She and her whole crew were led into Abreu's house, where they slept soundly in comfortable cotton hammocks hung all around the walls. Abreu and his family slept all together on thick woven matts in the middle of floor. *What a wonderful people the Taino are*, Fanny thought as she drifted off to sleep.

The next morning, they began preparations. The Moor laid out the ingredients for his bombs, but as he opened his sack, he discovered that some of his glass balls had broken.

"Curses! There is no way to replace these. They came from a glass blower I robbed in Venice. They were safe all this time. Vile corruption on the soul of the breaker of fragile things."

"Are you cursing yourself?" Lenton asked the innocent question and then wished he hadn't, as the Moor fixed him with a glare.

"Who else, you gormless twit. I did the breaking, I take the curse. Captain, we do not have enough glass bombs left. I am sorry I failed you." Fanny crouched next to him as he stared sadly at the broken balls on the ground. She was about to say something when Yahima, the youngest sister, fingering the pieces, held up a hand to Abreu, a thoughtful expression on her face. She spoke to him for a moment and then turned to the Moor and laid her hand on his knee. "*Tai guaitiao*," she began. Abreu translated as she spoke. "Good friend, I believe there is a solution to this accident. We have coconuts aplenty. They can be emptied and filled, the same as these little glass toys. Then you fill them with your strange powder, and you have coconut explosions."

"She's right!" shouted the Moor. "It will work. How did she know about all of this?"

"I told the plan to the whole tribe. They needed to know what was going to happen, just in case there were problems."

"Jolly good thing you did." The Moor jumped up and hugged Yahima. He stepped back immediately, thinking he might have crossed a line, but Yahima smiled and hugged him right back. Then she shouted what were obviously commands and people started running here and there. In no time, there was a large pile of coconuts in the center of the square. They were using what seemed to be handheld drills to bore a hole in the nut and drain out the milk. Then they were set around the fire to dry out.

"What is that tool?" Fanny asked Abreu.

"It is a sharpened bamboo nail, pierced by another piece at the top for a handle."

"Most ingenious. I think we need that on the ship. Our tools have a tendency to rust, as you well know, and bamboo certainly doesn't rust." They both laughed and sat down to help add to the growing pile of coconuts.

"Tomorrow, Lenton and I will go to the prison. We need a wagon and a mule. We also need a pair of those cassocks you sell to the priests."

"That has already been addressed. The wagon is at the head of the path to the road. We altered the cassocks last night and two of our finest thieves retrieved two of those strange round hats all the priests wear when they go outside. Fanny, Anacaona has a concern. Even though your Spanish and Italian are passible, she is afraid you don't look Italian enough. She would like to dye your hair, if you would let her."

Fanny remembered the story of her father and uncle having their red hair dyed as they were hiding with the Lowland Travelers in Scotland.

"I would be grateful for the help, as long as she doesn't use lye."

"Why would she do that?"

"I don't know. The Egyptians did?" Abreu laughed heartily and translated their exchange. Soon the whole tribe was laughing.

"Was I really that funny?" Fanny asked with a grin.

"No, it's just that the idea of using poison for dyeing is ridiculous to us. We make dyes from plants." He pointed to the red and orange pattern on Anacaona's apron. "This is from the annatto plant. The blue color comes from flowers and ground up seeds and rocks. The brown dye she will use on your hair is nothing more than boiled walnut shells, *tabako*, and some palm oil."

"Abreu, where do you get tobacco?"

"We grow it, and we smoke it. There used to be big smoking festivals where all the tribes would meet and exchange *cigarros*, but no more. No one is left. We have our own small festival here. Let me show you what we do." Abreu went to a small area next to a cultivated field. "That is where we grow the *tabako*. Then we roll it up and press it into a stone mold." He took a sharp-edged hoe that was leaning against a low fence and began to dig. Soon, he unearthed a stone ovoid mold that came apart in two pieces. Inside was a bundle of cured tobacco. Abreu cut the cotton strings that held it together, carried it to the ever-burning fire in the square. There, he wrapped it in a corn husk and lit the end. He passed it to Fanny with a flourish. She drew on it and almost choked on the smoke.

"First time, sir?" Q shouted from the other side of the fire.

"How could you tell?" Fanny choked back. Abreu gave her a sip of water from a cup made of coconut shell.

"I don't understand how such a creative and advanced people could be almost wiped out." Fanny was suddenly overcome with sadness.

"It is because we were always peaceful and friendly. When that devious rat Columbus brought the Spaniards to our lands, we welcomed them, and they killed and enslaved us all over these islands. A few other small groups of us also live in secret, deep in the jungle and on other islands. When I was first enslaved, I had come into Havana to bring medicines to the plantation workers. There was a terrible fever killing them, and they got a message to us asking for help. I was administering some tonics when the plantation master came upon us and beat me with a club. The next I knew, I was in the fields, harvesting sugar cane. The foreman watched me, his eyes always on my back. It took months for me to escape, but the only route to safety was on a Dutch slave ship leaving the harbor. You know the rest of the story. I will always be grateful to Captain Thorne for saving my life. I would have been killed on that slaver for helping the prisoners."

Fanny took Abreu's hand in hers.

"You have been invaluable to us, and now you are home. There is no way to repay you and your family."

"Yes, there is. Blow that prison all the way to kingdom come. That is payment enough!"

THIRTY-FIVE

A PRIEST & A PRISON

"I AM FATHER Ignacio Sebastiano. I have been sent here from the Vatican as an emissary from the Pope himself. I am now a guest of the Royal and Pontifical University of Saint Jerome of Havana. You have no doubt heard of me. Take me to the warden." Fanny had thrown out the two most impressive contacts she could think of, and it seemed to work. The guard at the gate of the prison was at a loss. This was clearly an important person. He would try very hard to accommodate him and maybe a good report would be given to the warden.

"I am sorry, Father, the warden is not here. He will return next week. If there is anything you need, sir, I will be happy to be of assistance. Corporal Abelardo Hernandez at your service." The guard ducked his head in his own version of a bow. Fanny already knew from Abreu's spies that the warden was away. That was the very reason they chose this day and this week for the raid.

"What I need is access to your prisoners. This boy is preparing to become a priest. Praying with the downtrodden and wicked will be part of his education." The priest strode imperiously up to the gate. "Well? What are we waiting for?" The guard scurried to open the gate and led the two priests down a stone corridor.

"I understand you have some English prisoners. How many of them are there? I was led to believe there were quite a few."

"Yes, sir. There were many, but most of them have died. The rest are in a common cell over here." Fanny looked through the window at a horrendous scene. Eight men were shackled to the wall with filthy straw on the floor and an overflowing bucket next to the door. They could just reach it at the end of their chains.

"And which is their captain?"

"The warden put him in a separate cell. He was afraid he might incite the others to violence."

Fanny looked through the window and choked back a sob. Will was in the corner, a filthy, emaciated shadow of the man she loved. *You are rescued, my love.* She tried to send her thoughts to him, but he seemed in a trance. She turned away and lifted her sleeve to her eyes.

"The stench in this place is horrific. It makes my eyes water. I will return in a day or two to complete our mission. You will have cleaned out the cells by then, or there will be consequences. Empty the buckets and change the straw. We cannot go inside them like that."

"Yes, sir, we will do just that." The guard ducked his head again and breathed a sigh of relief when the priest stalked out the door.

Fanny climbed in the wagon Abreu had acquired for them and clicked her tongue at the mule. The beast plodded slowly down the dusty street away from the prison. Fanny took a few deep breaths to control her emotions. She had seen Will. He was alive, barely, and she would have him free soon. It was almost too much to fathom. She made herself get back to business.

"Alright, Lenton. What did you see?"

"I can nick the keys from the guard, no problem. It's not too far between the two cells, and they are quite aways from the barracks, but we can't blow up the walls near the cells without hurting the prisoners."

"Right, good job, we will take them out through the barracks." said Fanny. "Here is what we will do. The sulfur bombs will take out the walls closest to the gate. The other bombs will take out the barracks wall that abuts the cells. When they go off, you grab the keys and open Will's cell. By then, our men should be in, so give the keys to Q, point him in the right direction, and then join me at the gate, where we will create a big distraction in order for the crew to get all the prisoners into the jungle."

The next morning, Abreu led the crew to the back of the prison. The Moor placed his little bombs carefully along the walls, according to Fanny's instructions. They all crouched in the jungle and waited for the signal.

Fanny arrived at the gate once again. She gave the mule's reins to one of the guards. "Hold this mule. Do not tie him up. It makes him testy." He took them in confusion, laying his musket against the wall. Fanny stalked through the gate, and the head guard greeted her again.

"Greetings, Father, we did everything you asked. The cells are ready for your worship to enter. They walked into the depths of the prison. Near an outside window, Fanny suddenly stopped and began shouting.

"The smell is no better! I shall report you to the governor. You are useless and incompetent!"

Outside the prison, Q smiled. "That is our signal. Light the torches and then step back." All along the wall, fire erupted as the men hurled their torches at the glass balls and the coconuts. The explosions came one after another. The conflagration was huge, more than anyone had expected. Orange and red flames shot toward the sky. On one side, a yellow fog began to collect. The stone walls tottered and fell. The Moor was elated that his little bombs had worked. He was sorry that Yahima wasn't there to see that her coconut bombs were just as effective as the glass ones. *She would have liked that,* he thought. Fanny had asked Abreu to tell the tribe to stay in the village. She said that making sure their existence stayed secret was a very high priority, and she didn't want to take any chances. She only allowed Abreu to accompany them because he knew the paths.

Just at that moment, inside the prison, everyone heard a loud explosion and then another and another. The guard jumped in fear, and Lenton took advantage of the moment and stole the keys from his belt.

"I smell sulphur. Run!" said Father Ignacio. "We must get out of here before we are poisoned." The guard began to run. Father Ignacio followed the guard to the gate. He turned and yelled to Lenton, "Hurry, we are in danger!"

Lenton unlocked the cell door and slipped inside. Will crashed his arms down as the head appeared.

"No, sir!" he heard the voice say and shifted his body at the last second. He lost his balance and fell back against the wall. He stared in amazement at a young priest. The boy touched his cheek where the chain had left a scrape and let out his breath with a whoosh. "We are here to save you, sir. We must hurry." In his hand was a ring of keys. Will sat in a daze as the boy found the right one and unlocked the chain from the wall and pulled it from the shackles. He helped Will to his feet. "I am sorry you will have to wear the shackles for now. We don't have time to take them off. Hurry, sir, we only have moments to spare." Just then, Q appeared in the doorway. Lenton handed him the keys. "This is the Captain's brother. The rest of the men are down that way, on the right." Q clapped him on the back and shouted, "Get to the front and do the next part of your job. Good work!" Will stumbled forward, and Q caught him before he fell.

Back at the front gate, Fanny stopped the assembled troops from charging into the barracks.

In her strongest priestly voice, she shouted. "*Peligro!* Danger! You can't go in; that is a poison fog. You must wait until it dissipates, or you will surely die." Just then, Lenton came flying through the gate, coughing, choking, and rubbing his eyes. "You see? I must take the boy back to the university at once. I will return with some medical staff in case of injuries."

As he climbed into the wagon, Lenton gagged and spat at the feet of some soldiers. They jumped back, and the troops milled about in disarray. They watched the priest jump into his wagon, cluck to the mule, and speed down the bumpy track. As they rounded a corner, Lenton peeked up. "How did I do sir? Was I convincing?" he asked.

"Most persuasive," said Fanny. "I particularly liked the part where you pretended to vomit."

"Ha, ha," crowed Lenton. "Maybe someday I will be as good an actor as you. Your priest was also most persuasive. But what exactly does that word, *persuasive*, mean?"

"It means that you are very effective at convincing someone to do your will."

Lenton's eyes narrowed. "Like you, sir. We will all follow you anywhere. Is that what you mean?"

"That is exactly what I mean. A good captain must be persuasive."

"I am going to work on that. I would like to be a captain like you one day." Lenton hummed happily as they continued down the track toward the jungle.

Inside the prison, Q remembered the drawing he had studied. He went through a filthy passageway and down some slimy stone steps. He opened a door, and it was like they were in another world. The entire back wall of the barracks was gone, and the jungle spilled into the long room. Will came out of his trance as he blinked in the bright light and began to flail with his shackles at the huge black man who held him. The man easily pinned his arms to his sides in a bear hug.

"Not now, Will, my lad. Now you are rescued, so let's be off."

Will was not a small man, but Q tucked him under his arm like a rug. Will was too confused and weak to resist. The rest of the crew were beginning to come through the door assisting the other prisoners.

The Moor came running down the corridor.

"There is a huge common cell where the prisoners are not shackled. Give me the keys. I am going to free them all. Chaos is a useful thing." Q tossed the keys.

"Hurry, Moor, make sure you don't get caught. Your big, hairy pirate presence would be hard to explain."

The Moor grinned ferociously. "Maybe I'll get a chance to wield my saber. It would be fun to take on a few of these Spanish swine. On the other hand, it would probably be too easy."

"Don't be an idiot. Unlock that cell door and get out!" He shouted to the crew picking their way over the broken stones of the wall. "Men, if they are too weak to walk, carry them. Let's make haste." They plunged into the jungle, letting the dense green foliage close behind them.

"There will be water and food when we reach the village, then we will head to the ship." Q said to Will in a soothing tone.

"Ship, what ship?" Will spoke for the first time.

"The pirate ship, *Bloody Rose*, sir. A fine ship and a fine crew. We sail proudly with Captain Frank Campbell."

Will struggled out of Q's arms and to his feet. "My wife's name is Campbell as well."

Q grinned, his teeth gleaming. "Is it now? What a strange coincidence to be sure!"

THIRTY-SIX

CELEBRATION & REVELATION

THE VILLAGE WAS in intense preparation for the arrival of the prisoners. Mats were laid all around the fire, a huge caldron of stew bubbling away over the flames. Anacaona directed large baskets of water and piles of thick cotton fabric to be placed within reach.

"These men will be in need of many things," she said in Taino. "First food, then medicines, and then washing and clean clothes." She went to a long shed and gathered plants and flowers. She sat with a very large mortar and pestle between her legs and began to grind them into a paste. "This will be for their wounds. I am afraid they will be dire. These men have been prisoners for two years, Abreu told me."

"Ana, what will happen to them now?" asked Luysa. "Will they stay here with us?"

Ana smiled at her sister. She had seen Luysa's interest in Q. She sat next to him when they ate and also helped him to pack the bombs for transport.

"I don't think they will stay, dear one. I think they will go back to their ship and return to wherever they are from." Luysa's face fell, but brightened again as Q emerged from the jungle, his arm around a very dirty thin man with long shaggy hair and a beard.

"Success!" shouted Q.

"Success!" Abreu echoed in Taino.

They sat all the bedraggled men on the mats, and the Taino men removed their shackles with stone hammers and metal spikes. Will looked around and was thankful that at least some of his men were still alive. His worst fear had been that they were all dead, and he could do nothing to stop it. A few women washed his face and body, taking particular care where the shackles had left festering sores. Someone handed him a coconut bowl full of soup. It smelled delicious, but he could only take very small sips. *How did this all happen?* he wondered. *Why did these people rescue them?* He remembered the black man who carried him mentioning something about a pirate ship, but he had been too dazed to follow what he was saying.

"How are you feeling, Captain?" Q knelt down beside Will and handed him a tiny bundle of leaves. "Anacaona says this will make you feel better faster. Put it under your tongue." Will did as Q asked. It tasted a bit like peppermint. The other men were doing the same.

"Who is Anaca . . . say the name again, please."

"Anacaona. She is the wife of Abreu and is the tribe's healer. They are also both chiefs. Why don't you rest until our captain arrives, and he will explain everything." Will wanted to argue, but something made his limbs loose and he laid back on the mat. All of the men were asleep almost immediately.

"What exactly was that?" Q asked Abreu.

"It is a mixture of plants that lets you sleep and helps your body heal. We use it whenever we are ill."

"Well, it worked fast, that's for sure." He looked around at all nine men sleeping peacefully while the women continued to dress their wounds. "I imagine when they awake, they will think they are dreaming."

A shout came from the jungle trail.

"We are here!" Lenton yelled happily. He and Fanny stepped into the square. The first thing Fanny saw was the nine men asleep around the fire. She drew in a shaky breath.

"It's alright, sir, they are sleeping. They are all well. Thin, hungry, and dirty, but well." Q knew Fanny's first thought would be of Will. "Here is your brother, sir," he said pointedly. He guided her to the fire, and she sat down next to Will's head. His beard obscured most of his face, but she knew every plane by heart. It was now clean and his ankles and wrists bandaged. She stroked his hair and steeled herself so as not to cry. She had done it. She had found him and now she would take him home.

As she sat with her head bowed, Abreu called out to the tribe and also the crew.

"Tonight, we will all rest, but tomorrow we will celebrate."

The next morning, the sun peeked through the tops of the pines. As it stained the sky red and pink and orange, the village began to stir. People emerged from their round *bohios* and began to work, gathering plants and vegetables, laying out wooden and stone tools and bowls, all in preparation for the upcoming festival.

Fanny had slept all night at Will's side and woke up just as his eyes opened.

"I had a dream," he said. "I dreamed my wife was here holding my hand. If only it were true." Fanny looked around. Her crew had gone to their hammocks in Abreu's house, and Will's crew were all still fast asleep on the mats by the fire.

"It wasn't a dream, my love. It's me. I am here." He looked at her through bleary eyes.

"Fanny? Fanny? How can it be you?"

"Darling, I will explain everything when we get to the ship. For now, I am your brother, Frank, and I captained the *Bloody Rose* here to free you from prison. Nothing else is important. Keep our secret, alright? The only ones who know are Q and Abreu's wife, Anacaona. Q is the man who carried you out. He is my quartermaster and my friend. She is the one who healed you, and my savior as well. She knew immediately that I was a woman and never said a word to anyone. Not even Abreu. Do you understand?"

"Well, *Frank*," he said the name with extra emphasis, "if you would be so kind as to help me up, I will wash so that I can greet and thank these people properly. Why is your hair brown?"

"It was part of a ruse to rescue you. I will explain later," said Fanny and walked him to her private bath enclosure. Once inside, with the curtain drawn, she threw herself at him and kissed him mightily. Being in a weakened state, he almost fell over, but Fanny held him tight.

"Frank," he said, "this is unseemly behavior for a brother."

"I see prison has not dulled your wit, only your mind," Fanny retorted. They hugged again, but then Fanny pushed away. "Darling, I have to be Frank for a bit longer. Please help me to maintain my disguise. All I really want to do is kiss you, but we cannot chance it." Will held her hand a bit longer, gazed into her eyes, and kissed her one last time.

Then he said loudly, "Get out of here, you daft bugger. I am going to wash and I don't want my brother gawking at my fine physique!" Fanny laughed and slipped through the curtain to join her crew. They gathered at the fire and drank out of clay cups. The drink was being poured by Abreu and several other men from pitchers with a long, curved handle. Both the pitcher and the cups were covered with designs that were intricate and beautiful, full of color and movement.

"What is this?" asked Jonas. "It tastes a bit like ale."

"It is called *chicha*. It is made from fermented corn, but don't ask how. You do not want to know." Abreu winked as he spoke. Gio wasn't put off in the least.

"Well, I want to know how it is made. It is delicious."

"Are you sure?" Abreu had a wicked glint in his eyes.

"Stop playing or sling your hook. I want to know."

Abreu took his time. "Well," he said stroking his chin, "it begins with ground corn. Then, the women of the tribe chew it up and spit into a large clay bowl. They boil it with spices and then let it ferment for a few days. The women will not let the men participate in this process, and they guard the final recipe closely." Most of the men stopped drinking at the word spit. They sniffed their cups and exchanged skeptical looks. Gio, on the other hand, was fascinated.

"The spit helps with the fermentation, right?"

"Right. Would you like some more?"

"Yes, please," said Gio. He held out his cup, and then swallowed it down in one gulp.

Lenton held out his cup cautiously. "It won't make me sick, will it?"

Abreu laughed. "It will make you well."

"Oh, what the heck," said Jonas and held out his cup. Q and Fanny followed suit. Will's crew didn't hesitate. They were happy to drink anything that wasn't rancid water. Will arrived, and Fanny handed him the cup that Abreu had refilled for her.

"Thank you, my brother," he said, clapping Fanny on the shoulder. "Men, this is my brother Frank and his crew. They took time out from pirating to rescue us. I know you are thinking that we hunt pirates, but these men are our friends and brothers. Let us raise our cups of whatever this drink is in honor of the bravery of our brothers and the amazing hospitality of the people of this village."

All the men, including the pirate crew, raised their cups high. "Cheers!" they shouted in unison.

"This is a very strange custom, but I assume it means thank you, so you are most welcome." Abreu translated Will's sentiment to the tribe. They shouted, "*Hahom, hahom,*" which Abreu explained meant *Thank you to you too.* "We will now prepare for the celebration, so why don't you all sit by the fire and share stories while you wait."

Fanny said, "That is a very good idea. The Taino set great store in storytelling, so I will tell you all this one." She proceeded to relate how they had arrived in Cuba, the rescue plan, and what would happen next.

"Wait, you blew up the prison?" Will shook his head in amazement. "How on earth did you do that?

"Moor," said Fanny, "would you like to elucidate?"

"Dunno, but I will explain." The Moor scratched his beard.

"That's what *elucidate* means, you ignorant goat slapper." Bill landed his insult with great glee, but the Moor for once did not rise to the bait, much to Bill's disappointment.

"You are just pathetic. Now, about my bombs." The Moor

went on to explain how they were made, how they were used, and how glorious it was when the walls came down, swirling in sulphurous yellow smoke. At the end of his recitation, all clapped and shouted, "Huzzah!"

Fanny shouted with the rest and then stood up again.

"I know that you are all very anxious to get back to your families, so here is the plan. We sail to the Cayman Islands. It is about two days away, with a good wind. We will put you off in a longboat with a sail a short distance off the coast. We can't enter into a main harbor because we are, in fact, as my brother mentioned, pirates, and the British would love to kill us all. There will be British vessels there, and you can find your way home easily. You can tell them you were imprisoned by the Spaniards, somehow captured by pirates, and then, for some unknown reason, released. We will be long gone by then, so even if you must name our ship, we will be safe."

"Thank you, Frank. My men and I will be ever grateful for the heroism of your men." Will looked at Fanny with an absolute straight face and said, "I myself must get home straight away. I promised my wife I would not die, and I am sure the delicate thing is in vapors over my absence." Fanny had to put her head down and pretend to cough. She was saved by the entrance of a magnificent procession.

Abreu and Anacoana led the tribe to the sound of strange, beautiful music. They were followed by men and women, some with drums, long and short wooden flutes, and various gourds, which they shook. Those without musical instruments carried weapons. As usual, they were all mostly naked. Their faces were all elaborately painted with bright colors and beautiful designs. On their heads were crowns of multicolored feathers, leaves, and flowers. It was clear that the women were warriors as well. Many of them carried weapons along with the men. There were large wooden clubs, stone axes, long spears, and tall bows and long arrows. As the musicians played what seemed to be a rhythmic and joyous song, Abreu and Anacaona led the group in a circular dance around their astounded guests. Their feet stamped and shuffled in an intricate pattern. They waved their weapons and their hands in perfect synchronicity with the music. Q could not take his eyes off Luysa as she shook a bow as tall as she was, twirling and bending like a reed in the wind. Q thought it was the most beautiful thing he had ever seen. All of the men were entranced by the beauty of the spectacle. Will stood next to Fanny and whispered in her ear.

"We are privileged to see this, aren't we?" One of the things Fanny loved about Will was that he often spoke aloud what she was thinking, and here he was doing it again, as if no time had passed. She surreptitiously squeezed his hand, he squeezed back, and they both grinned.

"Careful, you two, someone might see." Q had sneaked up behind Fanny and Will. "What kind of behavior is that for two brothers? Unless, of course, you are Italian. They are always hugging and kissing. Gio tries to kiss me on the cheeks every time I compliment his food. I couldn't make him stop, so I finally had to stop saying nice things about his cooking. Now I tell him it is all awful." Fanny and Will laughed together.

"Ah, Q, you are such a liar. You let him kiss your cheeks every meal."

"Don't listen to your brother; he exaggerates something terrible."

"Don't I know that to be true," said Will, and Fanny punched him in the arm. "Just like the days of yore."

"Shut up, you dunce, or I'll punch the other one!" Fanny cocked back her fist to punctuate her threat. Will lifted up both his hands.

"I surrender. But when I get my strength back, we will renew this battle." Fanny had been having so much fun bantering with Will, she had forgotten his weakened condition. She felt terrible, but knew she needed to keep the ruse in play with the men watching in amusement,

"Next time, I won't be so easy on you."

The dancing stopped, but the music continued as the Taino laid out a feast. The base of everything was some kind of delicious flat bread that Abreu called *cassava*. He told them it must be prepared correctly or it could poison you. Then he laughed and said not to worry, that his people had been baking this bread for hundreds of years, and no one had ever died. It was covered with a rich fish stew and sprinkled with nuts and dried spices.

"Eat gently, men," Will admonished. "After starving for two years, our stomachs are probably walnut-sized."

There was more food and more drink, and at the end, balls of shredded coconut covered with powdered cacao. As everyone laid back, sated and happy, Fanny once again stood up to talk, but this time, she addressed the Taino.

"Your hospitality, your bravery, your generosity, and your kindness are unprecedented. We owe you so much and do not have much to give you. However, we do have some small treasures that we will send back with Abreu when we return to our ship. Now, please, all of you get some rest. Tomorrow's trek through the jungle will not be easy, and we need to sail as soon as possible." The celebration wound down, and people headed to their hammocks. A few drifted elsewhere. Q and Luysa disappeared into the jungle. The Moor and Yahima stayed by the fire holding hands and whispering in their respective languages. Somehow, they understood each other.

Abreu called to Fanny from the porch of his house.

"You and your brother come and sleep here. I have some interesting news." He proceeded to tell them about a spy he had sent into Havana to check on the goings on at the prison. Most all of the prisoners had managed to escape, some into the jungle, and some into the bowels of Havana. The prison is shut down while they try to figure out how to repair the walls. The guards are all in trouble with the warden and the governor, and they still don't have any idea who was responsible for it all.

"I think you will be safe to sail tomorrow. They are only guarding the harbor in case someone tries to get out. Oh, and everyone is praising the heroic actions of Father Ignacio Sebastiano and his acolyte. They are saying that without his bravery, everyone might have died."

"Was that you, Frank?" Will looked at Fanny sideways and winked.

"Of course not. I am no priest. I am just a pirate."

"Don't be modest," said Abreu. "Captain Campbell planned the whole thing, and every bit of it worked."

"Captain Campbell, I would take off my hat to you, but I don't have one." Will bowed with a flourish, almost fell over, and they all laughed. Abreu led them inside to hammocks where Will was asleep almost as soon as he lay down. Fanny watched him for a moment and turned toward hers when Anacaona slipped up and took her hand. Once again, she pressed her hand to Fanny's heart, then Will's, then her own; then she disappeared across the great room in the semi-darkness. *How does she know these things?* Fanny wondered to herself. *And what made her my protector and friend?* It didn't matter, Fanny just counted herself the luckiest woman alive. She had found Will, made new friends, and was on her way home.

THIRTY-SEVEN

BACK TO THE JUNGLE, BACK TO THE SEA

IN THE MORNING, preparations were proceeding rapidly for the return to the ship. Will's men all had new bandages on their wounds. Because most of their shoes had either rotted or been taken from them, their feet were wrapped in palm leaves to protect them from the jungle floor. Because they were all still quite frail, Abreu's entire family, plus a few more tribe members, joined the jungle expedition. Abreu led the way, Fanny and Anacaona followed, and each kept her arm around Will. The Tainos and the pirates assisted and sometimes carried the rest of the men. Luysa and Q helped a very weak sailor, their hands touching behind his back. For some reason, the return to the shore was much easier, probably because they had cleared the path on the way in, but also because they encountered no spiders or snakes. By the end of the day, they had gone through the mangrove tunnel, passed the spring, and were at the edge of the marsh. The *Bloody Rose* was lit by the setting sun, her black hull gleaming and her flag atop the mast waving in the breeze. *She is a magnificent sight*, Fanny thought.

"That is a magnificent ship," said Will.

There he goes, saying my thoughts aloud again. God, I love him, Fanny thought, but out loud she said, "Yes, she is. Wait till you see how she handles."

"Ho, *Bloody Rose!*" she shouted. "Captain Campbell here. We are on our way."

"Aye aye, Captain," came the immediate reply from Jim. "All hands will be on deck."

They uncovered the two longboats hidden in the deep grass and loaded the men. Abreu uncovered a small dugout canoe that was underwater at the shoreline.

"We will follow you to the ship to make sure all is well."

"That is one heck of a canoe," said Bill. "How did you make it?"

While everyone loaded the boats, Abreu explained, "You pick a perfect log, char the inside with a slow burning flame, then carve out it out, and that's it. We hide them underwater so the Spanish can't see them, should they come into the bay. This is a very small one. Some of our canoes can hold forty or fifty people. When we all paddle, we are quite fast."

Bill shook his head in amazement. "I never seen anything like it, and I been a sailor all my life. Lenton, come look at this."

Lenton walked over and laid his hand on the canoe. He was just as amazed as Bill. "This is some great work. Look how the seat in the center was left higher than the rest. Did you carve this?" he asked Abreu.

"Yes, I did, and my wife helped." Anacaona didn't understand what was being said, but she knew it was something nice about her and pressed her forehead against Abreu's. The two of them launched the canoe together and when the longboats were boarded and afloat, the entire group of Taino paddled toward the *Bloody Rose* behind Fanny and her crew.

When they reached the ship, rope ladders were lowered all along the bulwark and Will's crew slowly made their way up to the deck. Fanny's crew clambered up hawsers and rigging lines the sailors on board had dropped over the side. Q and the Moor made it a race, but Lenton beat them all by swinging hand over hand up the anchor chain.

"I am so bloody glad to be back on the ship. I have had enough of jungle and land in general for the rest of my life." Bill didn't kiss the deck, but it crossed his mind.

Abreu's group were the last to come over the side, and the on-board sailors stepped back at the sight of naked, painted men and women.

"These are our friends," said Fanny loudly. "These are the people who helped us complete our mission. And this is Abreu's family." She indicated Anacaona and her sisters. "Without them, we would all be dead for sure." She leaned her head into Q and whispered something. Q nodded and began to issue orders: "Will, bring your men with me. I will show you where you will sleep. Abreu, give your people a look at our ship. Captain Campbell has some business with the crew."

Fanny gathered the men into a tight group. "As you know, we have a very, very rich haul from that Spanish galleon. We should never have been able to take her, but we did because she was slow, and her captain was stupid. What we have will make all of you very rich men if you choose to go back on land. I am asking you each to give up one tenth of a share for the Taino. As I said, they are the reason we survived. Also, I have already promised you two of my shares, so this should not be a painful decision. What say you, by a show of your hands?" No one hesitated, all hands shot up, their loyalty to Fanny obvious in their unanimous choice. "Thank you, men. I am once again proud to be your captain."

"Sir, what about Q? He isn't here to vote. It should be all of us." Jonas was hesitant to ask, but he wanted to make sure things were right.

"Thank you, Jonas. Q gave me his vote earlier, but you are a good mate to watch out for him."

"Nah, I don't even like him. Just wanted to see if I could get his share if he went careening off somewhere."

All the men laughed heartily. They knew that Jonas idolized Q and would do anything for him. Jonas was embarrassed. "Shut your holes. Yer nothing but a bunch of shrieking harpies from the crack of Hades." This made the men laugh even harder. Just then, the Taino reappeared from below deck. They joined in the laughter simply because they liked to laugh.

When the hilarity had died down, Fanny said, "Abreu, we need to weigh anchor now while the wind is fresh."

"Of course, Captain; we shall be leaving at once."

"Not yet. We, the crew of the *Bloody Rose*, have a small gift for you. Please take it with our deepest gratitude." Q stepped forward with a large chest in his brawny arms. Two of Abreu's men took it from him, holding the handles on either side. They staggered under its weight.

"Let's get some lines to lower it into the canoe."

Q took advantage of that moment to pull Luysa behind the forecastle. "I know you don't understand, but I will be back, I promise." He pantomimed as he spoke and hoped he was getting through. When she took his hands and placed them on her heart, he knew he had.

At the rail, Abreu grasped Fanny's hand and pressed his forehead to hers. Anacaona did the same, then wrapped her arms around Fanny and hugged her as well. She looked in Fanny's eyes and for the last time, placed her hand on Fanny's heart. Then she said, in English, very clearly, "My friend."

"My friend," Fanny repeated softly. By now, it was twilight and as the Taino were paddling away, Fanny shouted from the rail, "We will be back, my friends! Men, sails away!"

The crew was once again a precision machine. The anchor was weighed, the sails were released from the tops of the rigging by Lenton and three others who had scrambled up the mast, as agile as monkeys. Q stood at the helm, awaiting Fanny's command. "Q, we head north and then east toward the Caymans."

Q spun the wheel, and the *Bloody Rose* was under full sail in no time. She tacked her way out of the bay and into open sea. *Finally*, Fanny thought, *I can take a breath.* She stood at the rail, watching the stars race by.

Suddenly, there was a commotion at the hatch. Fanny slid down the rails and into the middle of a row on the gun deck. Some of Will's men were fighting with some of the pirates. Punches were being thrown, but at least no one had pulled a blade yet. "Enough!" Fanny shouted, her sword at the ready. "What is going on?"

Bill cried, "He called Lenton a sniveling bilge rat. Who does he think he is? Lenton was just trying to be friendly. Poor little sod." He was so angry his lips were curled back from his teeth.

"What is your name, sir?" Fanny stared down the sailor who had started it all, holding her yet-to-be-sheathed sword at the ready.

"None of your bleeding business, ya scabby sea bass." The sailor was clearly not in his right mind. He was looking at a deck full of pirates, all armed, and had just insulted the captain. Her men surged forward.

Will stepped in between the two groups. He had no weapon, but he spoke with unmistakable authority.

"His name is Seaman First Class James Pritchard, soon to be known as Seaman Third Class or perhaps no rank at all. This is my brother you are insulting. My brother, who sailed into danger to rescue your sorry self. He could just as easily have left you there, but he didn't. Now you are on his ship, spewing your venom, and making my whole crew look like a bunch of unthinking, uncaring ingrates." He turned to Fanny who still had her sword at the ready. "I am profoundly sorry for the behavior of some of my crew. It will not happen again." He gave a pointed glare around the room. "Will it, men?"

"No, sir!" They all saluted as he stalked up the hatch stairs. Fanny sheathed her sword and followed. In what seemed like a moment, they stood at the rail together.

They stood in silence for a moment, then Will said, "Is that your fathers' blade?"

"No. I wish it was. I couldn't figure out how to smuggle it on to my first ship. This one was provided to me by Captain John Thorne, the original captain of the *Bloody Rose*. You do know it's the same ship you saw years ago?"

"The one with the elegant dinner on deck? Really? This is it?" She nodded. "Isn't that the strangest serendipity of all times! And now you are the captain."

"You would have liked Captain Thorne a lot. He had a sense of humor and was decent like you. He also saved my life more than once."

"I would like to thank him if I could. What happened?"

"He fell in battle, saving one of his crew. It was a great loss. I am trying to live up to his legacy."

"The way your crew admires you, I would say you have."

Fanny cleared her throat. "Come to my cabin, Will. We have much to discuss." Fanny made an effort to sound casual in case anyone was listening, but inside her heart was pounding. He followed her silently. Q placed himself on the steps outside the door. He saluted Fanny. "I am taking the first watch, sir. You will not be disturbed."

"Thank you, quartermaster. Your diligence is noted."

Q winked as she passed by and shut the door.

"These are very fine quarters," Will said as Fanny turned the lock on the handsomely carved door.

"Well, as you know, I *am* a pirate captain."

"And as you know, I *am* your husband who adores you. What do you say to that?"

"I say, kiss me now!"

"Aye aye, Captain!" And after snapping a crisp salute, making her laugh, he did, for a good long moment.

Then he touched her hair, brushing it back gently from her forehead.

"Your hair is red again."

"Anacaoa helped me wash the color out that last night in the village."

"I'm glad. You look almost like yourself, just as beautiful as ever. I used to see you in my dreams. It helped me stay strong." He laid a kiss on the side of her neck. Fanny closed her eyes and gave a deep sigh and wrapped her arms tightly around him.

"I was afraid we would never be together again," he said.

"I knew we would. You promised, and you never lie. Now I promise that this is the last time we will ever be apart."

"I will hold you to that. Where are we going now?"

"To the Caymans to deliver your men and then home to Lymington. We may have to run a gauntlet of British warships, but we will make it."

"How ever did you find me?"

"It was Colin. Somehow, he made his way to us and told me where you were."

"He is a brave and valiant fellow. I owe him my life. Where is he now?"

"Home with Nate, Sara, and Joshua, waiting for our return." Emotion was about to overwhelm her, so she made a joke. "And all the chores you owe me are waiting there too." She shook a stern finger at him. He grabbed it and placed a kiss in the center of her palm. Fanny put her hand over her heart in Taino fashion. "I love you, my husband, but you know who will be missing you the most? Dolly, who loves you even more than she loves me."

"I have missed that big, black, furry beauty too, except when she cleans my face with her tongue." They both laughed, remembering their first and only morning together as husband and wife. "Does she love me more than you do?"

"Not a chance! I love you more than every wavelet in the sea. You?"

"Don't be daft! I love you more than all the raindrops that fall from the sky. Now, no more talking!" Suddenly, Will's eyes fluttered. He swayed against Fanny and almost fell. She caught him and helped him to lie down. He was asleep in an instant. She curled up beside him, her head on his chest, listening to his heartbeat. Moonlight touched the great glass window aft and a single moonbeam broke through, bathing both of them in a silvery glow, like two stars in a velvet night sky.

Fanny sat up and gazed at his face, grateful that he was sleeping peacefully. She touched his cheek gently, then slipped out the door. Q appeared silently beside her, a worried look on his face.

"Is everything alright, sir?"

"Oh, yes, Q. Everything is just fine. He is sleeping, is all."

"Captain Campbell, sir, I would like to say something."

"Of course, Q, and please don't be so blasted formal. We are friends and don't you forget it."

"Fine. Frank, my dear friend," he said with a twinkle in his eye, "the crew and I wanted to make sure you know that whatever comes next, we are with you. Whatever decisions you make, we back you, and wherever you go, we go too!"

"Thank you, Q. Please tell the crew I will do my best to live up to the trust you have all given me." Fanny took Q's giant hands in hers. She squeezed them tightly, then let go and made her way to the bow of the ship, hiding her tears.

She leaned against the railing and watched the dark sea rush past. She thought of Sara and Nate, of Joshua and Dolly, and the tears would not stop. *Mamma, Pappa, I found Will! I wish you were here with me. I miss you so much. I don't know how or when we will ever get home. What I do know is that this ship, this crew, and my beloved Will are going to help make it so. War is imminent. The British and the Spaniards are surely hunting us. Whatever the next challenges, we will face them head on, together. Together we are strong. We will prevail.*

The wind ruffled through her flaming red hair. She smoothed it back, brushed away the tears, squared her shoulders, and smiled as the *Bloody Rose* picked up speed and glided silently through the indigo night.

ACKNOWLEDGMENTS

IT MADE ME so happy to write about a strong, smart, and fascinating heroine. I could have never done it at all without the help of an entire village of people: friends, family, professional people, other writers, and researchers. This is a list of some of them. Including all who helped me would require another book. Thank you, all!

Bold Story Press for taking on a first-time author and holding my hand throughout the daunting journey of publishing. Emily for accepting my book; Julianna, Nedah, and Karen for shepherding it to the finish.

Roz for being my first reader/editor. You kept me on track and made my preliminary manuscript look good.

Aly for being my sounding board and the research queen par excellence.

Aly, Paul, and Lynne for reading it in bits and having wonderful insights and suggestions.

Iva for being my personal proofreader.

Emilio for all his pirate books.

Mark S. for legal assistance above and beyond.

Jeffery B. for being a friend and a mentor.

ACKNOWLEDGMENTS

Claudy for teaching a great workshop and encouraging my writing.

The most important person of all has been Maurizio, my wonderful husband. He let me run all sorts of crazy ideas by him out loud. He gave great feedback and let me know when I lost track. He encouraged me when I would shut myself in the office for hours on end. He would bring me snacks and coffee and make me stop for dinner, which was always great because he is Italian. He also helped keep the Italian parts of the book accurate. Thank you for being my heart.

ABOUT THE AUTHOR

BROOKS ALMY HAS always been an avid reader. As a child, her favorite place to be was under the covers reading by flashlight, where her fierce imagination was stirred by great tales from far away and long ago. This led to a varied career, from acting on Broadway and in TV and film to directing and teaching. For Almy, writing provides an opportunity to explore the power of words and story in a different genre.

She writes at home in beautiful Italy with a big black dog, a little black cat, and her wonderful husband, Maurizio, who inspires her every day. This is her debut novel.

ABOUT BOLD STORY PRESS

BOLD STORY PRESS is a curated, woman-owned hybrid publishing company with a mission of publishing well-written stories by women. If your book is chosen for publication, our team of expert editors and designers will work with you to publish a professionally edited and designed book. Every woman has a story to tell. If you have written yours and want to explore publishing with Bold Story Press, contact us at https://boldstorypress.com.

The Bold Story Press logo, designed by Grace Arsenault, was inspired by the nom de plume, or pen name, a sad necessity at one time for female authors who wanted to publish. The woman's face hidden in the quill is the profile of Virginia Woolf, who, in addition to being an early feminist writer, founded and ran her own publishing company, Hogarth Press.

www.ingramcontent.com/pod-product-compliance
Lightning Source LLC
LaVergne TN
LVHW041747060526
838201LV00046B/934